ADVANCE PRAISE

"An absolutely great book, I was riveted from the very first chapter." - *Cat's Guilty Pleasure*

"Oh, Ronan you mysterious sexy man. Brandy and Ronan have a spark like no others, and a couple that would honor the big screen." - *Lana's White Hot Reads*

"A stunning, suspenseful romance filled with murder, mayhem, secrets, lies, a distrustful hero who will never trust another with his heart and a fearful heroine who only wants love. Can Ronan keep Brandy safe and his heart intact without hurting her or will he lose it all? Loved it!!" - *Goodreads Reviewer*

"Talk about a wild ride. I went through all of the emotions while reading this, once I picked it up I couldn't stop. ... Danger. Suspense. Love? All. Of. It. Definitely a must read!" - *Goodreads Reviewer*

"SINNER'S GAME was a very suspensy + mysterious + sparky + adorable romantic suspense love story!" - *BJ's Book Blog*

SINNER'S GAME

NEW YORK TIMES BESTSELLING AUTHOR

J. KENNER

deepest kiss
entice me
hold me
please me
indulge me
delight me
cherish me
enchant me

STARK SECURITY
shattered with you
shadows of you-short story
broken with you
ruined with you

SEE MORE TITLES AT WWW.JKENNER.COM

SINNER'S GAME

NEW YORK TIMES BESTSELLING AUTHOR

J. KENNER

PROLOGUE

I didn't expect it. The way he looked at me from across
the room. All heat and lust and need. The way he cut a
path through the crowd, ignoring greetings from friends
and waiters offering him champagne on silver trays, his
long legs closing the distance between us. And with each
step he took, my heart pounded harder, my mouth growing
dry with anticipation.

I'd slipped away from the buzz of the reception for a
few moments of peace in the small alcove beneath the
stairs. Three walls forming an indentation with a phone
table and a chair.

But it didn't feel peaceful here now. Instead, it seemed
fraught with the kind of danger I craved, even if that was
something I didn't care to admit.

His gaze locked on me, and I reached back to steady
myself, my knees going weak.

"Brandy," he said, stopping only inches from me, so
close I caught the scent of his cologne, woodsy and mascu-
line. My heart pounded against the thin material of my

fitted maid of honor gown. My entire body tingled, desperate for his touch, and the strength of my desire made me want to race from the room.

But I stayed. Despite my flushed cheeks, I stayed in place. More than that, I looked straight at him, then drew in a shaky breath when I found him looking right back at me, too.

I swallowed, my pulse picking up tempo as Ronan leaned forward, one hand on the wall behind me, just above my shoulder, caging me between him and the small table next to me.

"I've been looking for you."

"Oh? Why?"

His eyes skimmed over me, and the tingle on my skin ramped up, making me feel edgy and shy.

"Because you look stunning," he said in that rough, sexy voice that was like music to me. "And I've drunk just enough that I decided to tell you so."

My stupid cheeks went even hotter, and I bit my lip as I smiled, praying that I didn't sink so low as to actually giggle.

I cleared my throat. "I—um, thank you."

"You're okay?"

"I'm doing good," I said, hating the lie. I was about a million miles from good.

I flashed him another quick smile. I miss you.

That last part, I didn't say. But I wanted to. Instead, I cleared my throat again. "Um, so except for Ellie's pre-book launch party, I haven't seen much of you."

"Work," he said without elaborating. "But no way could I miss today, what with being the best man." He paused, his eyes on my face. "You made me look good, *standing up there," he added, his gravelly voice going soft.*

My blush came back. "I doubt that." I'd had an excellent view of him from where I'd stood by my best friend, Ellie. And he'd glanced at me nine times. Not that I was counting.

"Well, I'm glad you're here now." I sounded like an idiot. Like I didn't even know this man who had once held me close in the protection of his arms. But that was months ago, and our lives were back to normal. Now we're back to just being friends.

I blinked, realizing with horror that I was about to cry. That's what I got for drinking champagne and getting sentimental. But it wasn't just the wedding. It was the loss of something I never even had.

It was the fact that our friends' wedding was over, and the magical lights that filled this room would be gone tomorrow. Everything would. Including the fantasy that Ronan could be something more to me than a friend. Because despite the way my heart had flipped when he'd carried me so gently to safety, I was certain that was all he'd ever be. All he wanted to be.

"I—I should go check in with Ellie," I said. "Maid of honor duty is a heavy burden."

His broad shoulders filled the space, blocking my exit from the tiny alcove. I moved to step around him, suddenly uncomfortable in this small, cramped space. His hand pressed to my shoulder, and I looked up, thinking he was going to move out of my way and say goodbye. Instead, I saw a wild heat in his eyes. A fire that had the power to strip away reason and completely destroy me.

"Brandy."

That was all he said, but I heard the question. Everything in me said I should run. Everything but my heart. Foolishly, I stayed. Even more foolishly, I whispered, "Yes."

The sound had barely left my lips when his mouth closed over mine and his arms pulled me close. We stumbled together until my back was against the wall, our lips locked, our tongues lost in exploration. His hand cupped my head, holding me close as he kissed me wilder and deeper than I'd ever been kissed.

Time stopped. I melted.

I'd had only one real boyfriend, and God knows that didn't end well. But even when things were good between us, I'd never once felt like this. Like my body was molten. Like I was a part of this man in my arms.

Like nothing could ever hurt me again.

I was wrong, of course.

What hurt me the most was him.

"I'm one day home from my honeymoon, about to turn right back around to go to New York, and you're telling me this now?" Devlin said. "Christ, Ronan. This isn't a good time for a vacation. I need you here. We talked about this a month ago. I need you on deck keeping an eye on things."

Devlin Saint leaned back in his desk chair in his huge office at the Devlin Saint Foundation. His green eyes stayed locked on Ronan as he waited for an answer.

With his Brioni suit and regal bearing, Devlin was the epitome of power and control. A man whose public façade hid a much more lethal version of the man.

Another man might be intimidated, but not Ronan Thorne. Devlin was a dangerous man, but no more than Ronan himself. They'd been as close as brothers since their days in the military, and they knew each other's secrets. Most of them, anyway.

"Do you honestly think I'm taking this lightly?" Ronan had been standing, but now he took a seat in one of the guest chairs that fronted Devlin's desk. He leaned back, stretching out his legs, as casual as you please.

A muscle in Devlin's cheek twitched, but he said nothing.

"Things are quiet right now," Ronan continued. "Tamra's more than capable of handling things on both the public side and behind the scenes. And there's not a damn thing on my active docket."

"Tamra's a capable woman," Devlin agreed, referring to the woman who'd been like a mother to both of them for years, and who now ran Devlin's businesses like a general. "But we have active teams spread out over five countries. And while I'm away, it's your job to be on deck."

"From which I'm taking a week of leave. Task someone else to handle it." He noted the way his friend scowled. Not so much with irritation, but with curiosity. "I'm sorry, man. This is my line in the sand. It's non-negotiable. Either I take temporary leave, or I leave for good."

Devlin's brows rose. "It's as important as that?"

"Do you think I'd be sitting here if it wasn't?"

His friend drew in a breath, his shoulders rising and falling. "No, of course you wouldn't. Take as much time as you need."

Ronan nodded, accepting the words as an apology. "Appreciate it. If all goes well, I'll be back in just a couple of days. But this is time sensitive. I've got a lead. If I don't jump now, who knows if I'll get the chance again."

Devlin studied him. "We can get the team on it. Whatever support you need."

"No. This is personal."

"Everything's personal," Devlin said.

"I'm handling it." The words came out sharper than Ronan intended. "Appreciate the offer, but it's not necessary."

Silence hung in the air, and for a moment, Ronan feared he'd have to make good on his threat. Then his friend nodded. "Fair enough. So long as you know I'll always have your back."

"Same." That was the kind of friendship they had, which was probably why guilt was stabbing away at his insides, because he'd never once told Devlin about Sheldon Cartwright or Michelle or anything about what went down all those long years ago.

He caught Devlin's eyes, saw the question brewing on his friend's face, and quickly schooled his expression into blank professionalism. Then he grinned. "Still happily married? Not tired of Ellie yet?"

"Ass," his friend shot back, but the retort was without heat. They both knew that Devlin was blissfully happy. Hell, he practically glowed.

When Ellie had first returned to Devlin's life, Ronan had feared the worst. The woman was a former cop turned reporter, after all. And that was all kinds of danger, especially since Devlin was the central figure in a web of secrets involving dozens of people. To the world, Devlin was nothing more than the multi-billionaire behind the humanitarian Devlin Saint Foundation. The foundation was real enough, its mission important to Devlin and all the staff.

But another organization lurked in the shadows behind the foundation. Devlin had created Saint's Angels to do good in a way that a humanitarian foundation couldn't. The SA was Devlin's passion and Ronan's, too. And he'd worked as Devlin's right hand from the beginning, taking the lead on numerous projects since Devlin had to be the front man for the legitimate foundation that worked hand-in-secret-hand with the shadowy one.

Where the Devlin Saint Foundation could finance rehabilitation programs for victims of trafficking, the ultra-secret Saint's Angels could go after the criminals themselves. Could hunt them down. Could take them out. Could rid the world of its vermin in a way that sanctioned law enforcement could not.

Only a select few knew about the organization, or that Devlin himself was a billionaire vigilante who lived in the shadows, his gun as much of a weapon as his checkbook. Ronan was right there beside him, the Angels' mission as important to him as it was to Devlin or anyone else on the worldwide, secret team.

Secret being the operative word.

Which was why Ronan had been less than enthusiastic when Devlin trusted Ellie and her two closest friends—Brandy and Lamar—with the secret.

Nowadays, Ronan would trust Ellie with his life. More than that, Ronan had to admit that he was a bit jealous of his friend. Not that Ronan was attracted to Ellie; he wasn't. But he couldn't deny the tug at his heart when he saw how happy the two of them were together.

He'd felt that kind of connection to a woman only twice in his life. The first in a past he'd worked hard to bury under a heart that had turned to stone. Or so he thought. Because recently, something dead inside him had started to bloom. Equal parts wonderful and terrifying.

But not something that he could or would cultivate.

Brandy Bradshaw might be temptation personified, but he knew better than to risk everything again. What was that saying? Once burned, twice shy.

He could rejoice in the fact that she'd become a friend. That he genuinely cared for her. That he'd always watch out for her.

But more than that?

Not now. Not ever.

And certainly not while Sheldon Cartwright was alive.

He realized he was looking at his hands, imagining Cartwright's neck in his grip. He lowered them, then shifted his gaze up to meet Devlin's curious eyes.

He cleared his throat. "Anyway, thanks again. I know it's inconvenient. But like I said, everything's taken care of. We're pretty light right now."

"Run me through it."

"A few things we're monitoring, but I don't expect them to pop for at least a month. We're still gathering intel." He took Devlin through most of the list, addressing the details of missions from Texas to Nigeria to Bangladesh without missing a beat.

"All sounds good. That everything?"

"Not quite," Ronan said. "I closed the matter for Colonel Seagrave." He hoped he sounded casual. That mission had gone off without a hitch. But it had also changed everything.

Alexander Seagrave was the commander of the Western Division of the ultra-secret SOC, or Sensitive Operations Command, and he often used black ops money to hire Saint's Angels for specific missions. This one had come in while Devlin was touring Europe with his bride. Identify and terminate the leader of a terrorist cell that was bankrolling their weapon purchases by kidnapping teenage girls to sell as sex slaves. Sadly, an all too familiar story.

Ronan had found him, followed him, and assassinated him. A sanctioned hit, but one that would blow back on Ronan if his finger on the trigger was ever known. The agency damn sure wouldn't claim knowledge.

He wasn't concerned about the risk. None of Saint's Angels were. They'd joined the organization because they believed in its mission to make the world a better place despite going directly against the establishment's rules.

Devlin had never shied away from telling Ronan about the horrors in his life that had led up to the decision to create the SA. His vile father and the people he'd hurt or killed. The empire in which Devlin had been raised. The lies he'd lived with.

Ronan knew all of Devlin's shit; it was only fair that Ronan should tell Devlin what he'd learned on the Seagrave mission and why he had to take time off.

And yet he couldn't say the horrible truth out loud. Because to do that would be to admit his role in Michelle's death all those years ago. Not to mention his own shame in not avenging her back when he'd had the chance.

Later. After he'd made it right—at least as right as it could be with Michelle long in a grave. Later he'd tell his friend everything, but right now, he needed to focus. Because Sheldon Cartwright had resurfaced. And no way was Ronan missing the opportunity to hunt the son-of-a-bitch down and put a bullet through his brain.

He drew in a breath. "Like I said, everything's running smoothly. And I won't be gone long."

"Good. And take as much time as you need. I was an ass earlier. I'd say it won't happen again, but I hate lying to my best friend."

Ronan managed a chuckle despite feeling that kick in the gut again. "Yeah, well, maybe one day I'll tell you."

"Or maybe you won't."

Some of the tension left his body. It was good to have a friend who understood him. He pushed up out of the chair.

"Heading out now?" Devlin asked, also rising.

"No. Flight's at eight tonight. You?"

"Los Angeles tonight, then heading to New York at the crack of dawn tomorrow. And why don't you just take one of the jets?" Devlin asked, referring to the charter fleet he personally owned, which was sometimes utilized by the Angels.

"Appreciate it, but I'm good." Sheldon Cartwright was part of a different life. The final piece before Ronan could put the past behind him. Now wasn't the time to start commingling his two worlds.

Devlin nodded slowly, clearly trying to figure Ronan out. "Fair enough, but if there is anything you need, don't hesitate."

"I know that, too."

He stood almost at attention as Devlin's steely gaze studied him, but Ronan knew he wouldn't find his answers. Ronan was too damn good at hiding them.

After a moment, Devlin's shoulders relaxed. "Want

to come over later for a quick drink before you head to the airport? Ellie'd love to see you."

"Can't. I promised Brandy I'd fix her sink."

"Oh?" The pitch of Devlin's voice rose. "How interesting."

"Mind out of the gutter, Saint," Ronan said, wishing his own thoughts hadn't gone in that direction, too. "She's got a drip."

Devlin grinned, and Ronan scowled. "No." He said the word firmly, as much for himself as for Devlin.

"No to the gutter humor? Or no to Brandy?" Devlin asked.

"Both."

Devlin circled his desk, curiosity in his eyes. "That's another explanation you owe me."

"Owe?"

"Another thing I'm curious about," Devlin amended.

"What's that?" Ronan asked, though he knew perfectly well.

Devlin tilted his head, almost as if he was surprised that Ronan was opening that door. Honestly, Ronan was too.

"All right," Devlin said. "I want to know why, in all the time I've known you, I've never seen you date."

"Sure you have."

"No. I've seen you pick up women in bars. I've seen you leave with them. I'm pretty damn certain you fuck them, and I know you have a membership at Masque," Devlin added, referring to an LA-based sex club where Ronan went when he needed to blow off steam. "But I've never seen you in a relationship."

"I already knew you were observant. But what's your point?"

"One, I'm curious as to why, but that's my problem." Devlin leaned against his desk. "You hardly owe me an explanation. But on the side that does touch me, Ellie and I both thought there might be something going on between you and Brandy."

"You thought wrong." Brandy Bradshaw might have wormed her way into his fantasies, but she wasn't the kind of woman who could decorate his bed with no strings attached. She deserved a hell of a lot more than that.

Strings.

The word stuck with him, dredging up buried fantasies from his subconscious. That innocent, scarred woman bound and begging for him. And Ronan teasing her mercilessly, letting the pleasure build until she pleaded with him to please, please, please let her come.

No.

Not her. Never her.

She was better than that. Better than him, a man who found pleasure in a string of women who could make him forget. Women he paid handsomely in order to ensure both obedience and discretion. Women he could push, who understood his need to face all those dark places. To go right up to the edge of their limits.

But actually getting close to a woman? Opening his heart and settling into a relationship? Not happening. As far as Ronan was concerned, that was the hardest limit of all.

"Like you said, Devlin. You know me, even if you don't know the why of it."

"Fair enough. But I also know what I saw at the wedding."

Ronan felt his chest tighten. He hadn't realized anyone had seen them in the alcove. Those few blissful moments he desperately wanted to regret but didn't.

"Yeah, well, it was a mistake. Weddings and wine. A bad combination."

"I'll never regret my wedding," Devlin said. "But I will regret my wedding day if it sets off a chain reaction that hurts that woman. Brandy is like a sister to Ellie. She's family. We're friends, you and I, and nothing will ever change that. Hell, you're like a brother. But I promise you, Ronan, if you hurt her, we're going to have a problem."

"You think I don't know that? I already told you it was a mistake. It's not going to happen again. There's nothing between us, and there never will be." He met his friend's eyes. "We both know that a woman like Brandy deserves a hell of a lot better than a man like me."

CHAPTER TWO

"**B**randy!"

I come to a stop at the sound of my name, then almost fall on my face as Jake, my thirteen-year-old Labrador who's convinced he's still a puppy, continues to gambol down the street. I tug on his leash, then turn to find Inez Santos waving at me from across Pacific Avenue, the main east-west street in the Laguna Cortez Arts District.

She's standing in the doorway of her boutique, The Escape, and we wait for a gap in the light traffic, then hurry to meet her.

"Hey, Jake," she says, crouching down and ruffling his fur. He flops on the ground, licks her hand, and generally acts like he's in heaven. "I don't mean to waylay you if you're in a hurry, but I wasn't sure if you'd seen the new display."

She rises as she speaks, then gestures to the store's huge display window. I gasp, one hand going to my mouth as I take in the absolutely breathtaking sight. "Inez, it's incredible."

"Not it. *You.* Those bags are all you."

The window is entirely devoted to BB Bags, my somewhat eponymous handbag business since it's named after me, Brandy Bradshaw. Or my initials, anyway.

She has all my styles on their own pedestals—the waxed canvas bags that are my original design, the cross-body bags, even the fancy cocktail bags I've recently added. Those she has in the center, and the lighting is set to hit them so that the shimmery material sparkles.

"I love it," I tell her. "You make me look good."

"Please. These bags sell themselves. Stock's already getting low." She grins, her pale blue eyes crinkling as she pulls me in for a motherly hug. "I'm so proud. And did I hear you've got a booth at the Expo?"

I nod happily, and she squeals.

"That is amazing. And coming up fast," she adds. "You must be so excited."

"I am. And slightly terrified."

"Nonsense. The Southern California Fashion Expo has launched so many careers. You're going to be the next big thing." Inez is about twenty years older than me and in incredible shape, with close-cropped short hair that would look horrible on me, but which she totally rocks. Inez was the first storeowner to stock my bags, and her belief that I'll be a huge success has never faltered. Which is a heck of a lot more than I can say about my parents.

"Thank you so much for everything," I tell her sincerely. "You've been my fairy godmother."

"I like the sound of that." She cocks her head toward

the door to her boutique. "Time for a coffee? I bought an espresso machine for the store. Oh, wait. I forgot you don't do coffee. Well, I still have a kettle for tea."

"Thanks anyway, but I can't stay. I want to get home and wash off the beach." I gesture to my capris, my exposed calves covered in sand. "I'm supposed to meet Ronan at four. He's going to fix my sink."

Her mouth tugs into a grin. "Is he?"

I roll my eyes. "You're not original. Ellie said the same thing when we had drinks earlier."

"I'm sorry I missed her. I want to hear all about her honeymoon."

"Blissful," I say. "I'm pretty sure she's still floating on a cloud."

"As she should be. Devlin's a wonderful man. Easy on the eyes, too."

I laugh. That's for sure. And Devlin is wonderful. But I can't help but wonder if Inez would think so if she knew his secrets. His and Ronan's and the rest of Saint's Angels.

As if she's reading my mind, she asks, "And Ronan?"

I pretend not to understand. "He took pity on me. I tried to fix it myself, but the stupid leak keeps coming back."

"I was asking about the two of you. He's easy on the eyes, too, and I saw you chatting at the wedding. Did I see sparks?"

"No sparks," I lie, grateful that she didn't see us in the alcove. If she had, she'd know that there were so many sparks we could have burned the place down. At the very least, I'd thought we'd ignited a fire. But apparently, I was dead wrong.

"Really? There's nothing between the two of you?"

I shake my head, smiling like everything is peachy keen. "We're just friends. Honestly, I'm surprised you think there's more. Sparks? Not even." I hope I sound fascinated and surprised. But since my acting skills are nil, I probably sound cornered.

If she notices my discomfort, she doesn't mention it. Just tells me we'll do tea and espresso some other time, then promises to tell me how customers react to the window display before waving me on my way.

Jake's already with the program, and he starts trotting east toward home. I shoot Inez a final smile, then let him tug me along, my canine escort leading me past all the cute boutiques, art galleries, restaurants, and gift stores that line this well-traveled street that forms the heart of our town.

The shopping area ends where Pacific Avenue terminates at Sunset Parkway. But across the street, Copper Canyon Drive continues to wind up into the hills toward my house. We head that direction, Jake leading the way. At our lazy pace, it takes about fifteen minutes to reach my street, and we pick up speed as we turn the corner, because now Jake's eager to get home.

We're four houses away when I notice the Range Rover parked in my drive. I frown, then check my watch. I'm not supposed to meet Ronan for another thirty minutes, and yet I'm positive that's him. Which means that instead of grabbing a quick shower and putting on fresh makeup, he gets to see me shiny and sweaty.

Yippee.

For a moment, I consider calling him and telling him that I'm still out running errands and asking if we can push our sink repair appointment by an hour. Then I can linger in the bushes so that he doesn't see me when he drives away. Because seeing Ronan while I look this scrungy is really not high on my list.

Which, of course, is stupid. We're only friends. He's certainly made that clear enough. Heck, it wasn't that long ago I saw him with that redhead in the alley, and wasn't that a hard dose of reality?

I scowl at the memory—her with her back to the brick wall, and him with his arms caging her in. And—

Stop.

The word fills my head, final and resolute. I nod with corresponding firmness. I'm going to unsee that moment. I'm going to completely forget about it. Ronan Thorne with that woman is *not* a topic I need to think about, because there's absolutely nothing between us, no matter how much I might have hoped there would be. And, dang it, I really had hoped there would be.

Except no, I didn't.

Because every time I get involved with a guy, it all goes to hell. And I really don't want to lose Ronan's friendship.

But I do want more.

I draw a calming breath, then sternly tell myself that want is not the issue. I want to eat massive amounts of chocolate on a daily basis. I don't because I know it's not good for me.

Except, okay, yeah, some days I do.

Even so, the concept still applies. I may want Ronan in theory, but I also know that anything between us will end badly. It always does with men. I'll freeze up and be all weird about sex because that's who I am. He'll hurt me somehow. Maybe not physically, but there will be pain. Because that's what always happens. And it only gets worse.

After all, things went wrong with my last boyfriend, and I almost ended up dead.

For my own safety, I should probably just stay celibate.

And yet there's still that lingering *want* hiding deep in my soul. A craving that I can't shake but have to ignore. Because at the end of the day, I'm not a stupid woman. I'm also not a masochist. But getting involved with Ronan would mean getting hurt. That's the pattern, and there's no reason to expect it would change. Isn't the definition of insanity doing the same thing over and over but expecting a different result?

And besides, all of my musings are moot anyway. Because despite that blissful night in the alcove, Ronan has never, ever made even a hint of a suggestion of a repeat. It was a one-off. A drunken wedding kiss. And a harsh reminder of why I need to keep my distance from men. Nothing good comes of getting close.

Well, nothing except the feel of his lips on mine and his arm around my waist and his large hand cupping the back of my head.

I close my eyes and sigh, lost in this memory that I want to forget. Because no matter how much I tell myself I shouldn't want—don't want—anything to happen with Ronan, that is all a big, fat lie.

"Brandy?"

I jump, then open my eyes to find the man in question standing in front of me, Jake's leash in his hand and Jake himself curled up at Ronan's feet.

"Are you okay?" His blue eyes are focused right on me, and for a moment, I lose myself in them.

"Brandy?" he repeats. His golden blond hair is just long enough to curl a bit, and his beard stubble tempts my fingers.

I can't seem to stop staring.

Stop. Staring.

I shake myself, my self-issued order ringing in my head as my cheeks go hot. "Sorry. What? Oh, yes. I'm fine. I was just thinking."

"Thinking?" His brows rise as the corner of his mouth twitches, and darn it, I actually swoon a bit. There's just something about this man. Not his looks— although they definitely don't hurt. He's tall and broad-shouldered with a chiseled face that's not too perfect, and all the better for his rough edges.

Ellie once described him as a Nordic god, and that sounds about right to me. Either that or an action hero.

Then again, considering his day job as an independent security consultant and his secret vocation as one of Saint's Angels, he truly is the latter. Just in real life and not on a movie screen.

Bottom line is that although Ronan is very, very easy on the eyes, what I find most attractive is that underneath all that dangerous muscle is a guy with a genuinely good heart and a very sweet demeanor. The guy who so gently carried me out of that horrible underground chamber, then tended my wounds and promised that everything would be okay. The man who whispered that I was beautiful at Ellie and Devlin's wedding, and that all he could think about was kissing me.

The guy who makes my heart flutter and my fingers ache to touch him even though I know I shouldn't.

The guy who right now is silently grinning at me, as if he knows exactly what I'm thinking. And, yeah, he probably does.

I clear my throat. "Yeah. Just thinking. About work." I expect him to call me on it. Want him to, even. Because despite the very long lectures I keep giving myself, deep down I still want to kindle this attraction. And I'm certain he wants the same.

Which is why I'm ridiculously disappointed when all he says is, "I guess that means work's going well. Congratulations. I saw the new display in the window at The Escape earlier today."

"Thanks." I swallow as I readjust my fantasies, reminding myself that this is good. I don't actually want anything to happen between me and Ronan. Didn't I just give myself that lecture? Am I really that wishy-washy?

Apparently, yes, I am.

I force myself to smile at him. "You're early."

"A little. I have a plane to catch soon."

"Oh. So you're going to fix my sink and run? I was thinking about making cookies."

"I'd love that. Raincheck?"

I force myself not to be disappointed. "Sure. And thanks for grabbing Jake. I didn't realize I'd dropped the leash."

"Well, you were deep in thought. About work," he adds. What I hear is *about me*.

I manage a little shrug. "Lots on my mind. Oh! I saw Mr. Big," I say, referring to my mysterious landlord.

"Yeah?" he asks as we fall in step together, heading

the short distance to the house. "How did you know it was him? I thought you'd never met the man."

He's right. I have a unique deal in that in exchange for ridiculously cheap rent, I act as a house manager. The only downside is that on the few occasions he comes to town and wants the house, I get a call from the property manager and have to vacate for up to a week.

It's all very mysterious and weird, but I assume he's some sort of celebrity and really wants his privacy. Considering the fab house, minuscule rent, great view, and South Orange County location, it's a small price to pay.

"I was outside Pacific Property earlier, and some guy came out. I didn't think anything of it until he started staring at me, then asked what I was doing there. He was almost yelling. It was freaky."

I reach for Jake's leash, and when he passes it to me, our hands brush. And right then I wish I'd paid more attention when my dad did repairs around the house. Because then I could fix my own stupid sink and not have to spend the next hour or so feeling like an awkward thirteen-year-old girl, tongue-tied around the cute guy.

I realize he's no longer beside me, and I pause, then turn around to find his eyes on me, a curious expression on his face. My cheeks go warm even as my whole body gets all shivery. This is it. This is when he finally says something about that kiss. That strange and wonderful kiss that has occupied too much of my brain space lately.

"Ronan?" I ask when he continues to just stand there.

"Where did you go?"

I blink, totally confused. "Go? We're going to the house."

He chuckles, the sound low and sexy, and I hate myself because I cannot shut this attraction off. "I meant in your head. You wandered off somewhere, but you were telling me about Mr. Big."

"Oh. Right." Stupid, stupid. "Had an idea for a new bag design. Got distracted. Anyway," I rush on before he can challenge my crappy excuse, "after chewing me out, he just walked away. And since he'd come from the property manager's office, I walked over and asked Gail who the weird guy was. She told me that he's my landlord."

"Seriously?"

I cringe. "Honestly, I think I liked it better not knowing how weird the guy is. I mean, why was he yelling at me?"

"Probably thought you were someone else. He doesn't know you any more than you know him, right?"

I shrug. "I guess that's true. Honestly, I never thought about it."

"Odd, though," he says, his brow furrowed.

I snort. "Which part exactly?"

"Just wondering why he's even in town. Were you supposed to have vacated so he has the house?"

"No." I frown because he has a point. "At least, I never got told that I needed to vacate." I'm actually a bit surprised that Ronan knows the details of how my rental agreement works. Yes, Ellie and Devlin know. And Devlin is Ronan's closest friend. But there's no reason that my living arrangement would come up in casual conversation.

Which makes me wonder if Ronan asked. And that makes me wonder why he would ask. And that makes me wonder about things I have no business wondering about.

I clear my throat, clearing my random thoughts in the process. "For all I know, he has other rental properties here. Or he was just driving through town and thought he'd check in. I don't even know why I'm thinking about it. I mean, if I hadn't asked Gail, I wouldn't have even known it was him."

"True enough," he says. We've reached the house, and now he stands off to the side as I fumble with the keypad lock. I push the door open, and once Jake's bolted through, I put my back against the siding so Ronan can enter first. He hesitates, though, and I think that he's letting me go first. So I step over the threshold at the same moment he does.

Our shoulders brush, and I stumble over my own feet. He catches me by the elbow to steady me, pulling me close as he does. For a moment, I'm mere inches from him, his hand pressed against my lower back as I regain my balance.

I'm tall, but I still have to look up to meet his eyes. When I do, I find him looking down at me, his ocean-blue eyes seeming to reflect my own desire right back at me.

I want to say something. To ask. I want to know what happened. Or, more accurately, why nothing happened after that kiss. But even though I open my mouth to speak, all I say is, "Ronan?"

A flurry of expressions crosses his face as he releases my arms, but I don't have the skill to interpret them. Frustration, maybe. Lust, definitely. Sadness, too, I think. But I'm not certain. How can I be certain?

"Ronan, I—"

"We should talk." His voice is low, as if we were in a sacred place. That's good, I think. Because surely that means we'll get to the truth. My fear, though, is that it's the truth that's going to hurt me.

I say none of that; I just nod as he gestures for me to go ahead. I do, moving down the entrance hall that opens onto the large living area. I shift to the left, walking alongside the pass-through bar that separates the large kitchen from the living area. My plan is to go grab a couple of water bottles, but before I manage another step, Jake bounds by, then starts barking and low-growling at something on the floor in front of the sofa.

From where I'm standing, I can't see what it is, as the floor is blocked by the sofa back. But I immediately recoil as my eyes go to Ronan. "We had mice last year," I say. "If it's another dead mouse, please tell me you'll pick it up."

He chuckles, and that breaks the tension a little. He brushes past me toward Jake, who's completely losing his mind, and I follow. Then Ronan stops on a dime. "Brandy, don't—"

"What?" I ask as I start to step around him. He grabs me, but it's too late. I've seen it. The man. The body. "That's Mr. Big," I whisper. And he's sprawled out dead in front of my couch, a bullet hole right between his eyes.

CHAPTER THREE

"Wait, wait, wait," my best friend Ellie Holmes—now Ellie Saint—says, leaning forward in that *I'm going to get deep into your thoughts* reporter way that she has. She pushes her wineglass aside, then props her elbows on our small, round table. She steeples her forefingers under her chin, her brown eyes boring down on me. "You're really and truly telling me that nothing has happened between you and Ronan since my wedding? Nothing?"

I lift my shoulders in a shrug, then focus on my glass of Chardonnay, wishing I'd ordered something tall and fruity so I'd have a straw to toy with.

Instead, I bend down to pet Jake. He snuffles, then licks my hand before settling his head on his paws and drifting off again.

We're on the patio at The Station, a sidewalk café on Pacific Avenue, the main thoroughfare in the Laguna

Cortez Arts District, and this is the first time we've had a chance to catch up since she and Devlin got back from their honeymoon.

"Are you serious?" she continues, in the kind of incredulous tone she'd use to challenge someone who'd just announced that an alien spaceship had landed on the beach. "I mean, you two kissed. I saw you, remember? You and Ronan in the alcove by the stairs. And it wasn't just a friendly peck, either. That kiss made *me* blush. And you know that's saying a lot."

My cheeks heat, and I look around, wondering how many people are tuned in to this particular conversation. "Oversharing much?"

"Come on, Brandy. What gives?" She tucks a dark brown curl behind her ear as she studies me. "It's not just the kiss that got me thinking that way, and you know it. I've seen the way he looks at you."

I shrug. "He rescued me." Ellie had been the real target on that horrible day, but I'd been in the wrong place at the wrong time. I fight a sigh, warding off the memory of how safe I'd felt in Ronan's arms when he'd carried me to freedom. "And you know I don't want to talk about that."

Ellie reaches across and puts her hand on mine. "I wasn't," she says gently. "I saw the way he looked at you *before*. And the way he's looked at you since."

I shift uncomfortably. Ellie may be my best friend, but that doesn't mean I want her dissecting my sex life— or lack thereof—at a sidewalk café.

She leans back with a frustrated sigh. "It's just that I really expected to come back and find out that you two were a couple. What happened? Were there not sparks?

Was he—oh, please tell me he's not an asshole with women. I mean, I had my doubts about the guy at first, but he's won me over. If he's a jerk like some of the other guys you've—"

I hold up my hand to cut her off. I don't have the best track record with men, mostly because it's rare to find a guy who can deal with my issues. But that never came up with Ronan. Probably because we never even got close to an issue-y place.

"Nothing happened," I tell her again, speaking slowly and clearly as if that will make a difference. "I told you. It was just a drunken moment during a celebration. All sorts of crazy things happen at weddings."

"True. But you also said you're seeing him later today."

"Hello? We're friends, remember? You think either one of us would let a stupid kiss get in the way?"

"So that's all it was? A stupid kiss?" Her eyes narrow as if she's going to challenge me, and I really don't want her challenging me. Because then I might have to admit to my best friend—not to mention myself—how much I wish that kiss had never happened. Because all it did was make me wish for things I know I will never have.

"That's all it was," I say, then take a sip of wine because my mouth is so dry.

"No sparks, no nothing?"

She sounds so disappointed that I almost correct her. Because honestly, there were plenty of sparks. But that's not something I'm going to share with Ellie. Not right now, anyway. Probably not ever. I don't want her telling Devlin and him telling Ronan. Because how awkward would that be? Me unable to get the man out of my thoughts, and him having moved on without a care in the world, thinking it was just one of those wedding things. A secret kiss with no strings and no purpose.

Good grief, I sound like a high school girl.

I give myself a stern mental shake, then draw a breath. "For the last time, it was no big deal. And, yes, he's coming by today, but that's because he's a nice guy and he's going to fix my faucet. And no," I add, "that's not a euphemism. End of story."

She holds up her hands. "Sorry. I didn't mean to push, really. It's just that ... well, honestly, I was surprised it took until the wedding for him to kiss you."

I'd been surprised, too, actually. Not that I'm going to admit that right now. Instead, I down the last of the wine, even though I'm a lightweight and know I'll feel it. "We're friends," I repeat. "That's all."

I don't add that even though I'm wildly attracted to him, I'd be crazy to get involved with anyone. At a few years shy of thirty, I'm hardly a poster child for success in the world of dating, I've got issues coming out of my ears, and no matter how attracted I might be to Ronan Thorne, I'm a billion percent positive that nothing's ever going to happen.

"Do you want me to talk to Devlin? He could have a chat with Ronan. See where his head is."

"You know we're not in high school anymore, right? Much less junior high. And I sincerely doubt that the same Devlin Saint who runs a multi-billion dollar phil-anthropic organization, not to mention an ultra-secret side hustle," I add in a low whisper, "is going to want to gossip about his best friend's love life."

Her shoulders dip as she sighs. "I know. I know. It's

just that I'm really happy now. Marriage is amazing. I want you to be happy, too."

I melt a little at that. Ellie's been my best friend since childhood, and though my high school years were no picnic, she truly drew the short straw in the life-and-family game. But everything's turned around, and now that she's blissfully, happily, gloriously in love, she wants the same for me.

I reach down to scratch behind Jake's ears as he snorts with pleasure. "I love you for wanting me to be happy, but you forget that not only am I happy, but I'm already in a new relationship that's taking off like gangbusters. And I'm not the kind of girl to have two luuuuvers," I add in a voice that comes out like a mix of a film noir heroine and a sarcastic teenager.

Her forehead crinkles with confusion, then her face clears as she laughs. "Okay. Fair enough. Can't have you dividing your attention. BB Bags deserves all your energy. For now," she adds in a *this isn't over* tone.

"For now," I agree, simply to get her to drop the subject. "And just so we're clear, that means no playing matchmaker. Not with Ronan. Not with anyone."

She starts to speak, but I don't give her a chance to get the words out.

"I'm serious. It would stress me out too much. The business is really taking off, and I don't have time for anything else. Which is just as well since we both know that I'm cursed in the relationship department."

"Stop thinking like that," Ellie says.

"Fine. Fine. But it's a moot point because Ronan is firmly in the friend zone, and there's no one else on the horizon, and I am not looking," I add, pointing my finger at her to make sure we're one hundred percent clear. "I have a booth at the Expo, and getting ready for that has my full focus."

"Hell, yeah, it does. I know how huge that is."

She's right. The Expo can open doors to clients and funders, and these days I alternate between completely nervous and totally psyched. It's coming up fast, and everything has to be perfect.

"Which is why," Ellie begins as she pushes back from the table, "I'll put a pin in the matchmaking until after the Expo."

"That is not what I meant."

She winks, then tosses a twenty on the table. "Wait for me here or come with?" Her new property manager—who also works with my landlord—is one block over, off the main shopping street.

"I'm going to finish my wine and check my messages, then we'll meet you there. You're still coming with us to the beach, right? You have to. We've barely had the chance to catch up and you're leaving again in, what? Tomorrow?"

"Driving to LA tonight for a late-night show," she says, "then flying to New York at the crack of dawn. But it's only a few nights. Still, it'll be nice to be in Manhattan again."

"And for a TV interview. It's ultra-cool. And I didn't know about the LA one. That's amazing."

"They squeezed me in as an afterthought because someone had to cancel. Honestly, I don't know if any of anybody even wants me to talk about the book or if they'll just focus the camera at Devlin and sigh."

"Well, he's pretty damn pretty," I say, which is the

understatement of all eternity. "But seriously, you are not an afterthought. And of course they want you both. The reporter and her subject—and now they're married. It's a great story from all sides."

"The journalist in me has to agree."

"Who would have guessed one little writing assignment would lead to a book and the love of your life?" I wonder if anything in my work life will ever lead to romance, but I doubt it. My work making purses and totes is a long way from Ellie's as a reporter. Especially since her research uncovered all manner of intriguing secrets.

Honestly, I'm not sure I'm wired to survive the kind of drama that Ellie and Devlin went through to get where they are now. But the truth is, I've never seen her happier, and I can't help but be a little jealous.

Ellie rises, then slings her purse over her shoulder. "Meet me at the management office, and I'll walk with you as far as the foundation," she says, referring to the Devlin Saint Foundation created by her husband and located a few blocks away on the beach side of the Coast Highway.

"Sounds good. See you in a bit."

As she heads out, I pull out my phone, then speed dial Cara, an old friend in Los Angeles who I recently hired as a virtual assistant. She answers on the first ring. "Hey, just going through the replies you sent to all my messages."

"All good," I say. "But I realized that we don't have the banner for the Expo yet. Can you check on it?"

"Already done," she tells me. "Tracking app says it's arriving at your place tomorrow."

"You're the best. Any calls?" The moment the words leave my mouth, I cringe. Because what I really want to know is if Ronan called. But only to confirm he's coming by to fix the drippy sink. Not because the talk with Ellie put him at the forefront of my mind.

"I haven't checked yet. I can call in and do that right now if you want to hold."

"No, that's okay. I'll either call in myself or listen when I get home." I decided early on to have a landline and an answering machine for the business. "Anyone who really needs me has my cell," I add, even as I silently assure myself that Ronan would have texted or called my mobile phone if he had to cancel. That he hasn't is a good sign, and I'm just being paranoid thinking that he'd blow me off by leaving a message at my work number.

Business handled, I finish my wine, leave an extra ten for a tip, then stand up. I feel weirdly powerful. Like I've finally got a grasp on the world.

Not my love life, maybe, but so what? I've got a career that's not only taking off but that I'm managing like a boss, friends I adore, and a dog who forgives all my quirks and oddities.

Why complicate all that goodness with a guy?

CHAPTER FOUR

I'm about half a block away from the restaurant when I realize I've got a crumpled-up napkin in my hand. I start to shove it into my purse, then see a trash can straight ahead. I hurry there, Jake padding beside me, and give it a toss. The wind catches it, and it falls onto the ground. I sigh, then start to turn around. Before I manage that though, I hear a deep voice. "Sorry, ma'am. I'm going to have to arrest you for littering."

I continue my turn, irritation flashing for a split second. By the time I'm facing him, though, I know exactly who's spoken. "Gee, officer, maybe we could work something out? Brownies for life? Cupcakes with thick chocolate frosting? Blueberry muffins?"

I swear he starts to drool. I know all of Detective Lamar Gage's favorites, after all.

"Well, it goes against my sworn oath as a detective, but yeah, I'll let you off for a basket of blueberry muffins," he says as he pulls me into a bear hug.

He's tall, but so am I, and I rest my chin on his

shoulder as I breathe deep, smelling his cologne, then push away, giving him a light smack on his broad chest. "You jerk. I thought you were out of town. You could have had lunch with us. You just missed Ellie."

Ellie and Lamar went to the Irvine Police Academy together and immediately bonded. She jokes that it's because she was the only woman and he was the only Black recruit, but I know it was because their personalities mesh so well. Both are smart and dedicated and completely loyal. She dragged Lamar into our friend circle, and we became a trifecta, with Lamar and me growing even closer when Ellie moved to New York to go to journalism school.

"I was in LA this morning interviewing a witness," he says, "but it took no time at all. The guy knows nothing. So now I'm back. Sorry I missed lunch." He glances down at Jake. "Heading to the B.E.A.C.H.?"

Jake's ears perk up, and I roll my eyes. "Don't bother spelling. He understands it all. Yeah, but I have to hit Pacific Property first to grab Ellie. Walk with me? Then you can go with us to the B-place later?"

"Wish I could, but I'll walk with you for a bit."

"Heading back to the station?"

"No. I'm off for the day. But I've got a late lunch date that may turn into post lunch fun, if you know what I mean."

As we walk, I give him a sidelong glance. "I know exactly what that means. And who's getting lucky?"

He chuckles. "Potentially getting lucky. And other than me? It's Darrell."

"Darrell? Someone new? Is it serious?" I hope it is. He's been mourning his former girlfriend for a while, and while I totally get it, I'm sad for my friend and want him happy again.

Lamar Gage is one of the coolest people I've ever met. A former child star, he gave it up as he got older because he wanted to be a cop—and he's a damn good one. I don't know how his parents—both tied-in to Hollywood—feel about that, but as far as I'm concerned, Lamar is living his best life.

"Not serious," he says, answering my question about Darrell. "I'm not ready for that. But he's a friend and there are benefits." He says the last with a smirk on his lips and a gleam in his eyes.

I sigh. In the time I've known him, Lamar has had more friends-with-benefits than actual relationships. "Honestly, I don't know how you do that."

"Well, there's this anatomical response. And just because we're both guys, I assure you the parts match—"

"You're hilarious. I mean, I don't know how you can casually sleep with someone. I don't get that at all."

He hooks his arm around my shoulders. "That's because you're special, Brandy. Don't let anyone try to shape you into anything else."

I hip-check him like he's being an ass, but the truth is I appreciate what he says. There are times that I wish I was made differently. More like Ellie who, before she settled down with Devlin, swore she was having a great time seeing as many people as she wanted to.

Of course, I knew that wasn't the truth. In her whole adult life, she never had a relationship before Devlin, just sex. For the buzz, for venting frustrations. Sometimes just for fun.

I spent many years worrying about my bestie. But

looking back, maybe that's my problem. I long for the deeper stuff, but at the same time, it terrifies me. That getting close part. The inevitable revelation of all my tragic secrets. Not that my terror is the only thing stopping me from getting close. The truth is that most guys aren't interested in dating after I make it clear there won't be any sex until there's something deeper between us.

Maybe I need to be more like Lamar—only in it for the fun.

Or maybe he's right, and I should stick to being me.

I guess at the end of the day, I don't have much of a choice. *Me* is all I've got.

I must make a face, because Lamar says, "What?"

I shrug. He studies me for a moment, then says, "Speaking of non-casual sex, what's going on in your love life?"

This time I wrinkle my nose. "Not a thing."

He stops on the sidewalk, and I have to tug Jake to a halt so as to not get too far away. "Oh, no," I say. "Not you, too."

"Me, too, what?"

I shoot him a scowl. "According to Ellie, the whole world seems to have been on the Brandy and Ronan train. Except for Brandy and Ronan."

"So there's no train?"

"Not one that's left the station. We're just friends," I add, over Lamar's snort of laughter.

He starts walking again, and Jake and I fall in step beside him. "And that's a good thing?"

"Moot point since it's the only thing."

He pauses, looking me up and down, his gaze so appraising I actually blush.

"What?" I demand.

His smile is slow and easy. "He doesn't know what he's missing, Brandy Bradshaw."

I squeeze his hand. "If I haven't told you lately, I really do love you."

"Yeah?" he quips. "Then why are you lusting after Ronan?"

"Jerk."

He chuckles as we continue on, now only one block away from Pacific Property. "Do you still need help getting your booth together? You know I'm cheap labor and—"

"What?" I ask, stopping beside him.

"Nothing. Just remembered something at work." He starts moving again. "Let's just keep walking. We don't want you to be late."

"There is no late. I'm just going there to meet Ellie. Lamar, slow down." I'm practically jogging to keep up with him. "What's the big hurry?"

But he doesn't have to answer. I see it all on my own, and I stop dead, Jake tugging at his leash.

Ronan.

He's in the shadow of an alley across the street, his back to me, but easy enough to recognize. He's standing in front of a woman with flowing auburn hair. He's caging her in, his hand against the brick of the building wall. I'm seeing him mostly from behind, but I can see part of the side of his face. He looks serious, and cozy, and his face is very close to hers.

"Brandy. Let's just go."

"Is he ... Who is that? Is he dating someone?" I try to sound casual, but I feel anything but. As much as I might say I don't want a relationship—as much as I swear that I certainly don't want Ronan—apparently that's all a big, fat lie.

I look up at Lamar, my head spinning as I try to put this all together. "We're friends. Why would I not know if he was seeing someone?"

Lamar looks like a kid who just lost his puppy. "Sweetie, I don't think he's seeing her."

"What do you mean?"

I watch as he draws in a breath, then I glance back at Ronan again.

I snap my attention back to Lamar; I don't want to see Ronan with that woman. "Lamar," I urge. "What's going on?"

"Brandy, honey, I know her. I've arrested her twice."

Slowly, I shake my head. I have no idea what he's talking about.

"She's a call girl, Bran. High class, sure, but Jacey Kane's a prostitute."

CHAPTER FIVE

"A call girl?" I repeat, forcing myself not to tug away from Lamar's arm so that I can look back at the woman in question.

But Lamar keeps with the forward motion, and that's fine. Because, honestly, I don't want to see that, anyway. No thank you very much.

Except now I'm wondering if Ronan saw us as we passed by. And if so, what on earth will I say when I see him next?

Nothing. It's none of my business.

"You okay?"

"Me? This has nothing to do with me. But I do need to hurry. Ellie, then the beach. And you have your date."

"I can reschedule if you need to talk."

I reach out and squeeze his hand. "I have the greatest friends in the world. Thanks. But I'm fine. Really."

He eyes me like he knows better.

"Really," I repeat.

Another moment passes, then he nods slowly. "Okay, but if you need to talk—you need anything—you call me."

"You got it. And if your lunch date doesn't turn into after-lunch fun," I add, grinning as I mimic his earlier words, "you should pop by. Ronan's coming at four to fix my sink." I try to sound casual. "If you come by then, we can all have a drink. Maybe I'll make cookies."

He hooks an arm around my shoulder and gives me a sideways hug. "Hard to turn down homemade cookies. I'll try and make it."

"Cool. No big deal if you can't."

"You're really okay?"

"Fine," I say, even though it's not entirely true. But I *should* be fine, so the answer is close enough to the truth.

He gives me another squeeze, then heads off. I watch him go, hoping he's really going to come by.

Before, the thought of being with Ronan made me nervous in the good kind of way.

Now I'm afraid I'll be a stuttering mess. Either that or break out into a lecture on the stupidity of sleeping with sex workers. Which would be bad since it's none of my business. Not even slightly.

Which begs the question of why he is so completely filling my head. And freakin' Jacey Kane, too.

A call girl? Seriously?

I draw a deep breath, then take in the area around me, trying to force him from my thoughts by filling my head with something completely different.

This street runs parallel to Pacific Avenue on the south side and is lined with equally charming stores, tasty cafés, and fabulous galleries.

It wasn't like that when I was a kid growing up here.

Back then, Pacific Avenue was the entire universe as far as the Laguna Cortez Arts District was concerned. When I was little, my parents would bring me to the seasonal festivals, and we'd wander through the booths that were set up in the cordoned-off street, then go grab ice cream or a meal at one of the many local restaurants. After, we'd head back to the car, always parked one or two streets over.

In those days, I felt so cherished being out with my parents. My childhood was full of love and laughter, and it wasn't until I was a teenager that all that changed and being with my parents became a chore. It still is.

Back then, I'd hold both their hands as we strolled Pacific Avenue, but disappointment would wash over me when we had to leave that vibrant street. Daddy would lead us north or south to whichever parallel streets had yielded a parking place. It was like leaving Oz, and I always felt let down when I climbed into the minivan.

Now the Arts District has expanded, and the parallel streets to the north and south of Pacific Avenue are chock full of darling local establishments. There's more traffic, too, but I'm okay with that because it means that business is booming. And as I pause in front of Vavoom, a new gift shop that commissioned an exclusive tote bag, I can't help but celebrate consumerism. After all, I'm in two—count 'em, *two*—shop windows in the busiest shopping area in town.

I pause, smiling as I take in the bag and my prominently displayed logo—two Bs back to back so that they form a typographic butterfly. Just seeing it makes bubbles of joy flutter inside me.

I'm ridiculously giddy, so much that I want to hold

out my arms and twirl down the sidewalk. I rein in the urge. Not only because I'd get strange looks, but also because I'd undoubtedly end up tangling poor Jake in the leash. That and the fact that the boutique is across the street from Pacific Properties, and I really don't want them reporting back to Mr. Big that his tenant is a ditz.

Even so, I'm totally twirling inside. Because I. Am. A. Successful. Business. Owner.

Seriously. How cool is that?

I take out my phone, then snap a quick picture of the bag with me in the window's reflection for later posting to social media. As soon as the shutter clicks, though, I realize I'm not alone. I turn, ready for another shopper to rave about my awesome tote, but the man isn't looking at the bags. Instead, he's staring straight at me.

"Ms. Bradshaw? Brandy Bradshaw?"

"I—yes?"

"I'm so pleased to have found you."

I wrack my brain, but I have no idea who this man is. He's clean-shaven, in his late thirties, and he's neither attractive nor unattractive. Honestly, if he hadn't spoken to me, I doubt I would have noticed him at all.

"I'm sorry, but have we met?"

"Forgive me. Protocol is not my forte. I'm Mr. White. We spoke briefly a few months ago. I had heard about you. I knew that I would soon be in need of a good, ah, designer. And we were introduced."

"Oh. Right. I apologize for not remembering." I still don't, but I offer him a bright smile. "As you can imagine, I've met a lot of people over the last year. It's all such a blur. Was it at a trade show?"

He nods vaguely. "What? Oh, yes, of course, yes.

And I understand it's unusual to approach you this way. But I have a sensitive project that I don't wish to discuss over the phone."

I start to ask him what could be that sensitive about purses and totes, but he barrels on before I can get a word out.

"I explained that to your assistant a few days ago. She called me back yesterday and said that you'd be in the Laguna Cortez Arts District today for lunch, then suggested that we meet in person."

"Cara did?"

"Cara?" He frowns. "I don't recall her name." He cocks his head, his eyes narrowing as he studies me. "I was under the impression that you were aware of the appointment. But if I've somehow offended you, I can—"

"No, no," I say as he hurriedly steps backward, as if he's just insulted the queen or something. "Really, it's fine." It's not, of course, and I make a mental note to have a long talk with Cara about forewarning me about stuff like this.

I force a smile. "I'd be happy to sit down and talk with you." After all, who cares how odd the guy is? This is a possible job, after all.

"Is now a good time?"

"I'm sorry, but it's not." I *could* talk to him now, but I have Jake, who's starting to get antsy, and a few other things already on my plate. Plus, I really like to have time to prepare. Another reason I'm irked at Cara.

Frowning, I rummage in my bag—a waxed canvas tote, very practical, and my very first BB Bag—then pull out a business card. "Just email me," I say as I extend it, and he snatches it from my hand.

"Thank you," he says. "I truly didn't mean to upset your protocol. Perhaps it was a mistake approaching you, but I want to work with the best. Surely you understand that."

"I'm flattered," I say, even though I want to tell him that he's laying it on a little thick.

"Do you want all the, ah, parameters in the email?"

"Um, sure. Just a brief summary. Enough to give me an idea what you're thinking of, but nothing detailed. Shorthand is fine. It doesn't have to be formal. I just want to be prepared when we talk."

"Of course. Shorthand. I completely understand."

"Great. After I review it, we can make an appointment to talk further."

"That's perfect," he says as he glances at my card. Then he meets my eyes with a huge grin. "BB Bags. Clever."

"Thanks." Considering my name's Brandy Bradshaw, and my business is literally making bags, I'm not sure it's really that clever. But it works for me.

He holds out his hands, his thumbs up and his forefingers extended like he's a little kid playing cowboy. "Ping! Ching! A BB gun. I get it. And *bag*. Like you're gonna bag 'em. Seriously. It's very clever. But with your reputation, I would expect nothing less."

"Oh. Well, thank you." The man is seriously odd, but he's a possible client, so I smile politely. "So, you know, email me."

Thankfully, he takes the hint. He puts my card in his wallet, says goodbye, and hurries off down the street.

From where he's curled up on the sidewalk at my feet, Jake lifts his head, then releases a quick bark.

"You said it. Come on, boy. Let's cross over and see if Ellie's done."

He rises, yawns, then shakes, happy vibes practically radiating off him. Possibly because we're heading to the beach, but more likely because stuff is happening.

Must be nice to be a dog.

I'm about to step off the curb to jaywalk when Pacific Property's front door opens across the street. I pause, expecting Ellie. Instead, it's a man I've never seen before. He's medium height with receding hair and a strong jawline. Not bad-looking, but not good-looking either. The kind of guy who fades into a crowd. I wouldn't have even noticed him, except I was looking for Ellie.

And the only reason I'm still looking is that he's staring right back at me, his eyes narrowed the way I stare down an ant who's found his way into my kitchen.

I tug on Jake's leash as I pause between two parallel-parked cars, not sure if I should stay or go as Mystery Man makes a beeline toward me. I'm about to turn and head the opposite direction just to get away when he stops at the little concrete island that separates the east- and westbound traffic.

"What are you doing here?" he asks, his voice low but sharp as he calls to me from across the westbound lane. I gape at him, confused, then realize that I must have misread the situation; he must be staring at someone else. But when I glance around, I realize there's no one else nearby. I'm about to tell him he must have the wrong person when he raises a finger, points right at me, then says, "Go. Now. You know you shouldn't be here."

I take a step back; this day is getting weirder and weirder. Obviously, both he and Mr. White have me confused with someone else. Or he's delusional. Either way, I'm not inclined to engage. I clutch my purse tighter, as if that will protect me. After I was taken, Lamar arranged for me to get a license to carry a small .22 caliber Ruger, and he takes me to the range weekly. I appreciate it, and it makes me feel safer when I'm alone in the house. But I can't bring myself to carry it.

Now I hope that wasn't a mistake, because this man has definitely crossed the freaky side of the line.

He glances from me to Jake, his scowl deepening. Then he shakes his head. "Sorry, sorry." He shoots me one final scowl, then turns, crosses the eastbound lane again, and stalks down the street toward the paid parking lot.

As soon as he's out of sight, Jake and I dodge the light traffic and sprint to Pacific Property.

Gail, the receptionist, glances up, then puts her pen down and gives me her full attention. "Wow. I wasn't expecting to see you here today."

"Who was—" I begin, but she cuts me off.

"Ellie's back with Mr. Crenshaw. You can go hang in the break room if you want. There's a bag of dog treats in there if Jake wants one. I have to get back to the asshole who caught his carpet on fire and thinks that the landlord should pay." She points to the blinking light on her phone.

"Sure," I say, making a note to ask her about Crazy Mystery Man later as I lead Jake to the small kitchen and grab him a treat. I also wanted to ask Gail if Mr. Crenshaw found Ellie a new tenant for her rental house, but I suppose I'll hear all about that from Ellie when her meeting ends.

For a while, Ellie had planned to live in her rental house herself, but all that changed when she and Devlin got married. Now they're together in a stunning house on the beach, filled with love and happiness.

I sigh. I'm thrilled for my friend, but the truth is I can't even imagine having a blissful household with a man who loves me the way Devlin loves Ellie. Or, rather, I shouldn't imagine it. Because the truth is that I do. Mostly at night in a delicious secret story that starts from when Ronan rescued me from that horrible basement and ends with him spooned up against me in bed, my body limp from making love.

That, however, is a fantasy I need to abandon. I've never even told Ellie. Why should I when I know it's never going to come true? Sure, I'd let myself hope for the first couple of weeks after the rescue, but Ronan never gave me any hint that his tenderness was based on anything other than his empathy for how terrified I must have been.

So I put that all behind me, but then he kissed me at the wedding, and my hormones started dancing again. Not to mention my confusion. But it's been a month now, and there's been nada in the way of any indication that he's interested. We're friends, sure. And that's why he's fixing my sink.

But man, I wish that was a euphemism.

More than that, I wish I was the kind of woman who could ask why he kissed me at the wedding but didn't pursue anything else. Because as much as I love my work, I really do want more. But after a lifetime of horrible experiences with men, I know better than to press my luck.

Bottom line? Even if I could conjure the nerve to tell Ronan how I feel, I wouldn't. Ronan's a friend. And I would never do anything to risk that.

"Hey," Ellie says, pulling me from my rambling thoughts. "Ready for the beach?"

At the familiar word, Jake pops to his feet with more energy than a dog his age should have.

"I think we are," I say, grinning at him. "Got a new renter?"

"No, the application didn't pan out." She sighs. "Soon, I hope." She shoots me a sideways glance. "Cara interested in moving to Laguna Cortez?"

It would be great to have my assistant living so close, but I shake my head. "I'm pretty sure she loves LA, but you can always ask her."

We head for the door, but I pause before pulling it open. I turn back to face Gail. "By the way, who was the man who left right before I came in?"

She bites her lower lip, as if I've just asked the most awkward question ever.

"What? Is he the kind of guy that just randomly lays into people?"

She frowns, her brow furrowing. "What? No, no. It's just..." She trails off, then sighs before bending low over her desk and gesturing me closer. "I'm not supposed to say, but that's Robert Matheson. He's your landlord."

CHAPTER SIX

"He probably had you confused with someone else," Ellie says as we walk the beach. "After all, you've never met the man, right?"

"True." I shrug. "You're probably right. Just confusion."

I'd given her the rundown on Creepy Mystery Man aka Mr. Matheson aka Mr. Big aka my absentee landlord as we walked the short distance from Pacific Property to the beach, and while she agreed it was weird, she was determined to convince me not to worry about it.

"Even if Mr. Crenshaw included a picture when Mr. Big got your application, I doubt he'd recognize you. Your hair was still short back then, right? Wasn't it a pixie cut, and mostly pink?"

She's right. When I'd returned to Laguna Cortez after a short stint as a buyer for a boutique in Los Angeles, I had a completely different look. I'd been coming off a crappy non-relationship with an LA guy who I thought was great but turned out to be a big jerk. Since that seemed to be a pattern in my life, I figured the only way to change the men in my life would be to change the me in my life.

So I went to a fancy salon, had my hair cut daringly short, then dyed it a pale shade of pink. It was fun and sassy, making me look like the kind of woman who flirted confidently and easily with men.

Except I was still me. There was no magical change in my personality. No movie montage where I suddenly morphed into a woman who was confident and comfortable around men.

Funny how that happens.

So I grew my hair out, kept only minimal color on the tips, and tried to convince myself that LA Guy's jerkiness was his flaw and nothing to do with me. Then I settled into my mostly-non-dating life.

All of which meant that there was really no reason for Mr. Big to recognize me at all. Ellie must be right. It was just a weird, coincidental case of mistaken identity. Freaky but benign.

"If it's really bugging you, why not talk to the management company? Mr. Crenshaw would surely reach out to him for you."

I shake my head, the idea mortifying. "And make him think that he freaked me out that much?"

"He *did* freak you out that much. Maybe he should be made aware of the excessive strangeness."

"No. No, it's fine. Jake!" I add, calling him back from where he's getting too close to the surf. "Frisbee!"

He bounds in circles, finds the fallen Frisbee again, then starts trotting back to us. As I watch him, a horrible thought occurs to me.

"What if..." I begin, turning back to Ellie. But I trail off, unable to let myself even think those words.

"What?" Ellie presses.

"Nothing," I say, taking the Frisbee from Jake and letting it soar again. I watch as it floats away, jealous of how carefree both the disc and the dog are.

"Brandy..."

"Sorry. It's just—I don't know."

She cocks her head and stares me down. "Give."

"Fine, fine." The words come out in a whisper, too horrible to speak aloud. "What if he's in town because he's moving back in? And he acted all weird because it was so awkward to see me before they give me notice."

"No way," she says, but I see the way her mouth curves down into a frown, and I know she's considering the possibility.

"No," she repeats, shaking her head. "Not going to believe it. And even if it is true, you know we'll find you a place. Besides, Gail would have said something, even if she wasn't supposed to."

"You think?"

"Absolutely."

I draw a deep breath, a bit mollified. "Okay. Right. My landlord might be a crazy person, but he's not evicting me. I hope," I add with a grimace.

"It's going to be fine," she assures me, which is sweet but hollow since she doesn't know the sitch any more than I do. "I need to run," she adds.

"Us, too. Jake!" I call, watching my four-legged bestie romp in the surf. "Come on, boy! Time to go!"

He trots back obediently, and I attach his leash.

"Oh, now he's sad."

I laugh. "Yeah, well, he may still have boundless puppy energy, but I don't." After over an hour of watching Jake romp in the sand and chase the Frisbee, my arm aches from the exertion.

"Call me later and give me an update on your sink." She winks, and I roll my eyes. Then she pulls me into a hug before reaching down to scratch Jake's head. "Take care of your mommy," she tells him. "Seriously, call me." She holds her fingers up to her mouth and ear as she starts to walk backwards.

I nod, and she waves then turns around and starts heading south toward the Devlin Saint Foundation, its façade rising up on the horizon a few blocks down the beach.

"Come on, Jake," I say. "Lead the way home."

He does that all-over wiggle thing, pleased to be in charge, and starts to tug me across the beach toward the street. I follow sluggishly. Walking on a beach is exercise all by itself. Add in a Labrador who thinks he's still a puppy, and I'm seriously dragging by the time we reach the intersection of the Coast Highway and Pacific Avenue.

That's okay, though. It's not a long walk home, and I'll still have time before Ronan shows up. At least enough for a quick shower and a cup of tea and a few moments relaxing on the back porch so that I can clear out my worries about my house situation.

Bottom line? As of right now, the day has nowhere to go but up.

CHAPTER SEVEN

The Present

"**B**ehind me."

I'm still staring at the body when Ronan gives the terse, whispered order at the same time as he steps in front of me. I look up, my breath shaky, and see that he's holding a gun.

That's when I realize he thinks the killer might still be here, and I clamp my lips together to keep from whimpering.

"Stay close." I nod, forcing my legs to move as he slowly leads us through the house.

"Do you really think someone could be hiding here?" I whisper as he looks in my bedroom closet.

"Could be?" he says from inside the walk-in. "Sure. Is it likely? No. But it's a possibility." He steps out, pinning me with his gaze. "I'm not taking chances with your safety."

I hug myself, pulling the warmth of his protection around me like a cozy sweater.

We move on, and he checks each closet, the bathrooms, every nook and cranny, including the garage and dozens of places I probably wouldn't think of, like the gap behind the water heater and the locked owner's closet.

It's full of empty shelves and a few file boxes stacked on a floor covered with ugly press-on tiles, unlike the beautiful wood of the rest of the house. Ronan opens the boxes, and I peer over his shoulder at what looks to be manila folders full of receipts.

Not exactly the Crown Jewels, but considering how quickly Ronan picked the locks, I guess it was never supposed to be a safe room.

Or maybe it's just a sign of how good Ronan is at his job.

It's also a reminder of how quickly things can go from good to bad. Because behind every door he opens, there could be someone lurking. Don't I know better than most people how things can flip with no warning at all?

I tremble as memories wash over me. A party when I was sixteen. A drink from a boy that sent my life spiraling. And more recently, rough hands yanking me from a car. A knife at my throat. That horrible, dark room.

And then Ronan's arms, carrying me to safety.

Without thinking, I reach out and take his hand, clutching it tightly.

He looks back at me. "It's okay. I won't let anything hurt you."

"I know." The words—so true—come automatically.

For a moment, his eyes are hard on mine, then he gives my hand a slight squeeze. "Good."

We've made a full circle, and now we're back in the living room. The body is on the other side of the sofa. I can see it, but at least there's an upholstered barrier between us.

"You're sure that's him? Mr. Big?"

"I'm sure. I told you. I—I saw him today."

"You said he was shouting at you," Ronan says as he circles the couch, moving toward the body.

"Yeah, he was. It was really freaky." I lick my very dry lips, my eyes on my dead landlord. "This doesn't make any sense. He shouldn't be in the house. I didn't get any notice he was coming. And he's definitely not supposed to be here dead!"

My head snaps up as I say the words, realizing how ridiculous they sound. "I'm a little freaked out," I admit.

"I'd say you have reason to be." He, of course, is perfectly composed, and his calmness works on me like a balm.

I draw a breath, then watch as he continues to examine the body, looking but not touching.

I lick my lips again, then ask the question to which I already know the answer. "That's a bullet hole in his head, isn't it?"

Of course it is, but until Ronan says so, I don't think any of this will feel real.

"It is. I'd say a nine millimeter. Close range. Possibly a .357."

"Oh. You just know that?"

"Yes," he says. "I just know that."

"Right. Of course you do." It doesn't matter. The guy's dead. But I'm rambling, craving the normalcy of conversation even though it feels like nothing will ever be normal again. Like it's me, and these things just happen. One bad thing after another and another for my whole stupid life.

A hot tear leaks onto my cheek. I reach up and brusquely swipe it away.

"This was a hit, right? Not like a regular break-in. And now whoever did this is gone?"

"That's what it looks like. One bullet. Nothing taken." He's speaking firmly and directly, which I appreciate. But there's also a gentleness to his tone, which I appreciate even more.

"But why was he even here? He's not supposed to be here when I am, and I didn't get any notice at all—*oh!*"

"What?"

"Maybe someone got wires crossed and he thought I *had* been given notice that he was coming. Maybe that was why he was yelling at me. Because he thought I'd be out of town? He probably knows I usually go to San Diego to visit my parents during his weeks."

"It's a possibility," Ronan says.

"We need to call the police. Lamar will be—"

"Not just yet."

My eyes go wide. "Why on earth not?"

He just looks at me. That steady, unshakeable gaze locked on my face. Then he straightens, pulls out his phone, and sends a quick text.

"Devlin?" I guess.

He nods.

I swallow, hugging myself as the reality of the situation bonks me on the head. "Do you really think this has something to do with Saint's Angels? How would that even be possible?"

"I make it a rule to never assume anything." His expression is deadly serious when he adds, "You got sucked into our world once before. Do you really want that again?"

"No." The word is a whisper, and I take an involuntary step back, as if at any moment someone's going to grab me and pull me back into that place. As if this entire surreal afternoon is just a precursor to more pain and terror and—

"Hey." Suddenly, he's rounded the couch and is standing right in front of me, his hands gently gripping my arms. "I'm so sorry. I shouldn't have brought that up." He releases one arm long enough to tuck a lock of my hair behind my ear. "Don't you know that I'd—Devlin, too— we'd give anything to be able to turn back time? To have kept you safe from all that."

"I know." A tear leaks from my eye, and I suck in a breath as the pad of his thumb swipes it away. "I do. It's just—"

"I get it. And it kills me to see you hurting and scared."

His words flow through me like warm cocoa. "You make it better," I confess.

For a moment, he says nothing, then he takes a step closer, his hands tightening on my shoulders. We're only inches apart. I can practically feel the air sizzle between us, and all I want is for him to hold me close and let me cling to him.

He leans forward, and I think that's going to happen. That he's going to sweep me close, and I can finally let go, shedding my fear in the safety of his arms.

But then he clears his throat and takes a step backward. "Right, well, obviously I don't know who did this, but I doubt it has anything to do with you or Saint's Angels. Even so, I'm not taking risks, so we get a handle on the situation and then we call the cops. Understand?"

I nod.

"Objections?"

I hesitate only a second, then shake my head. As soon as I do, he moves back around the sofa to the body.

"I'm going to check his ID. The body. You understand?"

"Yeah."

"Brandy," he says firmly. "What exactly do you understand?"

"That you're looking first. Before the cops. And—and if they ask, I never even saw you touch the body."

"I hate asking you to lie, but if there's the slightest chance that—"

"No." I cut him off, hugging myself. "You're right. You need to be sure. And there's hardly any possibility this has anything to do with you or Devlin or any of you guys, much less me. This is something else. He got in trouble somehow. Maybe he came here to get something out of that closet. Maybe he trafficks drugs. It could be anything. But it's not something tied to you or Devlin or Ellie or any of us. It's not," I say, my voice rising in panic despite my best efforts to remain calm. "Because, Ronan, I really don't think I can handle that again."

"Oh, angel...." He moves swiftly back to me, his hands closing on my shoulders. I want to melt against him. I want to absorb all of his strength. But I don't. I just stand there, afraid of the body on the floor. Afraid of the way this man makes me feel. And terribly afraid that some new darkness has slipped into my world and that this time, that darkness will break me.

"Hey," he says, his fingertip going to my chin and lifting it until I'm looking into his sky-blue eyes. "Whatever is going on, you can handle it. But I promise you, Brandy, you won't have to handle it alone."

"Thank you," I say, feeling like an idiot for not keeping my shit together. "It's just—"

"There's a body in your living room. You don't have to apologize for being freaked out."

"Right." I square my shoulders. "Who wouldn't be?"

He gently cups my face, and I resist the urge to actively lean into his palm. "You steady?"

"Yeah." I stay put as Ronan returns to my dead landlord. He squats down again, then pulls a pair of latex gloves out of his pocket and starts to pat him down.

"He's been dead for about an hour," he says as he gently turns the body and tugs the wallet out of my landlord's back pocket. I glance away, the process oddly ghoulish. "An ME will know for sure, but based on my experience and the way the scent of gunpowder has faded, that's my educated guess."

"You, um, just carry gloves?"

His fingers gingerly pull a mobile phone from Mr. Big's jacket pocket. "I keep a pair folded up in my wallet, yeah. They tend to come in handy."

"Oh. Right. Of course." I think about the kind of work he does. Dangerous work with the goal of taking down bad people even while staying outside the law. So, yeah. I guess habitually carrying gloves makes sense.

"Anything on the phone?"

Ronan shakes his head, then slides the phone back into Mr. Big's jacket pocket. "Locked."

"Too bad," I say. "It probably has his calendar. Maybe he's in town to meet someone and it got nasty."

"Possibly." Ronan shuffles through the wallet as he speaks. "Robert Matheson." He glances up at me, and I nod, then hug myself as I remember the way he'd yelled at me just a few hours earlier.

"That's Mr. Big's real name. At least that's what Gail told me. I didn't know it until today."

I shudder, remembering the way he'd come at me. "He was so freaked out when he saw me. God, Ronan, what if we're wrong and this really does have something to do with me?"

"How could it?" he asks reasonably. "Your first guess was probably right. Someone got wires crossed and forgot to tell you he was in town and you needed to get gone for a few days."

"Maybe. Gail would know. I just..." I trail off, shaking my head, then laugh a little. "I always thought I'd be better in a crisis. But every time something horrible happens, I go to pieces."

"You're doing great. Entirely in one piece," he says. "And for the record, according to the rule book, you're allowed to break down when confronted with a dead body in your living room."

"Section A, Part Three?"

"Exactly." We share a small smile. And for a moment —one tiny, wonderful moment—I feel calm again. I smile again as a silent thank you.

He stands, then returns to me. "We're going to figure this out. Do you believe me?"

I nod. How can I not believe this man?

He takes off the gloves, pulls out his phone, then dials. "Hey, Tamra," he says a moment later. "I've got a situation to deal with tonight. Can you do me a favor? I have a flight scheduled for seven. Commercial. ... What? No. Devlin offered, but this is personal. I just need you to call and change it for me. ... Yeah, tomorrow, before lunch. ... Great. Appreciate it."

He smiles at me as he taps out a text.

"Ronan, no. I'll be fine. Don't change your plans. I don't want you to—"

"Done," he says. "And I just told my people in Chicago that I won't be there until tomorrow. I'm not leaving you to deal with this on your own."

I start to protest, but he cuts me off, putting his hand on my shoulder. "Tomorrow is soon enough."

I nod, more relieved than I want to admit. Honestly, I don't even want him gone tomorrow, but that's just silly. "Okay, then. Thank you," I add, then jump as the doorbell chimes. Ronan's hand tightens on my shoulder, the pressure calming me.

"It's probably Devlin," he says, then glances at the clock. "You're not expecting anyone, are you?"

"No—Oh! Yes. Lamar. I told him we'd be here if he wanted to stop by." I wince a little at that. "I told him we'd have a drink and celebrate my non-drippy sink. Sorry."

"Not your fault. Sorry about the sink." He grins, clearly trying to lighten this whole thing up for me. I smile back, grateful.

The bell rings again, and I glance at the video feed on my security app. "Lamar," I confirm. "And he has the key code," I add. "If I don't answer, he'll let himself in, figuring we're so deep in sink repairs we didn't hear him ring."

"Shit." Ronan drags his finger through his hair. "Go answer the door."

I nod.

"And Brandy, we arrived right before him. Saw the body, checked the house. I was just about to call 9-1-1 when he rang. Got it?"

"I shouldn't just get rid of him?"

He shakes his head. "We can't keep this from the cops. And I'd rather Lamar be the first on scene than someone we don't know."

"Right." I hurry that way, then fling open the door and throw myself into Lamar's arms before he even has a chance to speak.

"You're here," I say. "Thank goodness you're here."

CHAPTER EIGHT

Thank goodness you're here.

Brandy's words rang in Ronan's head as he returned to the body, slid the gloves back on, then efficiently pulled out the man's phone again.

"Fuck," he muttered as his second attempt to unlock it failed as soundly as the first.

The curse wasn't directed at the phone, however. Instead, it was directed at Lamar, whose soft and reassuring tone Ronan could hear, though not the actual words.

But what did Ronan care that Lamar was the one comforting her? Lamar was one of Brandy's closest friends and a detective—of course she'd be relieved he was on site.

He sucked in air, not mollified, as he positioned the phone over the dead man's face, then grinned in triumph as the facial recognition software unlocked the device.

"Lamar. Good to see you."

Ronan recognized Devlin's voice, steady and professional as always. He didn't worry that Devlin would say something to tip Lamar off; Devlin was too much of a professional. He knew there was a situation from Ronan's text, and he'd play it cool until he learned what the problem was and who held what information.

Quickly, Ronan manipulated the dead man's phone, going into settings and turning off the lock feature. Then he stood and slipped the phone into his back pocket as he rounded the corner to see Ellie giving Lamar a hug.

"Hey, Watson," she said, calling the detective by the nickname that Ronan knew they'd had for each other since their police academy days, a complement to her nickname of Sherlock, the pair of names signaling the close relationship of the two friends.

Recently, that relationship meant that Lamar had been willing to bend the rules for Ellie's sake in order to protect Saint's Angels. But whether or not Lamar would continue to color outside the lines, Ronan didn't know.

And that made him more than a little nervous. In Ronan's experience, if things had the possibility to turn to shit, they usually did.

Lamar had his arm around Ellie's shoulder, and Devlin caught Ronan's eye, his brow raised just enough that Ronan could interpret the question—*any indication this'll blow back on us?*

Ronan shook his head, the movement so minuscule he doubted anyone but Devlin noticed it. But he knew Devlin understood—*nothing obvious, but still an open question.*

"The gang's all here," Lamar said, looking between Ronan and Devlin. "Why do I have a feeling there's more going on than a drippy sink?"

Brandy had been watching Lamar, but now she turned to Ronan, as if he was the only one she trusted to navigate these waters. He nodded his assent, her faith both flattering and terrifying him. She thought of him as some stalwart against the horrors of the world. A super-hero who could protect her no matter what the cost.

But Ronan knew better than most just how futile faith really was. More than that, he knew that even best intentions could go horribly wrong.

"It's bad," Brandy began, her hands shoved deep into the pockets of her capris. "It's my landlord." Her throat moved as she swallowed. "He's dead."

Lamar's eyes landed on Ronan. "And you called Devlin before 9-1-1? Hell, before me?"

"Are you really surprised?" Ronan had considered telling the detective the lie he'd fabricated for Brandy—that they'd just arrived and were about to call him and 9-1-1 when Lamar showed up—but decided the detective deserved the truth. Some of it, anyway.

"*Shit*." Lamar drew a breath. "Does this have anything to do with you?" He pointed a finger at Devlin. "Either of you?" He twisted, moving his hard glare to Ronan.

"Only in that it affects Brandy," Ronan said. "As far as we know, this has nothing to with our work."

"Work," Lamar repeated, his voice tight.

Ronan's entire body went tense. He'd never been completely comfortable letting the cop in on the secrets in Devlin's past or present, but Devlin had made that decision when Ellie re-entered his life. It was a decision Devlin believed in, primarily because he knew that the cop would never do anything to hurt Ellie, and exposing Saint's Angels to the world would do exactly that.

But Ronan had never been as certain. People hurt people for their own agendas all the damn day. And he didn't know Lamar well enough to be able to see his breaking point.

None of which mattered at the moment. Lamar was here, he knew the situation, and they were stuck with trusting him. So might as well make the most of it.

"The body's in there," Ronan said, cocking his head. "By the sofa."

Lamar knew the way, and Ronan fell in behind him. Brandy was right beside him, and as they drew closer to the body, she reached over and took his hand, squeezing gently. He squeezed back, wishing he had the power to make this all go away. Brandy was one of the kindest, sweetest, most genuine women he'd ever met, and right then, he'd be willing to go toe to toe with whatever power in this fucked-up universe kept throwing hardballs at her.

"Hey," she whispered. "Ronan, my fingers."

Shit. "Sorry." He relaxed his grip, mentally kicking himself.

"Jesus," Lamar said from where he'd stopped beside the sofa. He turned to face them. "You haven't called this in?"

"We barely beat you through the door," Ronan said, falling back on the lie. "I cleared the house. Was about to call when you rang the bell."

"Did either of you disturb the body?"

"No," Brandy said firmly, her grip tightening just slightly, and right then, Ronan wanted to kiss her for her loyalty. Then again, when didn't he want to kiss her? As far as Brandy Bradshaw went, *want* was never up for debate.

Lamar looked between Brandy, Ronan, and Devlin. "Anything else you can think of?"

Ronan shook his head, not bothering to look at the others. "Not a thing. What you see is what you get."

Lamar stuck his hands in his pockets and walked the length of the body before turning back to look at Ronan again. "I can't help you, and I might accidentally hurt you if I don't know the full score."

Ronan straightened, fighting irritation. "We're not asking you for help. We would never draw you into anything."

"You're not drawing me in. I'm walking. You're family, remember? You're like a brother to Devlin, and he's like a brother to me. And that means that things are different. I thought you understood that."

Ronan's gut twisted as he glanced between Brandy and Ellie, the latter of whom was looking at her friend with something like love. His gaze bounced next to Devlin, who was nodding slowly. Everybody was fully on board with Lamar. Everyone except Ronan, and he felt like the world's biggest heel for doubting this man they all trusted.

But that was the hard thing, wasn't it? The people you trusted the most could betray you. Honestly, it was a wonder he and Devlin were as close as they were. But they had a shared history and knew at least some of each other's secrets. Over the years, he'd come to trust Devlin with his life. But not everybody could be in that circle. Ronan had learned that one the hard way.

Maybe it was time to drop his guard around Lamar,

too. "I can't think of a reason why anyone with any connection to Saint's Angels would kill Brandy's landlord."

"Then why the hell is the man dead?" Lamar retorted.

From where he stood leaning against the kitchen island that doubled as a breakfast bar, Devlin laughed. "You'd be surprised how many dead bodies pop up in the world that we have nothing to do with."

To his credit, Lamar chuckled. "Can't argue with that. But it's damn odd."

"Especially considering the way he yelled at you earlier," Ellie said, her eyes on Brandy.

"I know," Brandy agreed. "But that doesn't have anything to do with Saint's Angels."

"Wait, wait, wait." Lamar held up a hand. "What the hell are you two talking about?"

"It was really bizarre," Brandy said, releasing Ronan's hand as she took a step closer to the dead man. Ronan watched as she studied his face, her posture going stiff as if to keep herself in control.

Finally, she looked up at Lamar. "Remember when I told you I was meeting Ellie at the property manager's office? Well, he was coming out when I arrived. And he totally went off on me."

"Went off? What does that mean?"

She relayed the whole story, and when she was done, Lamar stood there shaking his head, looking as baffled by the incident as the rest of them.

"Weren't supposed to be there?" Lamar said. "What could that mean?"

Brandy shrugged, then glanced back at Ronan as if for support.

"Neither one of us has a clue," Ronan said as he fought the urge to move closer and take her hand. She was relying on him to help her through this, and the cold, hard truth was that he liked it—and he hated it, too.

Because with every glance—with every brush of her hand against his—it was getting harder and harder to keep his distance.

He shook the thoughts off, turning his focus to Devlin and Ellie. "What about you two? Got a theory?"

"Nothing," Devlin said. "It's definitely odd, but I can't see any way that this ties in with Saint's Angels. If you get a hint that it's otherwise," he added to Lamar, his eyes boring down on the detective, "let us know. Otherwise, thank you for understanding why we needed to at least be here initially. And for understanding why what we do needs to stay in the shadows."

"I don't know that I do understand it," Lamar said. "But we've been through a lot together, and Brandy's alive because of your team. So you can trust that I will never break your confidence. But you've got me walking a hell of a tightrope, guys."

Ronan grimaced. That was damn true.

Lamar looked between Ellie and Brandy. "You know how much I love you two, and that I tolerate the both of you," he added, returning his focus to the men with the slightest of grins. "But I'm working without a net. And we all need to realize that if I fall, there will be some serious shit hitting the fan."

He was right. One misstep, and this one detective could bring down an entire organization. It was a terrifying realization, but a reality they would have to live with. And the truth was, so long as he stepped wisely, Lamar Gage could be a hell of an asset.

"We know," Ronan said, not waiting for Devlin. "Guess that makes you an unofficial member of the team."

For a moment, Lamar didn't react, and Ronan feared he'd moved too quickly. Then the detective grinned. "So when do I get my secret decoder ring?"

"We're backordered," Devlin said dryly, and they all laughed, the lingering tension fading. About Lamar's role, anyway. There was still the matter of a body in the living area.

"I need to call this in, and I don't want you staying in this house tonight," he added, turning his attention to Brandy. "You can stay with me at the condo."

For a moment, sweet relief flooded Ronan from the simple knowledge that he'd be far away from temptation. But that also meant that Brandy would be away from him. That he wouldn't be there to watch over her. And there was no one he trusted to do that more than himself.

"She's staying with me." He met Lamar's eyes. "You work the investigation. I'll make sure she stays safe."

For a moment, Ronan thought Lamar would argue. Then the detective nodded, his attention returning to Brandy. "You keep that Ruger in your purse, do you hear me? And you keep your purse with you."

"I'll keep her safe," Ronan said.

"I believe you," Lamar replied. "But I still want her armed."

Ronan nodded. Under the circumstances, he couldn't

argue the point. "All right. But just so we're clear, she's staying with me."

"Right. She is," Ellie said, so quickly that Ronan assumed she had matchmaking on the mind more than protection.

"You're all talking like I'm in danger," Brandy said.

"Not while I'm around," Ronan said. "We're just being careful."

Ellie frowned at both of them, then shifted her focus to Brandy. "Do you really want to stay alone after finding a body in your living room?"

"No," Brandy admitted.

"That's not the only thing," Lamar said. "You're probably perfectly safe. But there *is* a body, which means there's a killer. And that's not something I take lightly."

"Me either," Ronan agreed.

"Fair enough, but I'm really not worried," Brandy said. "Freaked, yeah. Worried, no. I mean, why on earth would anyone want to hurt me?" Brandy looked around the room, her eyes stopping on Ronan.

"I can't think of a single reason," he said. "But until we know you're in the clear, you're not leaving my sight. And that, angel, is non-negotiable."

"Anything else before I call this in?" Lamar asks. Devlin and Ellie have already stepped outside, and we're following them, clearing the scene around the body before the cops arrive.

I look to Ronan to see if he's going to say anything about the fact that he inspected the body. But he just shakes his head. Apparently, the trust isn't as warm and fuzzy as it sounded a moment ago.

"Okay, then," Lamar continues. "Are we clear? I'm going to tell them I arrived only minutes after you did. You hadn't even seen the body yet, and we all found it together."

"We know," I say.

"Just making sure," he says with an apologetic shrug as he taps his phone. I only half listen as he speaks with the dispatcher. The fact that Lamar's now standing in my entryway in full-blown detective mode is a little too surreal for my taste.

As Lamar moves toward the open front door to get a

better signal, I turn and find Ronan watching me. I flash a quick, awkward smile, then blink back tears when he comes even closer.

"Sorry, sorry."

"It's okay," he says.

I scoff. "I managed to keep it together all this time, and I have no idea why I'm starting to melt now."

"Adrenaline fade," Ronan says. "All your emotions are screaming for attention. It's hitting home what's happened. And that's going to be especially hard for you."

His tone is gentle but firm, without any sugarcoating. And he's right.

"So basically, you're saying I'm a mess."

"Pretty much," he retorts, making me laugh and cry at the same time. "Definitely a mess," he adds. He grabs a tissue from the box on the entry hall table, then holds it out to me. I take it, then wipe my eyes.

"You're going to be just fine," he says gently. "And we're going to get to the bottom of this."

"I know. Thanks." I force myself to stand straighter. "I should be able to deal with this. But ..." I trail off, not wanting to talk about how the sight of the body had me thinking about the time I was taken. Or the way the blood under his head made me remember the steady *drip, drip* of—

"Brandy?"

His hands are on my shoulders, and I want desperately for him to pull me into his arms. Because my deep, dark secret is that the only time I truly feel safe now is in my dreams, when he's holding me close and telling me that everything will be okay.

"Hey, angel, talk to me."

I look up at him. "Sorry, I—"

"Don't be sorry. Are you okay?"

"I'm—yes. Yes, I'm fine. The blood. It's stupid, but even though it's out of sight now, I can't stop seeing it—"

"Oh, hell," he says, and for a moment I think I've annoyed him. "I wasn't thinking. I should have gotten you away from the scene the moment we saw it."

"I—no. That's not on you. It's just—"

"Of course it's on me. Do you think I want to see you hurting? Reliving that day?" He takes me by the elbow and leads me into the guest bedroom that opens off the hall. Ellie's old room. "Sit here," he says, nodding to the bed.

"Shouldn't we be outside?"

"They can kick us out if they want to. Sit."

I do as he says and climb on, my back to the headboard and my knees pulled up. "It's okay, really. I'm fine. It was just a moment, and…" I trail off. We both know I'm not fine. Functional, maybe, but not fine.

"Here," he says, draping the throw from the foot of the bed over my legs. I pull it up to my shoulders, relishing the comfort as he sits on the edge of the bed beside me, so close I feel his muscular thigh brushing my hip. I want to slide down and curl up against him, but I don't. I just clutch the blanket tighter.

His hand rests lightly on my knee. "I'll go get the others. Let them know we're in here."

I treasure the *we*, happy to know he's planning to stay with me. "Okay." Then, as he's starting to rise, I add, "Ronan?"

He pauses, waiting for me to continue. "Yeah?"

"I—thanks for taking care of me. I'm sorry I lost it a little back there."

There's an edge to his voice when he says, "You have about a million reasons to be upset. All things considered, I think you're doing just fine."

Clearly, I'm not, but I have no intention of melting down in this man's arms, no matter how much I might want to. "It's just—I think about the blood, and..."

"Hey, it's going to be fine." He sits again, then takes my hand, and I cherish the contact.

"Promise?"

"One hundred percent." His gaze is steady, unblinking, and even though I know that's not really a promise he can make, I believe him.

"Thanks," I say. "I feel ridiculous. I should be handling this better."

"You're doing great. Really," he says, this time rising off the bed. "I'm going to go tell the others where we are."

I nod, watching as he walks away, this man with his broad shoulders so willing to carry my burden.

He pauses at the door and looks back. "And, Brandy, just so you know, I never break a promise."

He turns back before I can answer, but I feel my smile all the way down to my toes. The circumstances may be crappy, but I have to admit, I like this part of the mess. The Ronan part.

I hug my knees tighter as I wait for him to return. The house is well-made, but I can hear the whine of police sirens in the distance. Soon, there are footsteps in the hall and muffled voices. A moment later, Ellie comes in, Devlin behind her. I glance over his shoulder but don't see Ronan, and his absence feels like a scar on my soul.

"You doing okay?" Ellie asks.

I nod. "Yeah. I'm fine." I'm proud of how strong my voice sounds, but I don't want to lose it in front of Ellie. It would be a betrayal of Ronan's promise. Because why should I be freaked out knowing that he's looking out for me? "It's just very surreal."

"Can't argue with that."

"Where's Ronan?" I ask, trying to keep my voice casual.

"He was on the front porch making a call when the cops arrived. He's probably giving his statement. Lamar's doing all of us in turn. Dotting the i's, crossing the t's."

That makes sense. I roll on my side, then pat the bed. Jake's head pops up—he's only allowed on the furniture on special occasions, and when I pat again, he shimmies with joy, then bounds onto the bed. "Lay down," I tell him, and he stretches out beside me as I stroke his back, making him wiggle with pleasure.

An hour later, Lamar has finished taking everyone's statements, having called Ellie and Devlin out in turn, then coming into the bedroom for mine. "I'll skip Jake," he says, making me laugh.

When he heads out to talk to the LCPD team, Ellie, Devlin, and Ronan return. "How much longer, do you think?" I ask.

"At least a few hours," Ronan says. "The forensic team is working on the carpet, gathering trace. We're fine here, but I talked with Lamar, and you don't have to stay. One of the uniforms can walk you to your room so you don't get in the middle of the CSI team's work. You can pack some things, and we can get out of here. Lamar can lock up when they're done."

"I'd like that," I admit.

"I'm going to call Los Angeles and New York and cancel the interviews," Ellie says.

I gape at her, then at Devlin, who doesn't look surprised. Clearly, they talked about this outside. "No way," I say. "No freaking way."

"Do you think I'm going to leave you right now?"

I point to Ronan. "I've got this guy watching my back. And besides, it's not like this has anything to do with me. Right? I just live here. I don't even know the man."

"Most likely not," she concedes. "But we can't know that for sure."

"Doesn't matter," I say. "I'm not about to let you cancel this. This is huge for your book. You're being interviewed on three different national late-night shows and a morning program. Do you know what that's going to do for your book sales? I mean, one, you wrote a brilliant book, two, you're married to Devlin Saint of all people, and three, you're getting on freaking national television. I will absolutely not forgive you if you don't go."

She opens her mouth as if she's going to argue, then turns to look at Devlin.

"She's right, El. And she's in good hands," he adds with a nod to Ronan.

Good hands.

The words settle inside me, soft and warm. And right then, I wish they weren't just a metaphor for safety. I'm not a woman who's casual about sex, and unlike Ellie, I've never worked out my personal baggage by banging it out with a guy. I never even understood that urge. But right now—*oh, God*—I can see the appeal. Feeling safe. Feeling alive.

Forgetting.

I shake it off. *Not me. Not happening.*

And very much beside the point at the moment. "It's settled," I tell Ellie firmly. "You're going."

She scowls, then turns her attention to Devlin.

"I'm with Brandy," he says.

Her shoulders slump. "Fine. You win. But I want reports. Regular reports."

"Done."

The bedroom door is open, and since the room is near the front door, we can all easily hear the officer stationed there when he says, "I'm sorry, ma'am. This is an active crime scene. I can't let you in."

"I understand. Could you ask Ronan to step out? He called me."

Ellie and I exchange glances. That voice belongs to Tamra Danvers, Devlin's very efficient right hand for both the foundation and Saint's Angels.

Ronan and Devlin are already stepping out into the hall.

"And you are?"

"It's okay, officer," Ronan says. "We work together."

I'm on my feet now, too curious to stay snug in the bed. Both Ellie and I head to the doorway, peeking out as we look toward the open threshold where Devlin and Ronan are talking with Tamra.

She glances up, sees us, and smiles. An elegant woman with a single streak of gray highlighting her dark hair, she's the epitome of both compassion and competence. Right now, her expression is full of kindness and sympathy.

I haven't had a good relationship with my mother

since I was a teenager, something that breaks my heart sometimes, but mostly I figure that I simply have to deal with it. That's the thing about families. Sometimes they can tear you apart, and sometimes it feels like it's the most pragmatic relationship in the world. After all, it isn't as if you get to choose them.

Tamra, though, is someone I would choose. She's kind and supportive and will always protect the people she loves. I'm lucky enough to be in that group. What I'm not sure about is why she's here. Work, I'm guessing, since she told the officer that Ronan had called her.

Now I watch as Ronan hands her his phone. "I'm tied up here for a while, but I need to get some documents off of this before my trip tomorrow. Do you mind? Just copy them to the cloud."

"Not a problem. I'll be able to identify what you need?"

"I'm sure you'll have no trouble at all."

"All right, then. It should only take an hour or so. I'll email you when it's ready."

I frown, realizing that the phone's in a gray case. Ronan's case is black. At least, I think it is. And most odd of all, she hasn't mentioned how she'll get Ronan's phone back to him.

Which, of course, is because it isn't Ronan's phone at all. I glance at Ellie, who turns to meet my eyes, her brow arching up in a way that makes me certain that she picked up on that inconsistency, too.

It must be Mr. Big's phone. And I feel a flash of anticipation. Because, dammit, I want to know what's on there, too.

"Goodnight, Ronan," she says. She nods at the officer,

but her eyes are on me. I think I see a hint of excitement there, and it sinks in that Tamra is truly part of that world. While her official job is mostly admin and PR for the Devlin Saint Foundation, the bottom line is that she's as much a part of Saint's Angels as Ronan and Devlin. And she likes it that way.

Ronan lingers, speaking to the officer, whose back is to me. He must feel me looking at him, though, because he glances up. I lift my hand next to my ear, my thumb raised like an old-fashioned handset and my head cocked in a silent question.

His brow quirks, and I'm sure he's approving of the fact that I picked up on the small detail.

Honestly, I should be annoyed—he snuck that phone off Mr. Big without telling me or Lamar or anybody. But I'm not. On the contrary, all I feel is pride that I figured it out. And the warm satisfaction of sharing in Ronan's secret.

CHAPTER TEN

I sit quietly in Ronan's Range Rover as we drive away from the house that I've lived in without incident since I moved back home to Laguna Cortez after college and a brief stint working in LA. It may only be a rental, but it's home to me, and I'm not entirely sure how to handle this new fear that surrounds the place. This knowing that danger can so easily step inside.

I know the danger wasn't directed at me, but it's touched me, and I hate that I'm scared. More, I hate this feeling that I need to scrub it away.

With a sigh, I slip off my shoes and pull my feet up onto the seat so that I'm hugging my legs. When I do, Ronan glances over. "Are you okay?"

I turn my head and give him a bright smile. "Why on earth wouldn't I be okay?"

As I hoped, he grins at me. "No reason I can think of. We're taking a drive on a beautiful night, and we'll end up at my place with a fabulous view. What could possibly be wrong?"

"Can't think of a thing," I quip as he stops at a red light. "Thanks."

"What for?"

"For babysitting me. I could have stayed with Lamar."

"Not an option."

"Why not?"

He's been looking straight ahead, but now he turns to face me, and the heat in his eyes takes my breath away. "Because there's no one I trust more with your safety than me."

"Oh. Thank you." I wince; how lame a response was that? I want to say more—to ask him about the kiss. To ask why he began something he didn't intend to finish. But I can't seem to find the words. Or, more accurately, I can't find the courage.

As the light changes and we start moving again, I remind myself that my silence is a good thing. I don't do casual sex, and Ronan doesn't do relationships. The reason nothing happened after that kiss in the alcove at the wedding was because nothing could. Anything more, and it would have screwed up our friendship, and that would be a tragedy.

I look out the window to get my bearings, then realize he's heading for Sunset Canyon, the winding road that runs above the town and connects Interstate 5 to the beach.

"You live in the canyons?" For the first time, I realize that although he's been to my place dozens of times, I have no idea where he lives.

He shakes his head. "Near the beach. Just north of Devlin and Ellie's house, actually. But I wanted to show you something."

"Oh. What?"

He laughs. "Impatient much?"

I scowl, but it morphs into a smile. I sit back, my arms crossed over my chest. "Fine," I say, a tease in my voice. "Be all secretive. Fine by me."

"Good."

We glance at each other, both of us stoic until I break and grin. "Jerk."

"Ah, but you love me anyway."

I force a laugh but turn away. I know he's teasing and only means it as friends, but the casual words have hit something deep inside of me. And since it's not something I want to examine too closely, I'm relieved when he pulls off the road into a turnaround.

"What's here?" I ask.

He kills the engine and opens his door, the interior light illuminating his face enough that I can see the anticipation in his eyes. "Just come on."

I get out, then join him at the railing. We're well above the town now. A few lights from windows, streetlights, and headlights dot the twisty roads that lead down through the hills to the grid that forms downtown. Beyond the grid is a white-ish strip bordered by frothing silver—the beach and the surf slamming against it.

Past that, all I can see is the silvery ripple of the moon reflected on the black infinity of the ocean.

It looks perfect and fragile. Almost like a model. Something a city planner might make and keep as a trophy on a pedestal in their office. But I have no idea why he's brought me here.

"I wanted to give you something beautiful," he says

when I ask that question. "Something to contrast what you see when you close your eyes."

Tears sting my eyes, borne of the unexpected surprise that he realizes that. He's correct that Mr. Big has filled my thoughts since we found the body, but surely Ronan is used to that kind of thing by now. "Thank you," I whisper. "This ... this helps."

For a moment, silence lingers. "I'm sorry."

I shake my head. "None of this is your fault."

"You don't deserve this."

"Does anybody?"

"No." His eyes are hard on mine, and he gently puts his hand over mine. "But ... never mind."

"What?"

"Nothing."

I wait, not turning away.

After a moment, he sighs.

"I was just going to say that I don't like to see you hurting."

My smile feels fragile on my lips, and I can't quite meet his eyes. "I'm okay with you saying that."

He chuckles. "Good. Because it's true." He opens his mouth, and I think he's going to say something else. But then he turns his attention back to the view.

I frown, frustrated, and decide to take the plunge myself. "Can I ask you something?"

He shifts to face me, and although I know I must be imagining it, I think I see trepidation in his eyes. But when I look more closely, all I see is him looking at me. A trick of the light, I suppose.

"Ronan?"

"Yes. Of course. You know you can ask me anything."

"You've started calling me angel. Why?"

He runs a hand through his hair, and I wonder if the question makes him uncomfortable.

"It's no big deal," I add quickly. "It's only—well, you didn't do that before I was—well, you know. Before that time when you rescued me."

"No," he says gently. "I suppose I didn't. I'm sorry if you don't like it. I don't mean to be condescending or—"

"No! I like it. I mean, um, it's nice. I was only wondering what made you start."

"You did," he says with the flicker of a smile. Then he continues before I have the chance to ask what he means. "You'd lost so much blood, and I was so worried about you. I was staying in your room at the hospital, and—"

"You stayed in my room?"

"The first night."

"Why? The doctors told me that I was lucky. That you got me out in time."

His shoulders rise and fall. "I guess I wasn't ready to trust anyone other than myself. And you were sleeping. I wanted to make sure you had a familiar face when you woke up."

"Oh." My chest flutters from his words, and I have to stifle the urge to reach over and take his hand. "I—thank you. I didn't know you'd done that."

He shrugs as if it was nothing, but to me, it's everything.

"I watched you," he said. "You'd have a nightmare, and I'd hold your hand. Or you'd shift in bed, and I'd adjust your blanket. And every time I looked at you in that white hospital gown, with your hair on the white pillow and your skin so pale, I thought you looked like an angel. Beautiful and ethereal. Honestly, it scared me a little."

"Scared?"

"Angels aren't of this world. I was afraid the doctors were wrong, and I started talking to you. Talking to this angel in front of me and telling her to fight her way back. That we needed your sweetness here. With us." He runs his fingers through his hair again, then shakes his head. "I sound like some maudlin teenager. I'm sorry."

"Don't be," I say, fighting tears. "And thank you."

"What for?"

"Everything," I say, even though the word really isn't big enough.

For a moment, we simply look at each other. Then he clears his throat. "Listen, Brandy, about what happened at the wedding—"

I lift a hand, cutting him off. "It's okay."

"It's not. I—I crossed a line."

I lick my lips, turning away so that I'm looking out at the light shimmering on the ocean. I don't want him to see the truth—and the hurt—on my face. Because those words sound remarkably like *It wasn't you; I was just drunk.* "Like I said, it's fine." But, of course, it isn't, and I should tell him that. It hurt the way he walked away, especially since he never walked back again or bothered to tell me why. "It's fine," I say again, underscoring the lie.

"Well. Okay, then." He takes his hand away, and when I glance back, I see that he's slipped it into his pocket.

"I saw you with that woman." The moment the words leave my mouth, I want to kick myself. Not only is it none of my business, but I'm probably coming off as jealous. Which I'm not.

Except maybe I am. A little, anyway. And maybe a tiny bit hurt, too, that he'd rather hire a call girl than be with me. Which is completely stupid and hypocritical since he and all my friends know that I'm not wired for casual sex.

"What woman?"

"The, um, call girl," I say. "I was with Lamar. He recognized her."

"I see."

I wait for him to say something else, but he doesn't.

"It's none of my business."

"No," he says. "It's not."

My stomach twists, and I feel like the biggest fool in the universe. "Right. Yeah, well..." I hold on to the rail and look down over the town, hoping he can't see the way tears are welling in my eyes. "I'm really sorry. I shouldn't have said anything."

I don't look at him, but I hear his sigh clear enough. "It's okay. Really." His hand lands softly on my shoulder, and I close my eyes, slowly and hesitantly acknowledging that this thing I'm feeling is jealousy.

I really am so screwed.

"We should probably get going." His voice is soft. He squeezes my shoulder, then turns and heads back to the Range Rover.

I follow, then climb into my seat and wait for him to start the car. He does, but he doesn't put it into gear. Instead, he stares forward, his hands gripping the steering wheel so hard I can see that his knuckles are white even in the dim light coming off the dashboard.

I force myself to say nothing. After all, I'd started this by mentioning Jacey Kane in the first place. Instead, I slip my shoes off again and pull my feet up, then try to disappear into a little ball on my side of the car.

By the clock on the center console, it's been only a minute, but it feels like an eternity has transpired when he finally speaks. "It's about love for you, isn't it? Or at least trust."

I shift in my seat, as if a better view of his face will help me understand what he's asking. It doesn't, and I shake my head. "What is?"

"Sex," he says. "It was the opposite of trust when that prick drugged you. The boy when you were sixteen. You had no agency at all. No control. No consent. No trust."

My mouth has gone completely dry, and I can only nod. I want to tell him to shut up because I don't want to talk about the rape or about how my parents were so shamed that they packed us up and moved from Laguna Cortez to San Diego or about the little girl I had to give up for adoption when I was barely seventeen. A child I never wanted, but who is part of me, even though I won't ever get to know her.

But I don't say anything at all. There's something in his voice that I've never heard before. Something vulnerable. And I want to know where this is going.

"And that other guy. The one who broke up with you because you wanted to date him before fucking him."

I wince at the harsh words but nod. In my experience, that's pretty much par for the course with men.

"And we won't even talk about the other."

"Please don't," I whisper, trembling as the memories

crowd around me. All that matters now is that I survived. And that it was Ronan who rescued me.

"You're so strong," he says, "and you don't even know it."

"I'm not."

"Bullshit. Look at what you've been through, then look at what you've accomplished. You're an amazing woman, Brandy, and one of the things I most admire about you is that you know what you want and what you need. The way you approach your business. How fast you've grown it. How well you run it."

"Ronan…" There are tears in my eyes, and I'm not sure why. Maybe because I never knew that he thought about me like that, much less that he understands me.

"And with sex—you know what you want, and you demand it. You don't sleep around. You don't do casual sex. You need that connection. Sex isn't a release for you any more than it's an escape. It's a sacrament. It's trust. And I think that's great."

I start to say something, then stop. He's right, so what is there to say? That lately I've been wondering if maybe I'm wrong, and I do need the escape? I don't even know how to voice those words.

And I certainly don't understand why he's telling me all this.

He draws a breath, his attention shifting from me and back to the view out the windshield. "That's not me." He speaks so softly I can barely make out the words.

I wait, but when he says nothing more, I have to ask. "What do you mean?"

"Brandy, I don't date. I fuck. I don't need that connection—honestly, I don't want it. And sometimes the easiest way to keep up those barriers is to put money on the table."

I have no idea how I should react to this. Strangely, I'm not shocked. But at the same time, I'm more disappointed than I should be.

"It keeps things businesslike," he continues. "I don't like complications."

"Nobody does. But complications always find people."

"Yes," he says, his eyes steady on mine, "I suppose they do."

I rub my sweaty palms down the jeans I've changed into, trying to think of what to say. "You don't have to tell me this."

"Yes, I do."

"Why?" I ask, though I already know the answer.

"Because I was drunk at the wedding, and I was only thinking about what I wanted. Because you're sweet and beautiful, and I can't stop fantasizing about you in my bed."

"Oh." My entire body tingles, and I force myself not to move.

"I should never have kissed you. I'm sorry. I'm so damn sorry. Do I want you? Hell, yeah, and more than I want to admit. But that's as far as it goes. I don't do relationships. I don't do courtships or slow builds. Not now. Not anymore. *Shit*."

He turns away from me as if he's said too much. I start to ask what he means but stop myself. He's already told me more than either of us are comfortable with.

"I'm sorry," he finally says. "I shouldn't have put all of that out there. But we both know there's an attraction, and I'm not good at playing games or pretending like there's not. I want you, Brandy. I do. But you deserve more than a man as fucked up as I am, and nothing's going to happen between us. The sooner we both come to terms with that, the easier it's going to be in close quarters. Because until we're certain that you're safe, I'm not letting you out of my sight. Got it?"

He reaches out and takes my hand, then squeezes gently. "For what it's worth, I'm sorry."

The teenage girl that lives inside me wants to shrug it off and tell him that it's fine. That I'm flattered, but I'm not infatuated with him at all. But that girl is a liar, and he's just put the truth on the line for me. He deserves the same. "It's okay," I say. "I—well, you're right. I'm not wired that way. But I am attracted to you, so you're right about that as well."

"I took a wild guess," he says, and we both laugh, some of the tension leaving the air.

"But we're still friends?"

His eyes widen. "How can you even ask that?"

"I am asking," I say. "Are we friends?"

"Of course." He starts the car, then reaches to put it in gear, as if too uncomfortable with my question to stay still.

"Wait. Please, let me say this."

He closes his eyes, puts the transmission back into park, then faces me. "I know I'm a shit, Brandy. I don't need—"

"No. No, just listen." I pause, trying to organize my thoughts. "I don't have a great track record with men. And, well, even though I am attracted to you, I don't want more." Or, I add to myself, I don't *want* to want more.

"Because I suck with men, and I don't want to lose you. Or find out that you're a huge a-hole and have my illusions shattered."

His shoulders shake with laughter. "You might be surprised how many people think I'm a huge asshole."

"My point is that we're good. Really."

"Okay, then." He starts the engine again. "One last thing," he adds, putting the SUV in reverse. "I wasn't thrilled when Ellie came back into Devlin's life. I was afraid she'd put stress on his cracks and everything would fall apart. But he's stronger than ever now, and it's because of her. I'm grateful for that. He deserves her."

"They deserve each other," I say, completely confused as to why we're now talking about Ellie and Devlin.

"But there's another reason I'm glad she's back."

"Okay. What?"

He chuckles. "You. What conversation have you been following?"

I feel my cheeks warm as he continues. "If Ellie hadn't come back to town, I would never have met you. And, Brandy Bradshaw, that would have been a damn shame."

CHAPTER ELEVEN

"You're kidding me," I say as Ronan presses a remote to electronically open a thick wooden gate set inside a stone fence. "*This* is where you live?"

We've been driving through one of the neighborhoods nestled at the top of the hills that rise off the beach on the north side of town. It's an adorable neighborhood, and the western-most homes have stunning views of the ocean from where they are perched atop the rocky cliffs.

Most of these homes are small, having been built as charming getaways for movie stars who would escape south from Los Angeles back in the Hollywood heyday. They're all darling, but some of the properties have more gravitas, including the one that has always been my favorite. Until today I'd only seen it through binoculars while standing on the deck of my dad's boat. It's not accessible by walking north from the main beach because of a tumble of rocks that extend from the cliffs to the ocean. And you can't get a peek at the house from the street because it's behind this fence that has exactly zero points to peek through.

I know because I tried.

Basically, the place is completely private.

But now that the gate is opening, I have an unencumbered view, and I'm even more impressed than I expected.

The home itself is a darling white clapboard house surrounded by flowers and highlighted by a vine-covered trellis. It sits on one side of a gravel courtyard complete with a huge stone table that's perfect for outdoor dining. I don't see any windows on the street-facing side, but considering the property ends at the cliff's edge, I'm quite certain that the long back wall is one giant sheet of glass.

While the home and courtyard are more than enough to impress, it's the home's companion that captured my imagination as a child. A huge lighthouse that rises up from the beach below, seemingly carved from the cliff itself, then extends into the sky above.

I turn in my seat to gape at Ronan as he drives through the gate, following a path that seemingly dead-ends at the lighthouse. "You're full of surprises."

He chuckles. "I like to think so. And yes. I live here."

"Will you show me around? This is literally my favorite property in the entire town. If I'd known you lived here, I would have demanded a tour ages ago."

"I'm glad to know it's special to you. It is to me as well. And yes. I think a tour is in order. Especially since you're staying for a while."

"Right," I say, his words reminding me that this isn't a luxury vacation retreat. I'm here until my home is no longer a crime scene, the blood is cleaned up, and all the locks are changed. And, possibly, until I can find another place. Because who knows if Mr. Big's next-of-kin will want to keep it as a rental.

And, honestly, as much as I love my place, I may not even want to keep my house because I'm not sure if I'll ever be able to walk through the living room again without seeing Mr. Big's body on my floor. Maybe I should just talk to Ellie about moving into her rental.

Ronan still hasn't killed the engine, and I glance toward him, wondering why we're still in the car. Then he reaches up to the visor and pushes a button. Immediately, a set of camouflaged doors open in the lighthouse's stonework. He drives in, then parks the Range Rover next to a classic Mustang convertible. "We're here. Want the tour?"

"Are you kidding?" I scramble out, then let my eyes roam over the round room. It's a garage, for sure, but also seems to double as a workspace.

"I do some work on the Mustang," he says. "And I tinker," he adds, pointing to what looks like a woodworking area.

"You live in here?" I tilt my head up, trying to imagine the rooms above us.

"Not exactly," he says. "I use it as an office. I live in the house."

"I'm so jealous. This has been my favorite property for as long as I can remember. I used to beg my dad to take out our boat so I could look at it. Once I even swam to shore."

"Too bad I didn't own it back then. It's a private beach, you know. Would have been fun to catch you."

I smirk. "Funny," I say in a voice I hope sounds cool

and casual, even though the thought of Ronan catching me on the beach is more than a little appealing. "But we need to work on our rules. If we're just friends, then flirting is strictly—" I stop, mentally rewinding the conversation. "Own it? You *own* this place?"

"I have several properties around here, actually. The others I rent out."

"Really? I never thought of you as the real estate mogul type."

He chuckles. "I like to stay diversified." His eyes narrow. "What type am I?"

"Excuse me?"

"You said you didn't think of me as the real estate mogul type. So how did you type me?"

"Oh." I wave his question away. "I guess just not that."

"Bullshit. Come on. Tell me."

"Ronan..."

He takes a step closer, a teasing gleam in his eye. "Come on, or I won't take you up."

"That is incredibly unfair."

He shrugs, like *what can you do?* "So much of life is."

"You're evil, you know that?"

"It's a burden, but I bear it. Let's head on into the house." He turns toward a small door on the north side of the circular room. I stay put.

He pauses, his hand on the knob, then turns back to me.

"You're incorrigible," I tell him.

"One of my finer qualities."

"Fine. Whatever. The silent, sexy type. Satisfied?"

"Silent?"

"Well, not now. Though maybe you should try harder to live up to your reputation." I try to sound grumpy, but I know I fail. I'm too amused.

"And sexy." He punctuates the word.

"Do you know how many sexy men I've met who've turned out to be complete jerks?" I'm barely managing to keep a straight face.

"I guess that means I'm a breath of fresh air."

I can't hold back any longer. I laugh, then nod. "Yeah. I guess you really are. Thanks," I add.

"For what?"

"I don't know. For being silly with me?" The words come out as a question because I really don't know what I'm thanking him for other than being here and letting me —helping me—forget for a moment why I'm even on this stunning property.

"You're welcome," he says with soft sincerity, as if he understands all of that, even though I haven't said a word. Honestly, I think maybe he does.

"So how long have you lived here?"

"Do you remember when it went on the market about six years ago?"

I nod. "I wanted to tour the place, but you actually had to provide financial statements."

"I bought it. Moved in four years ago. Took about two to get her fixed up. I wanted to stay true to the exterior of both the house and the lighthouse, but both interiors needed significant work, especially from the standpoint of turning the lighthouse into an office. Ready for the tour?"

"Um, duh."

"Come on."

He uses a key code to open a locked steel door, revealing a winding staircase. I follow him up, feeling like I'm touring a European castle. "Do you have to maintain the light?" This is one of the few working lighthouses on the Southern California coast.

"The Coast Guard still does that, but only when necessary, which hasn't happened yet. It was retrofitted when I bought it, so the lamp lasts a very long time. But the place itself is all mine."

"That's really cool. I'm glad it's still functional. It's like a piece of history."

"Exactly what I thought when I bought it. Here we are," he adds, stepping off the circular stairs and into a huge, spacious room with mostly glass walls and modern furniture, including a desk that must be at least six feet long and a sofa that is practically begging me to sink into it.

"This is your office? Wow." I slowly walk around it, passing an interior wall that is lined with steel cases. "What's in there?"

"Weapons."

I let my eyes run up and down, then side to side, exaggerating how much space those weapons take up. "Must be a lot of them."

"Yes," he says. "There are."

Right. Tools of the trade, I guess.

I exhale, then walk past what looks like a workout area toward the glass behind his desk. "You sit with your back to the glass?"

"I do. But only up here."

"What kind of a vigilante are you? For that matter, how can you stand to not look at the view all day?"

"I like knowing it's there, and it's a reward for my work. Plus, I had the original glass replaced with bullet-proof glass. It's tinted in a way that makes it almost impossible to see through from the outside. Even at night when we're illuminated in here," he adds, moving up behind me.

I'm standing looking out, and I can see his reflection as he approaches and puts his hands on my shoulders. It's the two of us, so close I can feel his heat and smell the scent of his cologne.

"Hang on," he says, then pulls his key fob out of his pants pocket. He clicks it, and the room goes dark, leaving nothing in front of us but the moonlit ocean and the sky.

"Beautiful, isn't it?" He speaks in a whisper, his breath tickling my ear.

I nod, mesmerized not only by the view, but by the way he feels against me, his hands firm on my shoulders as if I mean something to him. Something more than a friend.

I can see our reflections almost like a shadow on the outside world, and I meet his eyes in the glass, then draw a shaky breath. I don't want to feel this way, as if the most natural thing to do would be to turn in his arms and kiss him. I tell myself I don't want it, and even if I did, I know I can't have it.

Isn't that what he said as we looked out over the town? That he doesn't do relationships?

Maybe that's okay.

I shove the thought from my head, knowing perfectly well it's only lust talking.

I can't do that. I can't trust knowing there's no future. Not after everything I've been through.

We're friends, though, and that's good. That's for the best. I know it. He knows it. But somehow, in this moment, that just makes me sad.

"Brandy? Did I lose you?"

I shake my head. "I was just thinking about this place," I lie. "It must have cost a fortune to renovate."

"More than the purchase price, yes. I think it was worth it."

I turn back to him, surprised. "I didn't realize independent security consultants made so much. Or is this from working with Saint's Angels?"

"Pay for the SA is just a stipend. No one is in it for the money."

I wait, but he doesn't elaborate, and since it's not really my business, I don't press. Instead, when he turns the lights back on, I let him give me the tour, explaining the tech, showing how the property is secure. "We do a lot of SA work up here. Some projects we don't even want to run through the foundation. Only a few on staff know about the vigilante work."

"And it's okay that you're telling me all of this?"

"Of course."

His words don't really surprise me, but they still make me feel special.

"We'll go up and see the light during the day. Trust me when I say it's painfully bright in there right now. And we'll take the stairs down to the beach in the morning, too. Because of the rock formations here, the beach is essentially private. You can't just walk north from the main beach by the Arts District. Even Ellie and Devlin can't walk here, and they're only a stone's throw away."

"I know," I admit. "I tried once when I was a kid. Bothered me then, but now I like the idea of privacy."

"So do I," he says, a small smile tugging at his mouth as he looks at me.

"What?"

He shakes it off. "Nothing. Mind wandering. Do you dive?"

"I have, but it's been ages."

"The beach has excellent diving and easy access. I think I might even have a wetsuit that would fit you."

"I don't know. It's been a very long time."

"You don't have to worry," he assures me, his voice low and rough.

"Oh. Well, I guess we could." I glance over his body, so much larger than mine, and once again, my mind goes straight to the gutter. Or, more accurately, to a bed.

What is wrong with me? Stress? Fear?

We talked about this not even an hour ago. Attraction, fine. Acting on the attraction? Not happening.

A fine and sensible plan, but apparently my libido is not yet on board.

It's that kiss. That magical kiss. I swear, he cast a spell over me that night, and I've been lingering under its dark, sensual magic ever since.

And I have to say, it's one heck of a spell. Because for the first time in my life, I understand the appeal of sex without strings.

And that's not something I ever thought I'd say. But I want to feel safe. And for better or worse, that's how Ronan makes me feel.

CHAPTER TWELVE

"So that's a no?" Ronan asks, making me realize I've been shaking my head.

"What?" My voice comes out squeaky.

"A no to SCUBA? Not that we'd really do it any time soon. I think we have different priorities at the moment."

"Right. Yes. Priorities. Probably best not to—you know, *dive in*—right now. Haha."

His brow furrows. "You okay?"

I nod, then shrug. "It's been a very, very long day."

"Oh, hell. I'm sorry. Of course it has." He cocks his head toward the door. "Come on. Let's get you settled in the house."

We head back down the stairs to the garage level where Ronan grabs the overnight bag I'd quickly packed. Then we head into the courtyard. "You've seen the best view," he says as we walk. "But tomorrow, I'll take you to the edge. It's stunning."

I nod, imagining standing on the edge of the cliff

looking down at the rocks and sand below. Honestly, it makes me a little dizzy, but I'm not sure if it's the thought of falling ... or the thought of falling for the man beside me.

I stifle a sigh, then follow him into the house. It's dark, but as I expected, the entire back wall is glass, giving the illusion that we could walk across the living room and then just keep walking into the water, our path illuminated by the glow of the moon.

Regretfully, I turn away from this astounding view.

"This is amazing," I say sincerely. I love the ocean. I was always jealous that Ellie grew up right on the beach while I was tucked away in the hills. And while I confess that I like the idea of stepping out my back door and digging my toes in the sand, there's something compelling about Ronan's place, too, with its lovely view and privacy from people who stroll along the beach through your backyard.

"Make yourself at home," Ronan says, dropping my bag by the door. He gestures to one of the chairs. "Do you want something to drink? Or would you rather I show you your room?"

"Later's fine. I think right now some wine would be great."

"Can't argue with that. Do you trust me, or do you want to come pick something out on your own?"

I offer him a small smile. "I trust you." He matches it, and for a moment, our eyes meet. There was an awkwardness before, but it fades in the moment. Right now I feel like I'm exactly where I'm supposed to be.

Then he takes off his jacket and removes his weapon from his belt holster, and reality snaps right back around me. *There's a dead body in my house, and I'm here because I might be in danger.*

Focus, girl.

I kick my shoes off and settle in on his sofa, my feet tucked under me and a soft afghan over my legs. The only thing missing is Jake, but he's at his favorite doggy day care. We'd dropped him off on the way to Ronan's, figuring I'd get him back once the house was no longer a crime scene. I'm hoping that will be tomorrow, but even if it is, I may go stay at Devlin and Ellie's when Ronan leaves for his trip. I'll go back home eventually, but considering I can't stop seeing that body, I think tomorrow may be too soon.

I draw a breath and try to return to the moment, banishing the unwelcome memories.

"This place is amazing," I tell him as I look out over the view. "It's not how I pictured you living, but after seeing you here, I don't think I can imagine you anywhere else now."

"Do you imagine me often?" There's a touch of heat in his voice, and it makes me feel even warmer than the blanket.

"Maybe," I say boldly.

I see amusement twinkle in his eyes. "Brandy Bradshaw. Are you flirting with me? I thought that was strictly off-limits."

I pull my blanket closer, then try to shrug casually. "We never said that. Not specifically. I mean, sure, you don't do relationships. And, yes, I don't do casual sex. But as far as I know, that doesn't add up to a prohibition on flirting. Besides, who says I was flirting? I was just answering a question. Telling the truth."

I can't believe I said that. Any of it. I am not this bold with men. Not ever. But then again, I've never been attracted to a friend before.

"I see your point," he says, coming over with two glasses of wine. "So tell me more."

"More?"

"How do you imagine me?"

"Oh." So much for being bold. Now I'm regretting starting this. My head is spinning, and I haven't yet drunk one sip. "I don't know," I lie, because in my head I can see him beside me so clearly, his fingers slowly stroking my arm. He moves closer to kiss me, and I close my eyes. But before I do, I see him smile, and it fills me up from the inside out.

I draw in a shaky breath. "I see you smiling," I say, which is as close to the truth as I can come without blushing furiously, then running off to hide in a closet.

"Fitting," he says. "You make me smile."

As if to prove it, the corner of his mouth rises in that sexy grin he has. I actually giggle, then take a long swallow of my wine to hide it.

When I've gathered myself, I indicate the house. "What I started to say was that I never imagined you in a house like this."

"Like what?"

"Like something out of *Architectural Digest.*"

He lifts a shoulder. "I like fine things," he says, his gaze roaming slowly over me. "Precious things. Beautiful things."

"Oh." I lick my lips, then clear my throat. "I, um, guess I always thought you seemed more of a cabin in the woods guy."

"You mean alone with nature?"

"I guess." I shake my head. "I don't know. Maybe you're just a mystery, Ronan Thorne."

"Is that bad?"

I take another sip of my wine. At this rate, I'll be lightheaded very soon. "No."

"Good." He finishes his drink in one gulp and puts his glass on the coffee table.

"Are you having more?"

"No," he says. "I don't think that would be a good idea."

"Oh."

"Just in case," he says. "Bad guys."

I nod, but we both know that wasn't what he meant. And I'm not sure if I'm grateful he's sticking to my rules or frustrated that he's not abandoning caution and pushing me out of my comfort zone.

"For the record, this *is* my cabin in the woods," he says. "I happen to like a view other than trees."

I think about it, and he's right. He's surrounded by a neighborhood, yet set off, secluded against nature and people by the cliff on one side and the stone fence on the other. "So I guess I imagined you right, but in the wrong setting."

"And here I thought you knew me." He presses a hand over his heart, making me laugh.

"Not a bad thing. I like the idea of getting to know you better." As soon as I say it, I regret it. That doesn't feel like casual flirting. That feels like going too far into dangerous waters.

To pull it back, I hold up my wine glass. "You have good taste."

"Actually, I just know a very good sommelier."

"Yeah, my sommelier is great too. His name's George. He works in the wine and beer aisle at Ralphs," I say, referring to the nearby grocery store.

"I think we can do better than George," Ronan says. "Tomorrow if you like, we'll go and let you pick out a bottle."

"Is that how you entertain all the women who come to your house after they find men murdered in their living room?" Immediately, I regret the words.

To my relief, Ronan only smiles. "No, only the cute blonde ones." He reaches out and curls a strand of my hair around his finger. "With adorable pink tips."

My cheeks flush, and I look down, once again fascinated by my wine.

He releases my hair, then leans back, turning in his seat to look more directly at me. "We never did fix that sink of yours."

"And I never made us cookies." I frown as I meet his eyes. "Is it bad that I still want to? Even more than I did before?"

"Now?"

I lift a shoulder. "You know me. It's what I do when I'm stressed."

"I could eat cookies."

"Well, we'll have to hit the store, because we're not going back to my place. Not only did the cops kick us out of there, but I don't want to eat cookies made from ingredients that were near a dead guy."

"Pretty sure it's not catching."

"That," I tell him, "is not the point."

"For the record, I agree. But we don't need to go out.

I'm sure I have everything you need. And while you make cookies, I'll grill some steaks."

I gape at him. "You? A bachelor action hero who can cook?"

"Are you maligning me with stereotypes?"

"I'm calling you an action hero. Is that maligning you?"

He chuckles. "No. I'll take that as a compliment."

"Good. Because it's meant to be."

"But you forget about Casey Ryback."

I shake my head slowly, having no clue what he's talking about.

"*Under Siege*. Fun movie from the nineties. Action hero and a cook."

"You are a fount of amazing facts. I never would've guessed."

"No, you just assumed that I was hollow and one note. Too wrapped up in my action hero, bachelor ways to even have flour and sugar."

I grimace. "You know that's not what I meant."

"Did I?" The twinkle in his eye gives him away. "Well, maybe I did. But it was fun egging you on."

"It was fun deserving it," I respond, laughing as I stand up to follow him to the kitchen.

I'm not sure if he started this whole banter knowing that it would soothe me, but whatever the reason, that's the result. My world may have been knocked off kilter, but at the moment, it feels very much back on track.

The house has an open floor plan, and once we reach the kitchen, he settles on one of the stools at the island. "I can pull out the ingredients for you, if you want."

"Nope. This is my jam. I've got it. Just tell me where you keep things."

"As you wish," he says, then settles onto the stool to watch me grab and mix together the ingredients for oatmeal raisin cookies, a recipe I make so frequently that I could do it in my sleep. To my surprise, he has every-thing I need.

Although, actually it's not a surprise. But it would have been half an hour ago.

"You're staring," I say as I use a wooden spoon to mix the batter.

I glance quickly in his direction, and I think I see a gleam in his eye when he says, "I like to watch."

I roll my eyes and focus on the dough. This is some-thing I genuinely love doing. It's soothing. The ritual of it. The creativity. Honestly, if I didn't love making bags so much, I could happily open a bakery.

For that matter, maybe I should start selling special bags filled with cookies. A half dozen in a little sleeve that you sling over your arm. It could be a thing.

"You're smiling."

I shake my head. "Just being silly. Thinking about designing a purse that's primary purpose is to carry cookies."

"Very innovative. And it's nice to see you smile."

"I've been smiling."

He shakes his head. "Not like this. Not since we found the body. Your smiles have been polite. Conversa-tional. This one is joyous. I can't say I blame you, but I'm glad to see it again."

I'm not sure what to say. Either about my mood or about the fact that he sees me so clearly.

So I simply nod, then clear my throat and get back to work. "You really do have a well-stocked kitchen."

"Action hero. Cook. Just like you said."

"You really cook? Or is this just for when you have women over? Cook them a nice meal before the, you know, whatever."

I want to call back the words the moment I've said them, but thankfully, he only looks amused. "The *whatever* is the good part. And I think I already explained that I don't do the dating thing. That means I don't do the cooking thing. Not for women, anyway. But I do cook for me."

"All the more reason to consider myself lucky, I guess," I say. "After all, I'm getting cookies."

"Yes. You are."

Silence fills the kitchen. I'm not sure what he's thinking, but my mind has gone immediately to all the things that I *don't* get with Ronan. Things I shouldn't want but do. Things that are outside my comfort zone but right now are so tempting. Maybe it's the reminder of my mortality. Maybe it's fear.

And maybe that's all just an excuse. But I want to be in his arms. I want him to kiss and soothe me. But I know that won't happen. Because what Ronan wants from a woman is a fast fuck. Scratching an itch and moving on.

What I want with a man is a future.

"—apple pie."

"Sorry," I say, only then realizing that I've wandered down a dangerous mental path.

"I said that I feel about pie the way you do about cookies."

"What's that?"

"I bake pies. To relax."

I lean back against the counter. "No way. Apple pies?"

"Apple and pumpkin are my favorite. But I've been known to go wild with cream pies a time or two."

"You wild and crazy guy. And here I thought you got all of your excitement rappelling down buildings or leaping from helicopters while you chase bad guys."

"Yeah, well, that's on equal par with rolling out the dough for a nice flaky crust."

"I've always believed that cooking was an extreme sport. Now I know. Still," I add, waving the wooden spoon at him, "between cookies and pies, cookies are the real art form."

"Woman, them's fighting words."

"Phhbt."

"Oh, now you've done it. We'll have a throw-down one of these days. My pies against your cookies."

I cross the kitchen and extend my arm over the island. "You're on."

He reaches forward and takes my hand. Our eyes meet, his full of heat and need. And in that moment, I can't seem to speak. I can't even seem to think.

I see his lips part, and I realize he's about to say something. That's when I hear the tell-tale *beep, beep, beep* of someone punching in the front door code. I yank my hand away, my eyes going wide. "You expecting someone?"

He slides off the stool, shaking his head as he frowns. "No."

At the same time, I hear a female voice say, "Ronan? You home?"

I turn, gaping at Ronan. I recognize that voice. "Reggie?"

As soon as I say her name, the woman herself strides into the living room, a backpack slung over one shoulder. She tosses it onto the sofa, looking as comfortable here as if it were her own home.

Oh dear God, is this her own home? Are Ronan and Reggie...

Tall and athletic, Reggie Taggart is another member of Saint's Angels. She has shoulder-length dark hair highlighted with cobalt blue streaks, deep-set eyes, and a hint of a Central-Mexican accent. I don't know what training landed her in the fold, but I do know she's seriously badass.

She's usually totally put together, but today, she looks slightly frazzled around the edges. I'm hoping that's from the job and not because she's annoyed at having walked into the house to find me cooking with Ronan.

I thought she lived at the hotel she manages, a job that's both a family business and also a cover for the work she does with the Angels.

But what if she actually lives here? What if she shares a bed with Ronan? I haven't seen her since the wedding. Have they started going out in the interim? Have they always been going out? Casual fuck-buddies? Serious dating?

"Brandy? Are you okay?"

She's moved through the living room to the island where Ronan is on a stool. Now she's peering at me, a quizzical expression in her dark brown eyes.

I shake myself out of it. "Reggie. Hey. What are you doing here?"

"Same thing you are. I'm working on figuring out what's going on with the body in your living room."

Some of the tension eases out of my shoulders. Of course, she's here about the body. And I need to pull myself together.

There's no reason for me to be tying myself up in knots. There's nothing between me and Ronan. Nothing except one exceptional kiss in a dark alcove. A kiss I'm starting to wish had never happened even though its memory is one of my favorite nighttime fantasies.

"Have you figured it out?" I ask. Maybe this nightmare is ending tonight.

"No. But I have a hell of a lot more questions." She shoots a sideways glance to Ronan, but from my angle, I can't see either of their eyes. Even so, it makes me feel edgy. Like they're having a silent conversation.

And once again, I wonder if they're an item. Either dating or friends-with-benefits or something equally naked and sweaty.

Reggie turns back to me and smiles, almost as if she's resetting the room. "So other than bodies in your living room, how've you been? I haven't seen you in a minute, but I heard something about a fashion show? Sounds cool."

I want to know about Mr. Big, but the lure of talking about the Expo sucks me in. "Yeah, it's very cool," I tell her. "Most applications to the Expo for businesses my size are declined, so I was amazed when they chose me."

A little tinge of worry settles in my gut. I still have a ton of work to do to get ready. I really don't have time to be away from my studio which is inconveniently located in the den, uncomfortably close to where we found Mr. Big's body.

"I'll try to come," Reggie says.

"What? Oh!" I force my thoughts back to the conversation. "You should. I go every year. There are a ton of booths, and I always find something darling, and—"

"Ladies," Ronan interrupts. "I could talk fashion all day, but I'm guessing Reggie came here about something other than this year's winter accessories."

Reggie's mouth twists, but she nods. "As much as I like this year's colors, he's right." She focuses on me. "We need to talk. You both need to see something."

"Oh." Dread washes over me, and I feel a little sick. I turn to Ronan, but his expression has turned to stone, and I can't read a thing.

I look between the two of them. "What is it? What's going on?"

"That's my question," Ronan says.

Reggie hops off her stool and fetches her backpack from the sofa. She pulls out a laptop, then opens it up, and I come around so that I can see the screen, too.

Her fingernails are manicured and deep red, and they fly over the keys as she navigates to whatever is so important.

"The files on the phone were encrypted," she tells me. "So Ronan asked Tamra to shoot them my way."

"He did?" I glance at him, and he nods. I hadn't even noticed him sending a text. "Stealthy," I say. "So you got through Mr. Big's security?"

"I did." She taps some more. "And to be honest, it was very high-end security. Made me wonder why he needs his phone so well-protected."

"And you found something," I say.

She shoots me a sideways glance. "Yeah. I found something. You're not going to like it."

"What?"

A single brow rises, and she looks at me for a beat before turning her attention back to the computer. Ronan moves to stand behind me, his hand on my shoulder as we both look at her screen. So far, there's nothing there. Then the screen pops on, and I realize I'm looking at my empty living room. Specifically, the sitting area with the couch by which we found the body.

"I don't understand," I say. "Who took that video?" The angle is from above, as if we're floating near the ceiling looking down.

"It's the security feed," Reggie says. "Streamed straight to his phone in real time."

"Security feed? But the house doesn't have any security cameras on the inside."

"Oh, yeah. It really does." She turns to give Ronan a wry glance. "You should probably tell Devlin there's some interesting footage of him and Ellie from when they stayed over back when all that mess was going on."

I reach a hand up and start rubbing my temple. "Are you serious? Everywhere?" I feel nauseous. Somebody's been watching me. Constantly watching me.

I press my hand to my mouth, afraid I just might throw up.

"You okay?"

"Not really," I admit, turning to face him. "How could he—why? Why would he do that?"

"I don't know," Ronan says. He nods toward the monitor, and I turn to see Mr. Big walk on screen as he says, "but if he hadn't, we wouldn't know who killed him. And I have a feeling we're about to see that very thing."

"True that," Reggie says.

"Oh, God, no. I can't watch that." But the words are barely out of my mouth when I freeze, my eyes riveted to the screen. It's Mr. Big, all right, wearing the same clothes he died in. The same outfit he'd been wearing when he yelled at me on the street. And then someone steps closer, entering the frame from the left.

I feel Ronan's hand clasp my arm as I see that the woman is holding a gun.

"What the hell?"

His voice is barely more than a whisper, and I second his words, my heart pounding in my chest because this bitch is about to murder my landlord, and here we are, watching it in color.

She cocks her head to the left, tilting her face up and smiling as she raises the gun. In that moment, the camera has her right in frame and perfectly in focus.

Oh. My. God.

I gasp, suddenly seeing what Ronan has already picked up on. I twist around, letting him pull me against him, his arms going around me as I cry out, my horror and fear muffled against his chest.

Not from the brutal murder. Not from the splatter of blood. Not even from the way the body falls, life gone in an instant.

I'm in shock because the woman doing the shooting is me.

CHAPTER THIRTEEN

———————

Ronan held Brandy close as she trembled against his chest, but his eyes stayed on the screen. How? How the hell was this even possible?

"It isn't me." The voice was small and scared and broke his heart.

She eased back in his arms and looked up at him, her face pale with shock, her eyes so full of pain that it took all of his strength not to pull her back against his chest and hold her close so that he absorbed all her pain and fear.

Instead, he cupped her head. "Dear God, angel, do you think I could believe that it was?" He shot a sideways glance at Reggie, full of reprobation and anger. She looked back at him impassively.

"I wasn't even there," Brandy said, looking between the two of them, her voice still full of panic as if he hadn't even tried to soothe her at all. "I was at the beach. The time-stamp says two forty-five, and I was at the beach. With Ellie. You believe me, don't you?"

"Of course," he said, his voice as calm and soothing as he could make it. "Of course I do. Try not to worry. This is going to be okay."

"How?" she snapped, her eyes shining with anger and fear. "How the *hell* will it be okay?"

He fought a wince as she broke free of his embrace, then started to pace. Brandy rarely cursed, and that harsh word cut through him even more than the tear that was tracing a slow path down her cheek.

What he wouldn't give to be able to take that fear away. To keep her safe, always.

She paced some more, her fingertips pressed to her temples, then spun around to face Reggie, her expression full of fury and hurt. "You could have warned me."

"No. I couldn't. You needed to see it."

"The hell she did," Ronan snapped.

"It was her, Ronan." Reggie's voice was at least as hard as his. "At least it damn sure looked like her, and you know it as well as I do. She looked straight into the camera. Take a step back, forget that you want to fuck her, and tell me straight out that if it had been anybody else wearing the body of another person, that you wouldn't have done exactly what I did."

He fought a wince. "For Christ's sake, Reggie."

"What? It isn't true? Because that's what it looks like from the cheap seats. And you know what it looked like on that video? Like Brandy nailed her landlord."

"Dammit, Reggie, I—"

"She's right," Brandy interrupted, then turned her attention to Reggie. "You're right. About all of it. But you could have told me. Given me some hint as to what I was going to watch. My God..." She trailed off, her hand going to her mouth, her throat moving as if she was going to vomit.

"I am sorry, Bran. But I'm trained not to trust anyone. You had to see it raw. And I had to watch. I had to be sure."

"And are you?"

Ronan watched the two women, both standing tall, shoulders back, eyes locked. He'd been afraid this would destroy Brandy. Instead, she'd fought back her initial horror and was stepping into the fray. The woman was incredible.

"Are you sure now?" Brandy asked again, taking one step closer to Reggie.

"Yeah," Reggie said. "I am."

"Why?" Ronan asked as Brandy's shoulders dipped with relief.

"What?" Reggie's brows rose. "Now *you* need proof?"

"Because she knows me," Brandy said. "She knows I couldn't ever do that."

"Honestly, no," Reggie said. "People surprise me all the damn time. I'm talking about the fingernails."

Ronan glanced at Brandy, who shrugged. "Fingernails?" he asked.

In response, she cued the file up again and ran it. "Subtle, but see? Fingernails. Brandy keeps hers short." She increased the size of the image, losing clarity but proving her point.

"I could have worn press-ons," Brandy said, making Reggie laugh.

"Yeah, well, I'll lay money you didn't. And that *is* because I know you."

"And you'd be right," Brandy said. "Thanks for that."

Ronan stepped toward her, moving behind her and casually slipping his arms around her waist, pulling her close. She didn't protest, and he was grateful for that. He had to touch her then. Had to feel that she was okay.

"If it's not me, who is it?" She twisted her head to look at him, anger replacing the fear in her eyes. "And how the hell did they steal my face?"

"Money," he said flatly. "That kind of mask used to be movie fiction, but the real thing is available now—if you have the thousands to pay for it and the time to wait for it. As for who, I don't know. But," he added, his voice as hard as steel, "I promise we'll find out."

"She shot him. Some bitch stole my face, walked into my home, and shot him. She's setting me up. But why?"

"I don't know," he said gently, then squeezed her shoulders. "But we're going to find answers. Do you trust me?"

She nodded, and the easy certainty in her response both flattered and terrified him.

Michelle had trusted him, too.

Michelle had never even known she was in danger.

His gut twisted, and he pushed the memories away, focusing instead on the woman in front of him. A scared and confused woman whose instinct was to turn to him for protection and strength and solace from her fears.

He'd failed Michelle; he wasn't going to fail Brandy.

"—call Devlin."

"Sorry," Ronan said, turning to Reggie. "What did you say?"

"I said we need to call Devlin." She stepped into the kitchen and poured herself a glass of wine, then took a long swallow. "Until we know otherwise, we should assume this has to do with Saint's Angels."

"Why?" Brandy asked. She moved out of his arms but continued to clutch his hand. "I don't have anything to do with SA, and neither did my landlord."

Ronan fought a scowl. "No, but Reggie's right. Anyone watching would know you're tight with Devlin's new wife."

"Exactly," Reggie said. "Could be a way to flush out members of the team or even a misdirect for something else that's going on. Get our resources focused on tragedy surrounding someone at the periphery over here," she said, holding out one hand, "then run off and hijack a school bus over there." Her two hands were spread wide, and she looked from one to the other. "Seems like a no-brainer to me."

Brandy shook her head. "No, no, no. If we call them, Ellie will cancel."

"Brandy," Ronan began. "We—"

"*Dammit, no.*" She drew a breath, as if startled by the force of her outburst. "I'm sorry, but this publicity tour is huge. For her career *and* for getting more awareness for the foundation. Ellie's worked so hard, and the DSF does good work, and I'm not willing to mess that up. Especially not for a hunch. And that's all you have right now."

Her bravery shouldn't surprise him—he knew well enough that Brandy had a well of strength she rarely tapped—but the force of her loyalty to Ellie and Devlin made him want to pull her close and never let her go. Had they said she was on the periphery of Saint's Angels? Hell, this made her an honorary member.

But even so...

"I understand what you're saying, but Reggie has a point."

"She has a *hunch*," Brandy repeated. "Okay, fine. Pursue the idea that this is somehow about Saint's Angels. That's fine. Just don't bring Devlin back. What's the matter?" she added, her eyes darting between the two of them. "You two can't work without Daddy at home?"

Ronan bristled. "Saint's Angels is Devlin's baby."

"Bullshit. You both put your life and freedom on the line with every mission. I've seen what you're capable of —both of you. I love Devlin like a brother, and I don't want to screw this up for him. For either of them. Not until we know if the SA is even part of this."

Tears streamed down her cheeks, and he had to fight the urge to reach out and brush them away. Instead, he glanced at Reggie, who looked as conflicted as he felt.

"You forget. I knew them both when I was a kid. They deserve some peace. Please," Brandy said, reaching out to squeeze his hand. "Please don't mess this up for them. Not unless we truly have to."

Ronan drew in a breath, then turned to Reggie. "Brandy's right. They deserve this time."

Slowly, Reggie nodded. "The truth is, if it gets hairy, they can be on a plane and back here in about six hours."

"All right," Ronan said. "So now we just need answers."

"Exactly," Brandy said. "Who the hell is dressing up like me? And for bonus points, I really, really want to know why."

CHAPTER FOURTEEN

The little prick was smarter than she'd thought.

Tiffany Shein pressed herself against the side of the industrial trash can, both annoyed and impressed that her still-breathing third partner had actually managed to track her to San Diego. She'd always believed that Alan Long was a bit of a dud. A good foot soldier, but not big on ideas or initiatives.

As far as Tiffany was concerned, his biggest assets were his cock and his skill with a knife. She and Robert had been in full agreement on those points when they'd brought him on to their team and into their bed.

"Jesus, Tiffany," he said, his low-pitched voice amplified in the cramped alley. "What the hell do you think I'm going to do? Kill you? I love you. You know I do. I've been searching for you ever since I heard the news that Robert was dead."

She stayed silent, listening as his footsteps receded. She relaxed—just a little. Maybe he was leaving the alley.

"You think I'm going to hurt you for taking him out?"

he said, the fact that he was louder now killing her hope that he'd backtrack away. "I would've done it myself, just so we could be together."

He stopped talking, the silence lingering like a gaping chasm. Despite herself, Tiffany felt a pang of regret. He was a bit of a dud, but at least Alan was a dud who could fuck like a pro.

"Come on, Tiff."

She heard his footsteps as he moved down the alley and held her gun tighter. "God, it kills me that you don't trust me. Seriously, babe, even if I wanted you dead, why would I kill you before you tell me where you hid the bonds? That was the whole point, right? That was why you killed Robert. But now we can be together. Come on, babe."

She winced, wishing she had some idea of how he'd found her. Did he use some sort of tracker? If so, what was it on? She'd ditched her phone and her purse, and she sincerely doubted that he'd managed to weave anything into her clothes.

Apparently, the dud was smarter than she'd thought.

"Can we just sit down and talk this out?"

His voice was a bit louder. *Closer.*

She lifted her gun.

"If you don't want to be with me, it's going to break my heart, but I can deal. I just need to know. Hell, keep the money. I mean, would I like you to give me even two percent? Sure. I got debts to pay. Would I like to lie with you naked on a beach? You better believe I would. You and me under the sun drinking vodka and living the good life. That was the dream, babe, and it still can be. We split the take, and we can live that way forever, no Robert in the bed between us. Be like a slice of heaven."

She didn't reply. But she planted her feet. Held her weapon steady.

She heard him sigh. "Come on, babe. I know you're unsure. But man, it was ballsy of you to take that brief-case. What do they call that? Windfall profits? And you've got more than enough to share."

He was right about that. They'd been hired to take out an Argentinian industrialist. A typical job for typical pay. The kind of job she and Robert had been doing for this particular client for almost a decade.

This one, though, had a new twist. Recover a brief-case the mark had stolen and return it to the employer, a man she knew only as the Cheshire Snake. Because of the additional task, he'd increased the payout by a cool five million.

Alan was a new addition to their team, but a third person was an asset, especially on these higher profile cases where the mark had a private security team.

Because the Argentinian was a horny prick, Tiffany was on point, with Alan and Robert providing cover, transport, and backup. The plan was to get close with the promise of getting naked. In disguise, of course. She wore her least used mask, one that she'd so far only used for small cons—no hits. Didn't want to learn too late that her fake face was splashed all over Interpol.

Since the mark was in London for a meeting, she'd oh-so-casually bumped into him in his hotel lobby, then offered to buy him a drink for being such a klutz. When he'd agreed, she'd suggested his room instead, biting her lip and lightly stroking her cleavage while she purred that they'd surely be more comfortable.

He hadn't even hesitated. Men were such predictable pigs. He took her arm, escorted her up, then dismissed his security team, leaving only his bodyguard in a chair outside his door.

When his back was turned to mix her a drink, she'd pulled out her silenced pistol and put a bullet in his brain. Easy as spraying a wasp.

She'd grabbed the case and was about to leave when something held her back. She was so good at her job. Always following orders. Always the good little soldier.

This time, she wanted to know the *why*.

That's why she examined the case, disabled the countermeasures—a gas capsule that would surely have knocked her out—then picked the lock.

Less than two minutes after Mr. Argentina had met his demise, she had the case open and was staring at almost three hundred million in negotiable bearer bonds.

And wasn't that interesting?

That was the moment that Tiffany had decided to keep the haul all for herself. Robert was beginning to bore her, and despite his enthusiasm in bed, Alan was a dim bulb. They wouldn't expect the betrayal—men trusted their cocks, not their heads—so they'd be easy to take out.

Her employer was a different story. As with most in her profession, they'd never met face to face. But once he learned that Mr. Argentina and his door guard were dead and the case was gone, he'd pull the hotel security feed. And that, of course, was why she and Robert always worked in disguise, utilizing the identity of the people who rented Robert's Laguna Cortez home. Years ago, they'd relied on makeup and wigs, but these days, *Mission Impossible*-style masks were real. Expensive as hell, but real.

And because of that, no one would know the killer was Tiffany Shein.

They'd be looking for Brandy Bradshaw, a vicious killer hiding in the guise of a pretty little seamstress. A killer who'd taken out an Argentinian industrialist and her wealthy landlord.

There would be gaps, of course. The real Brandy would likely have an alibi. Which was why Tiffany had added fuel to the Brandy-is-a-killer fire by directing a potential client referral—with the very lame alias of Mr. White—to the real Brandy. She'd even watched the exchange, from afar of course, when the confused little seamstress had given him her card.

Now, if need be, Tiffany could call in an anonymous tip about the man who'd tried to hire an assassin. Couple that with other incriminating evidence she'd planted, and Brandy the Bland would become Brandy the Bad.

It wasn't a perfect plan, but it wouldn't matter. The real Brandy would protest her innocence, but so what? With all the evidence, who would believe her?

And soon enough, Tiffany would be lying safely on a beach somewhere, enjoying her well-deserved wealth.

Of course Alan—silent, creeping around the alley Alan—had created another problem. He was supposed to have been at the house, too, so that Tiffany could take both him and Robert out at the same time. A meeting that Tiffany had carefully arranged, and that dim bulb Alan had blown off so he could hang with a friend in Palm Springs.

How he'd found her here, in Newport Beach, was anyone's guess. Maybe Alan wasn't as dim as she'd thought.

She sighed, biting back a curse as she calculated the odds. In the end, she tucked her gun into the back of her jeans and pulled her shirt over it. Then she stepped into the alley with her hands raised. "You're right, I don't have the bonds with me."

"So? What are we going to do?"

"What do you want?"

"Baby, I only want you. Don't you know that? Why do you think I agreed to our deal? Because I wanted to be in bed with Robert? It was all about you. It's always been about you. Share the bonds, don't share the bonds. I don't give a fuck. I just want you."

She smiled. "That's what I've always loved about you, baby. You do talk sweet."

"Can we just talk? Try to figure this out? Neutral ground."

She hesitated, then nodded. "The diner." She tilted her head to indicate the back door to the all-night diner through which she'd walked when she'd seen him come in the front.

"Head back in, take a table, have a chat?"

"Exactly."

He nodded, and they headed for the door together. Tiffany looked up, searching the alley for cameras. She'd done that already, but she had a tendency to check things twice. Even three or four times if it was really important. Not being caught on camera right now was key.

And then, as Alan, polite son of a bitch that he was, reached to pull open the door, she yanked out her gun and shot him right in the back of the head.

He dropped like a stone as she pulled up her black hoodie, tilted her eyes to the ground, and calmly walked out of the alley with one less target on her back.

I'm curled up on the couch when Ronan comes back from walking Reggie to the door. She's heading home to continue searching the security footage that Tamra downloaded off the phone. With luck, there might be something else that gives a clue as to who the other Brandy really is.

"He knew her," I say. "The person under the mask. He looked right at her like he knew her, and he for sure doesn't know me." I frown, remembering the scene outside Pacific Property. "He thought I was her. When he saw me on the street and demanded to know why I was there, that's what it was. He thought that I was her disguised as me."

Ronan takes a seat on the sofa beside me. "Agreed."

"And then I think he figured it out. He looked at Jake. He gave me that strange look. And that's when he bolted. He realized he was talking to the real me."

"Could be. We'll never know for sure."

I sigh. He's right about that.

"So were they fighting? He didn't approach me. It was more like he was scolding me."

"Not a fight," Ronan says. "Or if it was, they made up. The man on that tape wasn't scared. He was smiling until she lifted that pistol."

I nod, pulling my knees up and hugging them. I feel removed from myself as we talk about this. As if it's all happening to some other person. I guess in some weird way, it is.

"Who could she be?" I ask.

"I don't know. But we're going to find out."

I scoff. "She could be anybody. She could even —*Ronan*," I say, suddenly realizing.

"We have no way of knowing if she's really a girl. That could have been a guy. The footage—"

I start to get up, but he waves me down. "I'll get it," he says, obviously realizing I want the laptop that Reggie left behind. He brings it back, and we look at the footage again, but there's really no way to be sure if the person wearing my face is male or female.

I look at him, then shrug. "Square one again?"

To my surprise, he laughs.

"What?"

"Nothing." He sits on the coffee table so he's facing me directly. "Nothing except that you are an amazing woman."

"Oh." I hug myself tighter, sweet surprise running through me. "I—thank you. But, um, why the sudden praise?"

"I think most people in this situation would be screaming for answers and cursing the universe for not providing them."

"I'm screaming. Just really softly and deep inside."

His grin flashes. "I wouldn't doubt it. My point, though, is that you're coping incredibly well." He reaches for my hand. "I know how strong you are, Brandy. I've seen it, remember?"

I swallow, letting in a tiny flash of the horror of that day I'd been taken. A memory I try to keep pushed far away. One with blood and pain and fear.

"There's a difference between bravery and hiding," I say. "I don't let it in."

"Bravery is whatever gets you through it. Trust me, angel. You're brave. I saw it then, and I see it now. We're going to get answers, and you're going to get through this just fine."

I draw in a breath, relishing the feel of his hand around mine. "Thank you," I say. "You always see such good things in me."

It's true, I realize. He always has. Or maybe it's just that he makes me feel good things. Honestly, I'm not sure. I just know that I feel happy when he's around. And safe, and special.

"Want a refill on your wine?"

"I really do," I admit.

He starts to stand, but that's when I remember, and I reach for his hand, then yank him back. "Wait! I think I know how to track down the fake me."

He sits again, but he doesn't let go. Instead, he cups both his hands around mine. I glance at our joined hands and hear the tremor in my breath as I begin to speak. "Mr. White," I say. "I forgot to tell you about Mr. White."

My phone is on the table beside him, and I reach for it, then go straight to my emails. *Nothing.*

"Damn."

Ronan's brow furrows. "What's going on?"

I slide my phone back onto the table, then I begin to relay the strange story of the man who thought it was my protocol to meet randomly in the Arts District in order to get a quote for a job.

"Did he say what kind of a job?"

"No. But when I gave him my business card, he pretended his fingers were guns and laughed at my name. You know, BB. I thought he was just weird. But he said he was going to email me with the parameters. That was the word he used. *Parameters.*"

I can tell from Ronan's face that he's thinking exactly what I am—this man wasn't intending to meet me. He was intending to meet the fake Brandy. "He said he knew where to find me because he talked to Cara."

"Who?"

"My friend that I hired as a part-time assistant. I'm sure I've told you about her."

"Of course. Right. But did he say her name or did he call her your assistant?"

"I—oh. I don't remember. Hang on."

My phone is on the table beside him, and he passes it to me. I dial on speaker, and Cara answers on the first ring.

"Oh my God, I've been dying to know. What happened with Ronan and the sink? Please tell me you guys didn't stick with traditional plumbing."

"*Cara,*" I say sharply, certain my cheeks are going to burn right off my face. "Ronan's here with me, and you're on speaker."

"Oh. Right. Haha. I've got such a fucked-up sense of humor, don't I?"

I picture her cringing, and my eyes dart up to Ronan's face. At least he looks amused rather than mortified.

"Listen, I lost the phone number for Mr. White. Do you have it?"

"Who?"

"Mr. White. He called to talk about me doing a project. You told him he could probably find me in the Arts District."

"Um, nope. Not me."

Ronan and I exchange a glance. "He said he talked to you. Well, my assistant."

"Unless you've cloned me, I don't know what you're talking about."

"Okay. No problem. I must have gotten my wires crossed."

"No worries. Do you want to schedule time to talk about the Expo? It's coming up so fast. I've ordered a ton of flyers and some display stands, but I'm wondering if—"

"I'll email you a time, okay? We're, um, in the middle of something right now."

"Oh?" Her voice rises in pitch, and I'm sure my cheeks are burning. "No problem. I'm just really psyched about the Expo. I want it to be perfect for you."

"Yeah. I'm psyched, too," I say, trying to muster all the excitement I'd felt just yesterday. Somehow, the Expo seems significantly less important than it did just twenty-four hours ago.

We end the call, and I lean back against the couch again. "So that's it. He talked to someone who said they were my assistant. And somehow, that person knew that I was going to be in the Arts District. How?"

"The cameras, I presume. Whoever we're looking for was watching you. If you made plans with Ellie, they might have read your lips."

"I really don't like this," I say, voicing the understatement of the century.

"Neither do I. Someone's setting you up. A man who's willing to hire a criminal seen on a busy street talking with a woman who's suspected of killing her landlord. It doesn't look good."

"*Suspected*," I repeat. "I'm not a suspect. Am I?"

"Not to Lamar. But I suspect you're high on the official list."

"Oh, God…" I stand and start to pace. "And he has my business card, and if he does email me back, then it looks even worse."

I turn, then come up short when I find him right there. Without thinking, I put my arms around him, gratified when he does the same and pulls me close. His body is hard and warm, and I feel safe. Like how could anything hurt me if this man is protecting me?

Except that's just an illusion, and he won't always be at my side.

I pull away, feeling awkward, knowing that I want more from Ronan than he's willing to give. I bend my head, then talk to the floor. "I should call Lamar. Fill him in."

"What? No. Not yet. The less he knows, the less he has to lie."

I shake my head, looking up. "We have to tell him something. I need a place to stay tomorrow night. I'm not going back to my place yet. I'm not even sure I'm allowed to."

He frowns as he stares at me, his eyes full of confusion. "What are you talking about?"

"Well, I can't stay here. Maybe it's okay with you, but I don't want to be alone. And Lamar needs to know about my double if he's going to be the one looking out for me. Right?"

His expression stays blank, and I exhale, exasperated. "You're leaving tomorrow, remember?"

From the way he reacts, you would have thought I'd shoved a knife in his gut. "*Shit.*" He drags his fingers through his short, blond hair, making a few tufts stand on end in a way that makes him look even more like a Hollywood action hero. The kind who gets the bad guy ... and the girl.

I swallow, not liking the direction my thoughts are going, and liking even less the thought that he's going away.

"I'm not going anywhere," he says.

I shake my head, the words not processing. "You talked to Tamra. Changed today's trip to tomorrow. I heard you."

"And now I'm canceling it. It's held for years. It can hold a little longer."

There's a shadow in his eyes when he speaks, and I step toward him. "What was the trip for?"

"It doesn't matter."

"Ronan, I—"

"I said it doesn't matter." His voice is sharper than I've ever heard it, cutting off my protests.

He grips me by the shoulders, then meets my eyes. I

see heat there and determination. "I'm not leaving your side," he adds, making my heart flutter. "End of discussion."

I nod. I hate that I'm a burden. A mess that popped into his life and has to be dealt with. But there is no way that I'm going to argue with him. I want him beside me. If I'm honest with myself—and it is so hard to be honest with myself—I want so much more than that. I want him to kiss me and touch me. I want him to make love to me. I want to forget everything around us, and I want to do that in the circle of his arms.

I turn away, muttering a thanks as I start to drown under this wave of desire. *This isn't me.* I'm not a woman who does sex for escape. Who intentionally gets involved with a guy to whom relationships are anathema.

But none of that seems to matter. I want him. His touch. His protection. I want to lose myself in his kisses and forget everything that's going on around us.

I want it ... but I truly don't know what to do about it.

I draw in a breath and force myself to look up at him. "What do we do now?"

"We need more information," he says. "Matheson's phone had the images that fed from his security cameras. But those usually self-purge to save storage on your device. I'm betting that the footage also feeds to a hard drive that will have a historical record of everything any of those cameras have recorded."

"And maybe we can find an image where he or she's not in a disguise?"

"That's the idea."

"How would we know it's the shooter? I mean, if he's

standing in the living room talking with someone, how do we know that person's my double?"

"I don't know," Ronan says. "We're taking this one step at a time. And the first step? Tonight, I'm going back to your house."

CHAPTER SIXTEEN

"Y‍ou doing okay?"

I lift my head long enough to glance at Ronan, who's at least three feet above me. I cling tightly to the branch I'm using to steady myself, hoping I won't rip the small tree out of the steep hillside, sending me tumbling into the dark below.

"I'm climbing up the back of a cliff so I can break into my own house," I say. "I'm doing as well as can be expected."

I hear his low chuckle. "You didn't have to come with me."

"Um, yeah. I kinda did. One, I don't want to stay alone, even if your place is Fort Knox. But more important, I'm at the center of some freakish murder mystery, and no way am I just sitting back and letting other people figure out why. And by other people, I mean you."

"Would it help if I say I'm sorry?"

"Did you do anything to set this in motion?"

"No."

"Then you don't need to say it," I reply, struggling for purchase as I climb to the next position.

He extends his hand, and I take it, letting him tug me up the short distance to his side. I stumble a bit, and his hand goes around my waist, holding me tight.

"Steady. I wouldn't want to lose you."

I swallow, suddenly keenly aware of his proximity. I know he means lose me down the hill, but in that moment, I'm tumbling in an entirely different way, and I tell myself this isn't real. I need to pull it back. My emotions are all out of whack, my adrenaline through the roof, and I'm locked in the embrace of this man that I have been crushing on for a very long time.

But it's not real, and I know that. I *know* it. But despite all of that, I still want to fall into the ocean of his eyes.

"You steady now?"

I'm suddenly aware of just how tightly I'm clinging to him. I nod. "I should've gotten a place with a regular backyard."

"But then the neighbors might see us breaking in."

I meet his grin. "Well, there's that."

My home backs up against one of the more treacherous of the hills that rise above Laguna Cortez, and because of that, it doesn't have a useable backyard, just a huge balcony that extends out over the hillside.

There's a ladder that extends from the balcony to a small shed, though, and it's to that shed that we're climbing. "What do you expect to find in there?" I ask him, but he just shakes his head.

We're moving again, and I'm relieved when we finally arrive at the concrete pad on which the shed is seated. My body aches, and I'm thinking that my regimen of jogging and yoga really isn't cutting it.

The shed is locked, of course, but I have a key. I hand it to Ronan, and he slips it into the lock. Then he curses when nothing happens. "Are you sure that's the right key?"

"It's the key they gave me when I moved in. To be honest, I never tested it. I don't come out here." The county takes care of clearing the brush, so I've had no need to explore the cliff. I just sit on the balcony and soak in the view. That's enough for me.

"Can you just get a rock and break it?" I suggest.

"Picking it would be easier. I've got a set of picks in my jacket."

"Of course you do. I have a drone in my back pocket."

He smirks but doesn't respond. Instead, he gets to work with the little pieces of metal, pushing and twisting them until finally, the lock pops open.

"Nice," I say.

"I can teach you. It's a useful hobby. Surprisingly relaxing, too."

Before I can tell him I'll take him up on it, he's pulled open the door. "I still don't get why we're looking in here. Don't we want to sneak in through the patio door?"

"There might still be operational cameras, and since we don't know who's watching, I don't want to be seen. We'll go in if we have to, but I have a theory."

Since he doesn't volunteer more, I don't ask. I just follow him into the cramped space. He uses his phone as a flashlight, illuminating folding chairs and beach umbrellas, rakes and shovels, and two huge ice chests.

It's cramped, but the ceiling is high enough that we

can stand inside. Also, it's surprisingly clean. Especially the path that runs between the piles of items, ending at one of the ice chests.

"Something's off," Ronan says. "It feels staged."

I look around, trying to see with his experienced eyes, then gasping when I see it, too. "The stuff is dusty," I say, running my fingers over the top of a folding chair. "But this section isn't." I point to where we're standing—the path running down the center.

"Exactly." He moves the few feet to the chest, then pulls it out. "Well, hello there," he whispers.

I hurry to him and stand on my toes to peer over his shoulder, but I see nothing except the wooden back of the shed wall. "What?"

He traces an area where the empty ice chest was. "See it? The discoloration?"

"Maybe?"

"Hold the light." I do, and he runs his fingers over the wood. "Gotcha," he mutters right as I hear a *click*.

An entire section of the siding opens like a door, revealing a crawl space. "What the hell?" I ask. "How did you even know to look for this?"

"The floor of the owner's closet. It was different than the rest of the house. My guess is that all of the footage from the house feeds to a drive located beneath the floor in that closet. And since Mr. Big couldn't just pop in and ask you if he could grab it, he made sure there was exterior access for pulling the drive."

"You got all of that from ugly floor tiles?"

"I just thought about what I would do if I was trying to secretly access security tapes."

"Oh, God." I think about what's happened in that

house. There's no sound recorded as far as we know, so Saint's Angels should still be safe, but we already know there are images of Ellie and Devlin. Of me, too, I'm sure. With my last boyfriend. In the shower. Walking nude from my bathroom into my closet.

I shudder. "You don't think they're leaking stuff, do you? I mean, Reggie said there was that tape about Ellie and Devlin..."

"We'll do a search—see what we find—but I doubt it. That's risky. Someone stumbles across it, then the house is searched and those cameras come down. I don't think the point is to sell the tapes."

"What do you think it is?"

"I'm not sure. But I think it may be training. How better to become you than to watch you?"

"Oh." The thought makes me a little ill. Correction— a lot ill.

"You okay?"

I nod, then point to the crawlspace door. "So that goes to the owner's closet?"

"Wait here," he says. "I'll find out."

I shake my head, panic rising. "No. Ronan, no. Don't leave me here."

He studies me, then nods. "Stay close and quiet."

I nod, willing to do whatever it takes not to be left alone while he slinks off into the dark. We have to crawl, which is less than pleasant, but it's dry, and the light from Ronan's phone gives off enough of a glow that I can at least see that the tunnel is clean and we're not slogging through dead bugs.

After about five minutes, Ronan stops, then rolls onto his back.

"What is it?"

"We're under the owner's closet."

"Are you sure?"

He doesn't answer. Instead, he slides on his back a few inches, then whispers, "Bingo."

"What?" I scoot closer, then roll to the side so I can see the area upon which he's shining the light. That's when I see the small metal plate on the tunnel's ceiling.

"Hold the light," he says, passing me his phone. "Keep it shining up there."

I do, then watch as he uses a pocket tool to unscrew the four corners of the plate. He tugs it free to reveal ... something?

"What is that?" It looks sort of like a giant circuit board. Like what I found as a kid when I took apart my parents' old, broken computer.

"Something like that," Ronan says when I tell him my impression. "This is where they're storing all of the security camera feeds. I'd bet good money on it."

"So whatever they were up to, it might be on here? Like maybe they were using the house during Mr. Big's weeks to do illegal stuff?"

"Well, I don't think someone was dressed up like you for a costume party." He meets my eyes. "We'll know more after we look at this."

"Are we done now?"

"Yeah, we're done."

"You're not going in?" I ask, glancing up as if into the house.

"There might be a cop on duty. Or the police might have found a way to hack into a live feed and see me. Or your double might be watching as well.

We've already run a risk coming here, but that was one I can justify. I can't justify traipsing in there on the off chance we might stumble across more information."

We've already run a risk.

The words seem to hang in the air, and I look back, half-expecting to see myself rushing toward me on twisted limbs like that girl in *The Ring*.

"We should go," I say as he shoves the circuit board into the pack he wore as we climbed. "What if there's nothing on there?"

"We'll cross that bridge when we get to it."

"Right," I say. I want this over now. I want all the answers now. But I know that's not how this works. There may be nothing on that circuit board. But in the world Ronan lives in, that's the kind of thing you have to try.

And if he does find something hidden in the bits and bytes of that board we're stealing, I know he'll tell me. And that we'll deal with it together.

"How's it going?" I ask him forty-five minutes later when we're back at his place and he's hooked up the board to his laptop.

He frowns and shakes his head. "The encryption is out of my league. I need to get the team on it."

"Oh." I'm disappointed, but I get it. "Well, the bright side is that you don't have to keep working on it. Want to watch a movie?"

He glances at his watch. "No."

I try to hide my disappointment. It's been a long day, and I'm sure he just wants to go to sleep, but I want to spend time. Talking. Being normal. Ideally with a glass of wine and his arm around me telling me this is all going to work out okay.

But I don't say any of that. Instead, I get up off the couch. "No worries," I tell him. "I should probably crash. It's been a long day."

"Hey, hold up," he says, reaching for my hand. "I meant no to a movie." He taps his watch. "Isn't Ellie on that LA-based show in five minutes?"

"Oh, my God. You're right. I can't believe I forgot." I settle back in next to him, thrilled when he puts a pillow on his lap and tells me I can lie down if I want.

"Since you're tired," he says.

"Oh. Thanks." I snuggle sideways on the sofa, my head on the pillow, his fingers stroking my hair. My whole body reacts to the soothing motion, so much so that even when the camera follows Ellie walking onstage after the opening monologue, I have a hell of a time concentrating.

"She looks good," Ronan says. "Tons of confidence, not the slightest bit nervous."

"That's my bestie."

We watch as she talks about the research she did on her book, *Saints & Sinners*, which details the rise of the foundation—and the juicy secrets about its founder, Devlin Saint, who they bring on stage in the latter half of the interview.

To be honest, except for being able to tell them they looked great, I'm only half-watching. After all, I know this story. More to the point, I can't concentrate with the way Ronan is stroking my hair. I'm not even sure if he realizes he's doing it; he's probably tuned in to the program. But me? I'm hyperaware.

The light pressure. The way his fingers move my hair, making it brush lightly over my skin. The touch of his fingertips as he traces a lock to my arm, bare below the sleeve of my tee.

When he idly traces the curve of my ear, I feel a jolt of warmth shoot all the way through me, ultimately pooling between my legs, and it's all I can do not to moan aloud.

His touch is magic. Hypnotic. It's taking me away to a warm and safe place, and I just want to slide deeper and deeper. So much that when he finally clicks off the television, I'm startled out of what feels like a dream state.

"Is it over?"

"Did I lose you?"

"Just dozing," I say. *And fantasizing...*

"Come on," he says as I force myself to sit up. "Let's get you to bed."

He stands in front of me, his hand extended to help me to my feet. I take it, then stumble because my foot has fallen asleep, and I gasp from the unexpected tingling. His arm goes around me, holding me up as he steadies me. I look up, only to find him looking down at me, and my breath catches in my throat.

I never really believed in that time-stopping cliché, but it's true. I can feel the universe going on, the world turning, but I'm entirely removed from it. It's just me and Ronan and this moment, and if I could figure out a way to capture this feeling and put it in a bottle, I would.

"Brandy."

That's all he says. Then he bends down, his lips

brushing mine. A question that I greedily answer. *Yes. Oh, yes, please.*

I part my lips, my arms going around his neck. I rise on my toes, wanting to taste him. Wanting to touch him.

Just wanting him.

"More," I whisper.

"Brandy, are you—"

"*More.*" I take his hand, then tug him back to the couch. He sits, then pulls me into his lap. I'm straddling him, and I can feel how hard he is, and it doesn't make me nervous at all. It feels right. I feel ready. And oh, so alive.

His hands cup my rear, and I moan softly as he tugs me closer. He draws in a deep breath, and I move my hips, stroking him. Wanting to take us both further.

I close my eyes and hear my name, *Brandy, Brandy,* and it's only when I open my eyes and see that he's not speaking that the oddity of the moment washes over me.

"Ronan," I whisper, then jump as the next shout of *Brandy* from outside is accompanied by the sharp ring of Ronan's landline.

"Is that Lamar?" I ask, referring to the voice, at the same time that Ronan leans sideways and reaches to answer the landline.

I snatch up my phone. "He texted SOS. He's outside, shouting for me from the street. Good God," I add as I see a dozen texts and missed calls. "What's going—"

I cut myself off when I see the look on Ronan's face. "Understood," he says, then ends the call.

"What?"

"We're leaving. Grab whatever you need. I want to be out of here in five minutes."

I don't argue. I haven't unpacked, so I just grab my

overnight bag and my purse, then shove my phone into my back pocket.

"Why?" I say when I'm back in the living room.

"The cops found the footage. An SD card in the camera itself. And a picture of you blowing away your landlord. They'll look for you here. You're not going to be here when they do."

"Oh, God." A wave of cold fear washes over me, not just for me, but for Lamar, too. "He could get fired if they know he told us."

"For more than that," Ronan says grimly. "He called the landline from a burner I gave him a while back. Wanted us to know that it's not just the tape. He found a box of bullets at your place."

"Well, sure. I have the Ruger he bought me."

"That's a .22. These were 9mm. The same caliber that killed your landlord. And the box had six missing."

"I don't understand."

"Angel, he found it in your bedroom. Your underwear drawer. He stayed for the search, just in case. And he pocketed the box."

"He hid evidence?"

Ronan nods.

"But—but how did that even get there? Those bullets don't fit my gun, and ..." I trail off. I know perfectly well how it got there. "Why? Why is she setting me up?"

"Once someone takes the fall for Mr. Big's death, the cops will stop looking. You're the patsy, angel. We just have to make sure we keep you safe and hidden until we can prove that you're a victim, too."

CHAPTER SEVENTEEN

"This okay?" Reggie asks, ushering Ronan and me into one of the suites at her family-owned hotel. The SeaSide Inn is a charming little hotel on the Pacific Coast Highway near the Devlin Saint Foundation.

The room itself opens off of an atrium, the perimeter of which is lined with the various guest rooms. Ours is a suite—two bedrooms and a living area. And since Reggie's family owns it and she's part of Saint's Angels, we're registered under fake names. Even Lamar doesn't know where we are. Not because we don't trust him, but because we don't want him to have to lie.

"I've known Chief Randall all my life," I tell Ronan as soon as Reggie's left us alone. "No way will he believe I did this."

"Probably not," he says. "But it's not a question of belief. It's a question of evidence. And he has to run with that or screw his reputation."

"But I didn't do anything."

"Angel, I know." He comes to me, his hands on my

shoulder smaking me feel safe. I want his kisses again. I want that place where we were before Lamar interrupted, our bodies close, our lips touching, and our minds far, far away from the body in my living room.

I think he's going to take me there, and I tilt my head up to look at him, but instead of heat, I see storm clouds in those deep blue eyes.

"It's late," he says. "You should sleep."

"Oh. Right." I force a smile because there is no way I want him seeing my disappointment. I start to turn away, then stop. "Thank you for keeping me safe."

"I'd do anything for you." His voice is soft, but the words are solid, and I feel the weight of them like armor around me. At the same time, though, I know they're not true. Because tonight I realized what I do want—maybe it's not how I usually am, and maybe it's terrifying, but I want Ronan. I want his touch. I want sex, the closeness and comfort that comes with it. Ronan has been my everything ever since he carried me out of hell, and even though I know he doesn't want forever, I'm still certain that I want now.

But I can't tell him that. I can't seem to conjure the words.

So I just offer him a smile, then turn and go into my bedroom.

I undress, slip naked between the sheets, and try, try, try to go to sleep.

It doesn't work.

I can't get my mind to stop whirring. Full of lusty thoughts and needs.

I roll over, drawing my knees up as I clutch my pillow. The truth is, I don't know who I am anymore. I never used to be a woman who wanted sex simply for sex's sake, and now here I am.

Except, no. That's not true. I do want more. But I know he doesn't, and I'm willing to take less simply to be with him. Because with Ronan I don't just feel safe, I feel like *me*. Like he's the person who completes me, just like in that movie. But he's still pushing me away because he thinks I want more than he can give.

Maybe I do.

But maybe I'm also okay with not getting it. If the choice is a part of Ronan or no Ronan, I guess I want what I can get.

I order myself to get out of bed. To go tell him all of that. But somehow, I can't get my body to move. So I just stay there, wanting and longing. Imagining his touch. His kisses.

And somewhere, lost in the melancholy of unfulfilled dreams, I finally drift off to sleep.

I DON'T REMEMBER FALLING asleep, but I wake to voices.

I grab my phone, then squint at it, surprised to see it's three in the morning. I sit up, alarmed. Have the police found us? Is Ronan trying to hold them at bay?

But no, that doesn't make sense. He'd have given me a warning before letting them in, and the police can't just break in. Can they?

Curious, I slip out of bed, grab the hotel-provided robe, and shove my arms into it. I fasten it tightly around my waist, drag my fingers through my hair, then pad barefoot to the door. I lean close, trying to make out words, but all I can hear is Ronan's voice. That and a soft muffle that might be a woman.

I frown, curious, then put my hand on the knob. Ronan wouldn't risk my safety, which means this must have something to do with the mystery of Mr. Big.

And that means I want to know what's going on.

I draw a breath, open the door, and walk into our communal living area. Immediately, I wish I hadn't.

"—you're really not going to Los Angeles? Who knows when you'll get a chance again? It's a miracle we tracked him from Chicago, and now he's so damn close."

The speaker is a woman, and she's sitting at the table so that I'm seeing her from the side. Her long red hair flows over her shoulders. She wears a dress with spaghetti straps, leaving her shoulders and arms mostly bare. Her bare feet are kicked up on another chair, stilettos in a pile on the floor. From this angle, I can see a long stretch of toned thigh that I imagine leads up to absolutely nothing under that dangerously short skirt.

And, of course, there's Ronan, right in front of her.

"I can't," he says. "Not right now."

He hasn't seen me yet. Neither of them have. He's wearing sweatpants and no shirt, and he's pacing in front of the dining table.

"Are you fucking kidding me?" She stands, that tiny dress barely enough for decency, and I feel my temper spiking as she crosses to stand in front of him, blocking his way. There's something about her that's familiar, but damned if I can place it. Doesn't matter, though. Unfair or not, I'm jealous as hell—and wildly curious as to what's going on.

I ease back a bit so that I'm standing in the dark crevice formed by the door and the frame.

"You've already paid me."

"And I'll get my money's worth," he says. "But not tonight. Not until I'm sure Brandy's safe."

I stiffen at the sound of my name.

"Do you really think you'll get the chance again? I'm not—"

"*Oh!*" I take a step backward, surprised by the sound of my own voice. I didn't mean to speak, but the realization of who she is just hit me with such force that the word was knocked out of my lips.

They both turn, and instead of being mortified, Ronan actually smiles. "Brandy, I thought you were asleep. This is Jacey Kane. Jacey, meet Brandy."

"Nice to see your face," Jacey says. "Makes it clearer why this guy's being an asshole," she adds, gesturing to Ronan.

"Oh." I have no idea what she means by that. "Thanks?"

She chuckles. "I should go, but it was nice to meet you." She turns back to Ronan, then wags her finger back and forth, indicating the two of them. "Soon. You and me."

"Yes, yes." He shoots an uncomfortable glance in my direction, and I quietly seethe.

"All right then," she says. And with a quick wave, she disappears from the room.

"Sorry we woke you up," Ronan says.

"Are you freaking kidding me?" My voice comes out way louder than I'd intended, but really? I mean, *really*? "I thought this was supposed to be our secret hideaway," I add, even though I really want to call him out on the Very Big Thing now lingering between us. "But you go and invite *her* here?"

He tilts his head to the side. "Brandy." His voice is infinitely soft and oh, so gentle. All of which pisses me off more.

"Don't *Brandy* me. I mean, come on, Ronan. I mean, I understand if you regret what happened between us at your house—I mean, I can live with that." I swipe a tear away, angry with myself for getting emotional. "But to then just back away slowly so that you can hire a call girl for a little—what do you call it?—*stress relief*? I mean, how do you think that makes me feel when we came *this* close to... to..."

I can't finish. The stupid tears are coming with a vengeance, and when he moves closer to me, I actually bat him away with my hands like I'm seven years old or something.

"Hey, Brandy, no. There's nothing between Jacey and me."

"Of course not. You *pay* her so you can avoid those damn strings."

"Not her. Not ever."

I want to call bullshit, but when I look up, I see the truth in his eyes. I wipe my nose with my sleeve. "But then what was she—"

"She works for Saint's Angels."

"She—really?" I blink, wrapping my head around that as I wander toward the sofa. "So she's not really a prostitute?"

"She is, actually. Her choice. But she doesn't think anyone should be forced into that life. She started helping us. Mostly feeding intel when she hears rumors about trafficking, that kind of thing. She's also served some time for cyber crimes, and she's proven to be a big help when we need some hacking done."

I sit, curling up in the corner, the robe pulled modestly over my leg. "Was that why she was here? Bringing intel?"

"Something like that. I didn't know she'd be coming tonight. I would have given you a heads-up."

"It's okay." I can't quite meet his eyes, and I'm sure I'm blushing when I say, "I'm sorry I flew off the handle. I had no right."

"Yeah," he says. "I think you did."

My heart flutters. "Really?"

He sits beside me, then takes my hand. The robe shifts, revealing my knee. "Really."

"Oh." I swallow, my pulse feeling suddenly prominent in my throat.

"What's in Los Angeles?"

"You heard that?"

"I thought your trip was to Chicago. The trip you cancelled, This the same? She found someone you were looking for?"

"It's not that big a deal."

That's what he says, but he doesn't look at me as he speaks.

"I don't believe you." He's still holding my hand, and now I squeeze his. "I don't want to take you away from something important. You should go. It's an easy drive to LA, so if it's important, you should go. Just leave now. Call Reggie. She can take over. I mean, she lives on site, so it's no big deal, and we both know she's a badass."

He almost laughs. "She is at that."

"Then go."

"No."

"Please," I beg. "Don't make me feel like some obligation you're stuck with."

He pushes off the sofa, then starts pacing. "Is that what you think?"

"Well, yeah. You want to go—it sounds like Jacey worked really hard to find this person—and you're staying because of me."

I have no idea what the bigger picture is, but that much I'm sure of. I blink back tears, feeling like the weight of the damn world is on my shoulders. I don't understand any of this, but I know I'm at the center of something very, very wrong. And because I'm in a trap, Ronan's stuck in here with me, too.

"This is my fault," I say, pushing up off the couch because I need to move, too. "And I don't want to be the reason you—"

"No." His sharp word cuts me off, and he stalks back toward me, so close I take an involuntary step backward, then another until my back is against the wall.

He stands right in front of me, his hand on the wall above my shoulder. At first, he simply looks at me, his expression so sad and lost it almost breaks my heart.

But then it clears, and all I see is fierce determination. "No," he says again. "Do not apologize. None of this is your fault. Not one single, goddamn thing. Do you understand that?"

"But—"

He silences me with a kiss, wild and hard and

punishing, as if he's trying to capture everything that he feels in this one moment.

I don't know what's going on in his head, and right then, I don't care. This is what I want. This is what I've been craving. The feel of this man next to me, the warmth of his lips on mine, and oh, how I want to get lost in it.

But then, without any warning, he lurches back, breathing hard. "I want you," he says. "I have for a very long time. But I don't want to push."

"You're not," I tell him. "And I know you think I want to take it slow, and that I only want to be with you if it's going somewhere. But that's not true. Not anymore. I've done that, and I still got hurt. I know you won't hurt me, Ronan. I just want..."

I trail off, trying to gather my courage.

"Tell me, angel. I need to hear you say it. I need to know you're sure."

I draw in a breath and lift my chin. I'm aware of my entire body. Every cell humming, heat rushing through me. I push away from the wall so that I'm standing right in front of him.

"You said that for me sex is about trust. A sacrament." I draw a breath, and with my heart pounding in my chest, I untie the sash on the robe. It falls open, and with one quick shrug, it slides off my shoulders to pool on the ground, leaving me naked in front of him.

"Please, Ronan," I say. "I trust you."

CHAPTER EIGHTEEN

"Brandy..."

His heart pounded from the shock of what she'd done. That she was standing now, naked and trusting, right in front of him. Her arms hung at her sides, and there was no modesty in the way she met his eyes.

He wanted to ask again if she was sure, but he knew the answer. Knew that if he slipped his fingers between her legs, he'd find her slick and open for him. He wanted to taste that heat. His tongue on her clit. His hands clutching her ass as his knees pressed against the floor, and she came for him, his mouth on her pussy as she screamed his name.

He craved it. Craved *her*.

But first, he needed to touch her.

"Ronan, please." His name was barely a whisper, but to him it felt like a prayer. He took a step toward her, mesmerized by her eyes. The way she watched him. The way her lips parted.

Slowly, he traced the tip of his finger over the curve

of her shoulder, relishing the way she closed her eyes and whimpered, as if forcing herself not to beg for more.

He felt the smile touch his lips. He wanted her to beg.

He was going to make her beg.

Slowly, he finished the path. Down her arm, over her fingers, then easing to her hip. He followed the curve up to her waist, his gaze tracing the path of his hand over her smooth, perfect skin. He eased his way up to her left breast, cupping it in his palm as his cock grew painfully hard, desperate for the feel of her.

He teased her nipple between his fingers, then almost came when she gasped, her head tilting back as those sweet lips whispered his name.

"You're so fucking beautiful," he said. "And this ... oh, baby, I love this." As he spoke, he traced his fingertip on the tattoo of a small feather that marked the swell of her left breast. He'd only seen a hint of it before—she'd have to reveal a hell of a lot of cleavage for the full feather to be revealed—and in the moment, it seemed as if the feather was a gift for him alone. A sign that they were about to fly, borne away on a wind of lust and passion.

"Ronan."

That was all she said, but there was so much passion —so much *need*—in her voice that it was all he could do not press her up against the wall and take her hard and fast, certain that her need matched his own.

No. Not her. Not Brandy.

Not like that.

"Ronan, please." Her words were breathy, and as he watched, she lifted her hands, cupping her own breasts in what had to be the most goddamn sensual thing he'd ever seen. His cock ached, and all he could think about was her. Losing himself inside her. Making her gasp with pleasure.

Making her scream his name before shattering all around him, her pussy throbbing from the force of the orgasm he'd give her.

He pushed away, his fingers running through his hair. *Get a grip, man. Get a fucking grip.*

He backed away two steps, putting space between them. "Brandy, angel, you don't want this."

"I do. Please—Ronan, please. I know what we talked about. I know what I said, and I know you're just trying to be a gentleman, but don't push me away." She took a step toward him, then another. Then she reached for his hands and—so slowly he almost came right then—she placed his palms on her breasts.

"Take what you want," she whispered. "Please. I'm scared, and the world is spinning, and I don't want to beg. I only want—"

"What?"

She licked her lips, then met his eyes straight on, her gaze never wavering. "To forget. Please, please, Ronan. Please help me forget, even if only for a few moments."

His heart twisted. He could understand that. Hadn't he been trying to forget for his whole damn life?

"Close your eyes," he whispered. She did, and her easy obedience was as much a turn-on as her naked body. He dropped slowly to his knees, his hands on her hips to hold her in place. Then he bent forward and traced the tip of his tongue along the juncture of her thigh, tracing the one side of the V that marked the way to heaven.

She trembled in his arms, and he held her tight.

Steady. Then he moved his head and repeated the motion on the other side, only this time, he didn't stop. This time, his tongue teased her clit even as he slid one hand between her thighs. He slipped one finger inside her as his tongue wreaked havoc on her clit, then another and another until he had three fingers in her pussy, and he was stroking that sweet spot, working her pussy and her clit and making her rock her hips as she moaned, begging him to *please, please, don't stop*. Then begging him to let her sit because her knees were too weak.

But he was relentless. He didn't stop. He had to taste her. Had to feel her explode. He held her tight, even when her pussy clenched around his fingers. Even when she started rocking. Even when her knees collapsed and she cried his name and he had to move quickly as she fell into his arms, her legs going limp.

He straddled her then, his hand cupping her face as he looked into her eyes. She was completely naked, and he was still in sweats, his cock about to burst out of them. He was breathing hard, trying to rein himself in, but when she reached for him, then tugged on the waistband with a whispered "please," he decided to tell control to take a flying leap.

He wanted her, dammit. And it was clear she wanted him, too.

"Brandy," he said.

"Ronan. Please."

He didn't need any more convincing. He peeled off the sweats, joining her naked on the floor. He straddled her, his cock brushing against her belly as he held himself over her, the sensation so damn erotic it was a wonder he didn't come right then.

"Tell me what you want, angel."

"I—" She turned her head, and he saw the red blush stain her cheeks.

He bent forward and kissed her, claiming her mouth, making her moan. "You said you trust me. So trust me enough to tell me what you want."

Her teeth grazed her bottom lip. "I want what you want."

He grinned. "Nice, because I want to fuck you. I want to bury my cock in you and make you scream. Eventually—not tonight—I want to fuck that pretty little ass, too. But tonight, I want whatever you want. And, angel, I want to hear you say it."

He bent closer so that he could whisper in her ear. "Tell me," he urged. "Talk dirty, and make me hard. Trust me enough to say anything to me. Because I promise you, I want to hear it."

He heard her shuddering breath. Not fear, he thought, but excitement.

"My breasts," she whispered. "I want your mouth on my ... my clit. And I want your fingers on my breasts."

"As you wish," he said, sliding down her body, his fingers teasing her nipples, twisting and playing as he kissed his way lower until he reached her pussy. He tightened his grip, giving her nipples a tug as he sucked on her clit, making her gasp and arch up.

"Again," she whispered. "More," she begged.

"Tell me," he demanded.

"My clit," she said. "Tease my clit with your tongue. And I want your fingers in me, too. Finger-fuck me, Ronan, but keep your tongue on my clit."

He moaned, too turned on for words, loving how

quickly and eagerly she demanded what she wanted. He eagerly obliged, his fingers inside her, his mouth on her clit and one hand teasing her rock-hard nipple.

He felt the beginning of her orgasm, and his cock ached to be inside her. But this was her show, she was calling the shots, and unless she—

"Ronan, please. Please fuck me."

Thank God.

His wallet was on the table, and he fumbled for it, then cursed. "I don't have a condom."

"It's okay. I'm on birth control. Are you—"

"I'm clean. I swear."

"I believe you. Ronan, *please.*"

He was too close—too turned on—to be gentle, but she was more than ready for him when he entered her. When he was deep inside her, he rolled them over so that she was on top of him, riding him as his fingers continued to tease her and her tight pussy worked his cock in a way that was driving him utterly insane.

He couldn't remember the last time sex had been like this. Both intimate and fun, playing as much as making love. And so desperately powerful.

Why would it be? When did he ever really make love?

He pushed the thoughts aside, not interested in regrets. Not now. Not with this woman taking him to places he desperately wanted to go.

He opened his eyes and found her watching his face, her expression so full of joy and passion that he couldn't take it any longer. That was it. The final straw that drove him over. He lost it, spilling deep inside her even as she exploded, too, her pussy clenching around his cock until they were both spent and limp, her body falling to stretch out on top of his.

"Wow," she whispered, and as far as Ronan was concerned, that pretty much said it all.

He moved just enough to pull the blanket off the sofa to cover them both as they stretched out on the floor. They stayed that way, curled up against each other, just breathing, until he stared to fear they'd end up asleep on the carpet.

He pushed himself up on his elbow, trying to combat sleep. With his other hand, he idly traced her curves, stopping to admire the tattoo once again. "Why?" he asked.

"I guess I wanted to be someone other than who I was. Someone who would surrender, like a feather in the wind."

"Surrender with me."

"I already did that. I liked it." She reached up to touch his cheek. "I never managed before. Not until tonight."

The words humbled him. "Thank you," he whispered.

A smile flickered on her lips. "I think I'm the one who should thank you. Ronan, I've never ... I mean, I've had orgasms. But not like that. Not like my body was going supernova."

"You're welcome," he said, unable to stop grinning. "But I was thanking you for your trust."

CHAPTER NINETEEN

Y*our trust.*

His words humble me. "You have it," I say. "I trust you completely. I have for a very long time."

I don't quite meet his eyes, afraid I'm giving too much away, even after the incredible intimacy we just shared. I've never been that open. That vulnerable. Never talked like that with a man. "I liked it," I admit. "The talking part."

"I know," he says. "I could tell. I liked that you liked it."

He shifts, then climbs to his feet, completely comfortable in his nakedness. He holds his hand out, then helps me rise. "I think a bed will be more comfortable," he says, then leads us to my room.

He pulls back the covers for me, and I climb in. For one brief moment, I worry that he's going to leave me and go to his room, but he simply slides in beside me, then holds me close. And right then, I want nothing more than to stay this way forever.

Silence lingers, then I whisper, "The trust thing—I don't think I could have been like that with anyone else."

For a moment, he says nothing, and I'm afraid he's fallen asleep. I turn to face him, only to find him looking at me, his expression so tender it makes me ache.

"Talking dirty?"

I nod, suddenly shy now that I can see him.

"You liked it."

It's not a question, but he deserves and answer. "Yeah," I admit, feeling my cheeks burn. "I really did."

The corner of his mouth twitches. "Why?"

I can't quite look at him when I answer. "It felt sexy. And I liked that you liked it."

"I liked it very much." He strokes my hair. "You've never talked like that before?" His voice is low. Sensual. "Never told a man to fuck you? To suck your clit?"

My cheeks burn from the question, but I shake my head. "No. Not even close."

He doesn't say anything. Not right away. Instead, he rolls over, then moves on top of me, straddling me. He's hard again, and his cock presses against my belly, making me ache with need, wishing he would just slide down a bit and thrust inside me.

"Never?"

I shake my head.

"Thank you," he whispers, and there's such sincerity in his voice that I have to blink to hold back tears.

"I liked it," I admit again. "With you, I liked it a lot."

He bends closer, his breath hot on my ear as he says, "Tell me what you want now."

"I want your fingers on my clit. Please, Ronan. I want you to make me come again."

"Greedy, aren't you?"

"For you? Yes."

He kisses me hard, his tongue teasing me in the same rhythm as his fingers between my legs, sliding deep inside me, then teasing my clit until I'm squirming beneath him, yet unable to move. He has me trapped. Helpless. And I hear myself cry out.

He starts to pull his hand away. "I'm sorry, I didn't—"

"No." I reach down, holding him in place. My heart is pounding in my chest. "Don't stop."

He hesitates only a moment, then his fingers tease me more, his mouth by my ear whispering, "Come for me, baby. Come on, angel," until my entire body is under his control and a new orgasm breaks through me.

I arch up, astounded by the power of the pleasure that crashes through me, and for a moment, all I can do is breathe.

When I come back to earth, I roll on my side. "Only you," I say again.

"Because you trust me. Because it is a sacrament. A promise that I will never hurt you. You have to know you'll be safe. And with me, you know that."

"Yes," I whisper, thinking that Ronan's trust feels a lot like love, and damned if I'm not sliding into it. "I do trust you." I prop myself up on an elbow. "I've never had that before. Knowing for sure that a man won't hurt me." *I think I have it with you.*

I don't say that to him, though. Instead, I ask, "That's not what you need, is it? It's not safety that you're looking for."

"No," he says. "I need control. Trust, too, but for me it's about the control."

"Maybe that's your own kind of safety net. You pay for sex, right? It's safe because there aren't complications. And you have control because you're the customer."

He looks away. "Yes," he says. "You're right."

"Do you belong to those clubs?"

"Clubs?"

"Sex clubs. I may not be that experienced, but I also don't live under a rock."

He grins. "Fair enough. Yes." His brow rises, and he slides his fingers down, then slowly fills my pussy. I whimper as he asks, "Do you want me to take you to one?"

"No," I say, because that's not what I yearn for. "But I like the way we fit. You liking that control. Me liking to feel safe. I don't know what you do at those clubs. What you need. But whatever it is, Ronan, you can have it with me."

"Oh, angel," he says, then draws me to him. He kisses my forehead. "What you do to me."

I close my eyes and snuggle close, astounded by how open I am around this man, and at the same time, too sleepy to think deeply about it.

I'm just drifting off when my phone chimes, signaling an incoming email.

I groan—I'd forgotten to silence it. I reach for it, then gasp.

"Ronan," I say. "It's from Mr. White."

CHAPTER TWENTY

U ntil Ronan and Reggie led me to it, I had no idea that there was a secret tunnel that started at The SeaSide Inn, crossed under the Pacific Coast Highway, then emerged in a subbasement at the Devlin Saint Foundation.

"It makes it easier to move people if they need to get to a meeting without being seen," Reggie explains as we step out of the corridor and into the foundation.

The corridor is not only well-hidden, it's well-protected, with multiple locks and codes required to pass through the series of doors before entering the subbasement through the back of a maintenance closet.

We move away from the closet, then jog quickly up the stairs, exiting on the third floor before taking a back hallway I've never seen before into the research room. Ronan leads us through this library that's open by appointment to the public, twisting through the stacks until we reach a private room.

He knocks three times, the lock beeps, and we enter

the room to greet the team members that Ronan has summoned for this mission. As soon as Reggie, Ronan, and I are in the room, Tamra shuts the door and locks it behind us.

"I don't expect anyone to interrupt, but better to be careful. Hello, sweetheart," she adds, reaching for my hand. "How are you holding up?"

"I'm doing okay," I say, surprised to realize it's the truth. I should be a basket case, but I have Ronan's strength to draw from, and that's keeping me centered. And sane.

We're here to plan out the mission for meeting Mr. White. His email had been lacking in those parameters I'd asked for. All he'd said was that he was requesting a meeting to discuss a job in Riverside County that required my particular brand of expertise. He asked that I reply with the location and time so that we could discuss the specific itinerary and fees.

So we had, with Ronan responding with a location that, apparently, Saint's Angels has used once before. As soon as the email was sent, he texted Tamra, who immediately pulled this team together.

In addition to me, Tamra, Ronan, and Reggie, there are five others sitting around the long conference tables. I recognize Charlie McKay and Corey Pennington—called Penn—from Ellie and Devlin's wedding. They both usually work out of state, but when Ronan reintroduces us, he explains that they've been in town to meet with a source.

The other three operatives are new to me. Derek Perez, Nova Freeman, and Shane Houston, all of whom joined Saint's Angels after retiring from a covert military division.

I look at Ronan, a little freaked out. "I'm just meeting the one guy. Do you really think we need an entire battalion?"

He comes over and cups my chin, looking deep in my eyes. "I'm not taking any chances with your safety. Understand?"

I see Tamra's brows rise, but I don't care. Right then, I want to put my arms around him and cling to him until I can once again block out the strange reality of my current situation.

But I don't. As much as I like this feeling of Ronan taking care of me, he doesn't do relationships. And as much as I enjoyed last night, I know well enough that sex without commitment won't work for me over the long haul. I bent my rules because Ronan makes me feel safe, and I trust him with my fragile heart. But I don't expect to be afraid forever.

I knew it was only temporary when I said yes last night. And now, of course, I have to live with it.

"Angel?"

"Yes. Sorry. I understand."

"You meet Mr. White with cover, or you don't meet him at all. And you need to do it. We need to know what Mr. White knows about this person who stole your face."

"I know. I understand. I just—" I glance around at all of them. "I wasn't expecting such a big team. I think it's finally hitting home what I'm in the middle of."

"A safety net," Nova says. A Black woman with a cultured British accent, she leans forward, her bead-adorned dreads brushing the table. "Thinks of us as your safety net, and rest assured that we won't fail you."

"Everyone on this team is an exceptional asset," Ronan says. "I don't expect anything to go wrong, but no one sitting at this table has stayed alive by expecting the best. Rather we plan for the worst."

"The worst," I repeat, my eyes darting to Tamra, who gives me an encouraging smile. "Okay. Yeah. That makes sense." I take a deep breath. "But could we start out by talking about the best? I mean, we sent that reply with the meeting location, so the first good thing to happen will be that he shows up at all."

"Correct," Derek says, stroking his orange-red beard.

"And then what? He comes, he sits down. But what do I say? What do I ask?"

"We'll rehearse everything," Ronan says. "But basically, you're playing a role. And based on everything he's said to you on the street and in the email, he thinks you're an assassin. You said he was acting nervous on the street. Of course he was."

"Which means you have the upper hand," Shane puts in. He has long hair swept back into a ponytail and a patchy scruff of beard. I have no idea if he surfs, but I can easily imagine him on a board.

"Exactly," Derek says. "So you'll ask him for more details about the nature of the job."

Ronan is the only one still standing, and he comes behind me and puts a hand on my shoulder. "Assure him that you chose the location because it's a place where you feel comfortable talking freely. Tell him you need to know everything in order to give him a quote. You need the target and a time frame. All the specifics."

"Stay business-like," Penn adds, his broad, stocky frame filling the chair. "But see if you can find out how he first heard of you."

"Only if it seems natural," Ronan adds. "Getting intel isn't on you. We'll take care of that."

"How?"

"You'll be on comms, remember? We'll hear everything."

I nod, running everything we've just talked about over in my head. Maybe it's not that scary after all. I'm no actress, but even I should be able to pull this off.

"Okay," I say. "I can do this."

"Yes, you can," Shane says, and the others nod.

Ronan gives my shoulder a squeeze as he passes beside me to reach the head of the table. He presses a button, and part of the surface pops up, revealing a keyboard. He taps, then a screen descends on the far side of the room, the DSF logo prominent as the computer boots up.

I settle into one of the chairs, but only half-listen as Ronan runs through the mission specs for each of them. Everything is for my benefit, true, but I have nothing to do with manning a post or checking comms. I'm the one being guarded, no matter how much they sugarcoat it with how easy my job will be. The bottom line is the same—I'm the one meeting with a man who thinks I'm an assassin.

I know it's only a mission to gather intel. And I know that the fact that these five operatives are going to be there as well isn't a sign that Ronan expects danger. It's just the way they do things, especially when a civilian— me—is in the midst of all of this.

I close my eyes, thinking about what Ronan said earlier.

We plan for the worst.

I'd heard those words at the beginning of this meeting, and I'd cringed. As if there was something unusual about them. Some portent of doom.

As if every single day, almost every person on the planet doesn't do exactly the same thing. Fastening a seat belt. Locking a car door. Putting on sunscreen. The revolutionary act of simply owning a first aid kit. Plan for the worst, after all.

And isn't that also exactly what I've been doing for years in the dating world? Holding back emotionally and sexually because I fear that the worst will happen? That every guy is a Walt who'll take advantage of me or a jerk who'll tell me to get lost if I don't want to put out on day one. Or day fifteen.

I can see how planning for the worst is a solid approach if you're expecting to encounter a paid assassin. But is it really the best approach for going through life? Have I been too caught up in protecting myself that I'm not actually being myself?

Which, of course, raises the question of who am I, really?

And the answer is that I don't know.

Brandy Bradshaw, fashion entrepreneur is easy. But the other me? The one that craves someone to love but is scared to give her heart?

I'm not sure I really know her at all.

I hug myself, and Tamra must think I'm cold because she hurries to my side and drapes a sweater over my shoulders.

It's such a kind and simple gesture that I reach back and grab her hand. *This is family,* I think. *These people I've come to love.*

I think about how little my own parents did. Running away after a rape turned into a pregnancy. Acting like I was an embarrassment they had to hide, then not even giving me the grace to spend a moment with my own child before handing her over to the adoption liaison.

That bastard Walt had violated me, but I'd been the one who was punished. Not by society, but by my family.

I love my parents—I do. But I no longer have illusions about who my family really is. That's Ellie and Lamar. Devlin and Tamra and Reggie.

And Ronan. Always Ronan. He knows it, too. I'm sure of it. But what he doesn't know is the depth of my feeling. Because I've moved way beyond physical attraction and friendship, and I haven't a clue what to do about that other than hope that he feels the same way, too. That there's more between us than just one night of incredibly awesome sex.

I've opened my heart to him, but I'm not sure if he understands how much. More than that, I'm not sure if he wants me like that. Someone to love, not just someone to fuck.

Considering all he's told me, I doubt it. Which means that once all of this is over, he and I will be over, too.

The thought hangs over me, black and dark.

"So how is this going to go down?" Shane asks, the question tugging my attention back to the meeting. "I understand we're not acting unless there's a threat, but what's the endgame? Just to make sure Ms. Bradshaw's safe during the meet? Or are we bringing him in?"

"As soon as Brandy's conversation with Mr. White confirms that he's truly not hiring Brandy Bradshaw to make custom bags, we'll move in. We'll detain him, and we'll question him."

"Detain him?" I ask. "You can just do that? And where? Here?"

"Here? Goodness no," Tamra says, as if I suggested desecrating a church. "We keep the foundation out of the SA activities as much as possible. Minimal co-mingling. A meeting like this on occasion? That's fine. Interrogating a reluctant source? Not so much."

"Which is Tamra's way of saying we have a place," Nova says. "A few miles from here. As for whether or not we can do that ... well, you know..."

She trails off, obviously not understanding that, no, I don't know.

"Can is one of those words that can be interpreted any number of ways," Ronan says. "But the bottom line is that if we can get him in an interrogation room, we can be assured of getting answers. Assuming this isn't all about purses after all."

"No," I say. "The email talked about a job in Riverside County. I don't know what that could have to do with my bags. Besides, there's something off about him. That stuff with gun-fingers in the street? That wasn't normal." I twist in my seat to look at Tamra and am relieved to see her nod in agreement.

"All right, then," Ronan says. "You heard the lady. Expect quick confirmation that Mr. White is in the market to hire an assassin. We'll grab and bag, then take him to the shed for interrogation."

"The shed?"

"Think of it as a code name."

I nod. I consider protesting that I don't want this entire decision on me, but I stay silent. After all, it's not. Ronan would never go against his own instincts. And by labeling this as my call, he's drawing me into the circle of this team.

I turn to look at him, only to find him looking right back at me. *Thank you*, I mouth and am rewarded by that slow smile I find so damnably sexy.

The meeting lasts another hour, then everyone heads out with instructions to meet again tomorrow. Everyone except Ronan, Tamra, and me, who linger behind.

"How much information do you think we'll actually get out of Mr. White? I mean, what this person does and how, maybe, but will he have a clue as to why they look like me?"

Ronan shakes his head. "Doubtful. But I think that answer's pretty clear."

I lick my lips, then draw a shaky breath. "They're setting me up. For killing Mr. Big."

"Yes," Ronan says. "But I don't think that's the primary goal. Those masks cost a fortune. If all they were going to do was be you so they could kill Mr. Big, why bother with the disguise? They could have just walked in and done it. Worn a hat to avoid the house cams. There's no reason to make it so complicated."

"Then what?"

"Most likely, they were working as partners. They pulled a job using that identity, and the one in your face double-crossed him."

"Why?"

"My guess would be money," Tamra says. "That's usually the go-to motive."

I say nothing, just slide back down into my chair as I wonder what the hell I've gotten in the middle of. "This is all because I rented the perfect house. I wanted to live in that lovely place with its beautiful view, and I never questioned why it was such a great deal."

"This is not your fault," Ronan says. "Not a single bit of it."

I shrug. I know he's right, but that doesn't change the fact that there's a killer wearing my face.

I frown. *Wearing my face...*

"What is it?" Ronan asks.

I look between him and Tamra. "Surely people must know it's a mask. I mean, it's one thing to model me. But smiling? Talking?"

"You'd be surprised," Ronan says. "We commissioned a mask like that once. I didn't wear it. One of our men in Paris did, but I was over there. It's a process to put it on. It covers the neck and chest. And an adhesive is used around the eyes, mouth, cheeks. That way the mask moves, too, mimicking the wearer's expression. If I hadn't known, I'm not confident I would have realized."

"This is messed up."

"It is," he says, coming over and putting a hand on my shoulder. "It really is."

I look between him and Tamra. "What about the circuit board? Has that helped? Did we find any images with what she really looks like?" I'm hoping there's crystal clear footage of her putting on the me-mask and am wildly disappointed when Tamra shakes her head.

"There must be alternate storage. Either that or they

moved everything to the cloud. The files from the house go back years. We still haven't cracked the encryption sufficient to actually see clean images, but I doubt they'll give us much help."

"Keep at it," Ronan says. "We can't rule it out until we're certain we can rule it out. Actually, give Colonel Seagrave a call. His people might be able to get past the encryption faster."

"Of course," Tamra says. "I'll go call him right now. And, sweetheart, you'll do fine tomorrow," she adds to me before leaving the room.

"Colonel Seagrave?" I ask.

"He runs a covert military organization. Occasionally, he hires Saint's Angels for off-book missions. You know what that means?"

I nod. Basically, it means that on occasion, the military hires mercenaries. People they'll disavow if the mission goes wrong. This is one of the benefits of growing up in a world ruled by film and television. I know pretty much exactly how that stuff works. But I never expected to really be in the middle of it.

That thought must show on my face because Ronan reaches for my hand, then gives it a gentle squeeze. I tilt my head to look up, wishing I could float away on the ocean of his eyes.

"You okay?"

"I'm nervous," I admit.

"It's my job to worry, not yours. I'll be right there with you, remember? Right in your ear. I'll tell you what you need to say."

"That's a good thing? What if he realizes that someone's feeding me lines? I don't know anything about this man. He might be just as dangerous as my double."

"You're going to do fine." He's holding both my hands now, and I see a muscle twitch in his jaw as he holds me captive in his gaze. "I promise you, Brandy, I won't let you down."

CHAPTER TWENTY-ONE

I won't let you down.

Hours later, the words still rang in his head. His promise to Brandy. His redemption for Michelle.

As if he could ever be redeemed. As if he even deserved to be.

He was in the hotel's gym, beating the shit out of a speed bag, his hands moving at least as fast as his frenetic thoughts.

He'd been working out for an hour. Trying to exorcise the memories. Trying to convince himself that this time that promise would hold true. Because, dammit, he couldn't lose another woman he loved.

Loved.

He dropped his arms, the bag still vibrating from the power of his punches.

He loved her.

He hadn't asked for it. He didn't want it. But there it was. She'd claimed his heart, goddammit, and that simple fact scared the shit out of him.

"Fuck."

"What's wrong?"

He spun, startled to see her behind him. "I thought you were asleep." It was past midnight, and she'd crashed right after the meeting.

"Tried. I guess I'm too wired. Well, too nervous," she added with a shrug.

"You shouldn't leave the room. What if a cop saw you? Recognized you from a warrant?"

"Then don't give me a reason to leave."

He opened his mouth to retort, decided she had a point, and held out his hand to her.

"Come on," he said. "Let's get back. Have a glass of wine, maybe put in a boring movie. You'll be asleep in no time."

She hooked a strand of pink-tipped hair behind her ear. "You don't have to take care of me."

"I like taking care of you," he said, surprised by the truth behind the words. "Besides, isn't that why you're here? Because you want me to?"

He expected her to deny it, so when she said—very simply—"Yeah, it really is," he recognized another facet of Brandy Bradshaw that tugged at his heart—the woman faced things dead on. And she was honest to a fault.

He met her eyes, savoring her mischievous grin. "Come on." He held out his hand, his heart flipping a bit when she took it so casually, as if this was no big deal. It was just the way they were together.

"I wish I wasn't so nervous," she said as they walked the short distance back to their suite.

"I'd be surprised if you weren't." He opened the door

and ushered her in. "If I could send someone in your place, I would."

She lifted her brow. "So how much are those masks? Why don't we put in an order, and you can be me?"

He chuckled, thankful that she could joke about it. She was scared, sure. But she was dealing.

Brandy Bradshaw was a hell of a woman and so much stronger than anyone—including her—realized.

"Go get in bed," he said. "I'll get some wine."

Her brows rose. "I'm supposed to be getting sleep so I'm fresh tomorrow."

"Uh-huh. And how's that working out for you?"

She laughed. "Good point."

"At any rate, I'm planning to behave."

"Well, now I'm just disappointed," she quipped, making him laugh.

He pointed at the door to her bedroom. "Go. In bed."

She whipped off a little salute and headed that way while he toweled off, then went to the kitchenette to grab two glasses, some napkins, and a bottle of Pinot Noir.

When he returned, she'd abandoned her jeans for just a T-shirt and underwear and was sitting up against the headboard, the covers a heap at the foot of the bed.

He'd changed into shorts before going barefoot to the gym. Now he put the wine on the bedside table, slipped into bed beside her, and passed her a glass.

"Thank you." She took a sip. Then another. Then a very long swallow that drained the glass completely.

"Thirsty?"

"I want to feel it," she said. "I want it to float me off to sleep. I'm so tired, but I just can't. Too worked up. I can't turn my brain off."

"I know the feeling well. Come here. Lean back." He indicated his legs, now spread to make room for her. She didn't hesitate, and he helped her ease over his thigh until she was between his legs and leaning back against his chest. He stifled a moan, her bare legs against his were like a brush of temptation.

"Close your eyes."

She did, her head back so her hair brushed his shoulder, and he was lost in the scent of her.

He wanted to calm her. Soothe her. More than that, he wanted to feel her. To know that she trusted him in her bed as much as she was trusting him to keep her safe in the world.

He started with her breasts, his palms cupping them, stroking softly over the material of her T-shirt.

"Ronan..."

"Tell me to stop, and I will. Otherwise, close your eyes and enjoy."

He held still for a moment, giving her time to answer. When she stayed silent, he bent to kiss the top of her head, even as his fingers slid down, lower and lower over her tee until he met the strip of warm skin right above the elastic of her panties.

Slowly, he slid his fingertips beneath the elastic, relishing the way her body went tense in his arms, in sharp contrast to the way her hips tilted up, as if urging him to continue. He did, stroking his fingers over her waxed pussy, loving the feel of her soft skin against the callused tips of his fingers.

With his other hand, he cupped her breast through her shirt, her nipple hard between his thumb and forefingers. He tightened his grip, rolling the nub as his other hand slipped lower, making her moan as his fingers found her slick, wet core.

"You like this," he murmured. "It makes you wet when I touch you. When I take what I want."

"Yes." Her hips moved, as if to draw him inside, but he didn't comply. Instead, he lightly teased her hard clit, then traced his fingers along her vulva, craving the sensation of sinking deep into her warmth, but holding back to claim the pleasure of driving her just a little bit crazy.

He twisted her nipple, and she cried out.

"Does it hurt?"

"A little." Her voice was breathy. Hot. And damned if his cock didn't get even harder.

"I'll be more gentle." He wanted to take her to that place where pain turned into pleasure, but not until she was ready. And if she was never ready? Well, that would be okay, too. So long as he could touch her.

"No." The protest was barely a breath.

"No?"

"Harder. Please. And ...just harder."

He took his hand off her breast, then smiled when she whimpered. "It's okay, baby. Trust me." Then he tugged up the shirt so his hand was on bare flesh. Her nipple was so damn hard, and he did as she asked, twisting it until she arched back, crying out his name as her hips rocked in time with the way he was teasing her breast.

He hadn't expected this. Hadn't thought she would be so responsive. So open. Not after everything he knew about her past with men.

She trusts you.

Dear God, she trusts you.

He continued to tease her nipple, making her squirm against him in a way that had her ass rubbing against his cock, and making him so damn hard. With his other hand, he continued to stroke her pussy first teasing her clit, then sliding two fingers deep inside her.

She cried out, her core tightening around his fingers as he licked the curve of her ear. "That's it, baby. Tell me you like it."

"Oh, yes."

"Tell me what you want."

"More." The word was like breath, and as she spoke, he pinched her nipple tighter, making her arch back, her hips gyrating as she fucked his fingers.

"Oh, baby, yes." He slowed down, sliding his fingers free so he could stroke her clit, but she reached down, directing his hand back to her core. And how fucking hot was that?

"Touch yourself," he ordered.

"What?"

"Play with your clit," he said. "I want to watch you touch yourself. I want to feel you tighten around my fingers as you come."

"Ronan..."

Her hips were moving, and he doubted she was even aware. She was so damned turned on, and the fact that he was the one taking her there made him so hard. He wanted to lift her onto his cock. To lube her up and fuck her ass as she sat on his lap and he finger-fucked her pussy.

"Yes," she moaned, and he almost lost it then, her word coming in such perfect time to his thoughts.

"Touch yourself," he repeated, then felt himself grow even harder as she moaned and squirmed against him.

It took every ounce of his strength not to role her over and bury himself inside her, but this was about her, about making her feel. About making her forget.

He continued stroking her. Teasing her. Taking her close to the edge then pulling back when he felt her body tighten. Over and over until she was begging him, her entire body on the edge as she whispered, "Please, please, Ronan, please." And only then, with his name on her lips did he finally let her go over, his fingers playing her like a finely tuned instrument until she shattered completely, crying out as her body rocked and trembled, his cock going even harder with the sound of her pleasure.

When her body stopped shaking and her breathing evened, she turned in his arms. Her face was flushed, her eyes glassy. She slid down until her head was on the pillow, her hand urging him beside her until they were face to face, her lids drooping as a soft smile tugged at her mouth.

"Thank you."

"For the orgasm?" he teased.

"For making me feel good. For watching out for me. For protecting me."

His heart skipped a beat, and he cupped her cheek. "I always will, angel," he promised. "Always."

CHAPTER TWENTY-TWO

I may have fallen asleep in bliss, but I wake up in fear.

It's the day.

The day I go meet a guy who is most likely trying to hire an assassin. Suddenly, this doesn't seem like such a great idea after all, and I hug the pillow closer, drawing strength from the scent of Ronan and the memories of last night. The way he'd touched me. The way he'd teased me and made me come. What had started out so tender had turned into something incredible, his fingers leading me into unexplored territory, making me feel alive and used and wanted.

And scared.

Not of the day that's head of us and the rendezvous with Mr. White. But of the reality that once this is all over, Ronan will be stepping back into his life, and I'll be going back to mine. Each to our opposite corners. Alone.

I opened that door. I told him I could play by his rules. Not needing commitment—not even wanting it. And I meant it in the moment. I wanted him, after all.

But now I'm wondering if I was a fool. Because how on earth am I ever going to get this man out of my system?

I sit up with a sigh, then hear Ronan's voice filtering in from the main living area. He's probably on the phone, doing whatever it is that he's doing to make sure I'm safe.

Right. The fake me. The dead landlord. The sketchy meeting in just a few hours.

I have a lot to worry about other than where Ronan and I go from here.

First and foremost, I have to get through this day.

I'm not sure what a high-end assassin would wear, but I don't have a lot of options, anyway. I do have a sundress and a thin sweater to cover my shoulders. That seems reasonable enough. I figure any self-respecting assassin is going to try to blend in, and what's more blendy than a sundress in a beach town?

I lay it out on the bed, then head to the bathroom for a long, hot shower, part of me hoping that Ronan will finish his call and join me. I know I shouldn't be disappointed when he doesn't, but I am.

When I'm at the point of risking that my skin stays permanently pruney, I get out, then wrap myself in the hotel robe before I head into the other room for coffee. He's still on the phone, but his wide smile and the heated twinkle in his eye erases my lingering angst, promising good things to come later. A reward for surviving this day.

Emotionally, I mean. Because I'm really, really not thinking about the possibility that I'm putting my life in danger by pretending to be my double.

I turn on the tea kettle for me, then refill Ronan's coffee cup, earning me a wide smile.

"That's good. Yeah, I want at least three hours lead time. ... I don't want to take any chances. ... Okay. Terrific. ... See you at the rendezvous."

He ends the call, takes the coffee from my hand, then sets it on the counter before pulling me into his arms. He's dressed only in sweatpants, and I press my hands to his bare chest, remembering the way he felt against me last night.

I can't help but touch him. More than that, I can't help but wish we could go back to last night. I would much rather lose myself in his arms than go on this particular mission. I admire what he and Devlin and all the other Angels do, but that's not a world I ever wanted to be part of.

How ironic that I'm now right in the middle of that particular brand of chaos.

"I woke up without you." The moment the words leave my mouth, I wince. I hadn't intended to say that.

He chuckles. "Nova called. She wanted to check on our timeline. Make sure everything's in place. She's exceptionally thorough."

"I like that in her. Exceptional thoroughness today sounds like a really good plan."

He cups my head, then brushes a kiss across my lips. My whole body seems to go soft, and all I want is to drag him back into the bedroom so that I can lose myself.

"Later," he says, squeezing my ass and making me wish I hadn't bothered with the stupid robe. "Unless you want to join me in the shower?"

"Tempting," I admit, wishing I'd waited. "But I think one today was enough. I'm going have some tea and get dressed."

As he heads into his bathroom, I slip an Earl Grey teabag into a cup of hot water, then head back into the bedroom. I shimmy into my dress, slide my arms into the sweater, and slip my feet into the white flats that I brought with me.

Even though we shared my bed last night, Ronan is showering in the room that is technically his side of the suite. That means my bathroom is free, and I go in there to put on my makeup. I don't tend to wear a lot, but I lay it on heavy today. I'm not Brandy, after all. I'm a badass assassin, and that requires a makeover. Honestly, I wish I'd brought a black tank top and leather pants.

The latter, however, would have required a shopping spree.

Less than an hour later, I'm back in Ronan's Range Rover and fighting my nerves as we head south. The meeting place is an abandoned hotel at Sandy Point, a beachfront area about fifteen miles from the Laguna Cortez city limits.

For decades, a high-end resort had been located there, but the main building was destroyed in a fire about three years ago. Apparently, there had been financial shenanigans, followed by an arson investigation and some arrests.

It's still tied up in litigation, and the property is essentially abandoned. The beach stays empty, too. Unlike the better beaches to the north and south, the waves on this stretch of the coast aren't great for surfing, and there's no reef to make it of interest to divers, either.

The resort's restaurant shut down as well, even though it wasn't damaged in the fire, and without that draw, there isn't much reason for anyone to come to this stretch of beach, not with Laguna Cortez so close to the north and Dana Point just a short drive to the south.

Bottom line, it's a terrible location for any kind of coastal recreation.

But it's the perfect place for this operation.

The charred hotel is a ruin now, but parts of it still stand, the cinder blocks and metal framing having survived the fire. That's where Nova is stationed. She's already in her place when we arrive, three hours before the scheduled meet with Mr. White.

I look up to see her standing at the edge of the mostly collapsed roof and waving down at us. Ronan lifts a hand, and she gives him the okay sign. Her job is to act as a lookout, and if it seems as if Mr. White is going to do anything funky, she's got orders to put a bullet in his head.

According to Ronan, she's one of the best sharp-shooters in the world. And I can't help but think how lucky I am that she's watching my back. Literally, as I'm going to be sitting at a table on the restaurant's patio facing the opposite direction.

The others are stationed in various spots. Charlie and Penn are closer to me, covering the abandoned restaurant itself, one watching the front in case Mr. White enters through the main entrance and makes his way to the patio that way. The other is on the roof, looking down at us, camouflaged by the siding, but hopefully having a sufficient view to watch us from above.

Derek is on the beach, posing as a local out with his German shepherd. "He comes with his dog to a lot of missions," Ronan tells me. "Arnold used to be a police dog. He loves the work, and he's good at it."

I glance over and think about how much I miss Jake, who I know is romping and playing at doggie day care. I wish I could go meet Arnold, but I know that I can't. So I satisfy myself with one quick look, then continue following Ronan.

We'd followed a winding, dilapidated driveway from the Coast Highway to the resort, then parked in its now sand-covered lot. The sidewalks that used to lead to this restaurant have long since been covered by sand and debris, and there's sand in my shoes and in my hair. I know it doesn't matter, but I'm already uncomfortable enough, and I'm feeling very antsy as I follow Ronan up the weathered steps to the patio dining area.

Ronan leads me to the table the team picked out—one that Nova can see from the resort, Derek can see from the beach, and Shane can see from his station on a small, anchored fishing boat. Charlie and Penn, of course, are even closer, and are also watching me like a hawk.

Ronan points to a bench that runs along the wall that the patio dining area shares with the main restaurant. I'm assuming it was used as a place to seat patrons while they waited for a table. It's about three tables away from me, but with a clear line of sight. "That's where I'll be."

"You sure he won't think anything about a homeless guy here?"

"I doubt he'll even notice me." He takes off his backpack and starts pulling out various tarps. "I'll be lying down under all of this. He'll think it's just a pile of debris, but if he realizes I'm a person, you can act surprised. And don't worry, I'll be able to see you just fine." He holds up one of the tarps and sticks his finger through a slit that he's made in the material.

Although he did shower, he didn't shave, and he intentionally messed up his hair and is wearing ill-fitting clothes that Reggie pulled from the lost-and-found. Even if Mr. White does notice him, he looks enough like a homeless person that he shouldn't draw too much attention.

He glances around, then taps his earpiece. "Everyone in position?"

I'm not wearing mine yet, so I don't hear the response, but Ronan seems satisfied.

"We've got full coverage," he tells me. "And Nova's got eyes on the walkway, too."

"The walkway?" I turn in my chair so that I can see the cliff that rises up behind the restaurant. At the top of the cliff runs this section of the Pacific Coast Highway. But it's at least a two-story drop from that roadway to the beach below. A wooden walkway has been built into the cliffside, leading up to a scenic overlook.

Personally, I wouldn't get on it. I doubt it's been maintained since the fire, but I'm glad to know Nova's keeping an eye on it.

All in all, between the cliff, the highway, and the ocean, this is a very secluded location and perfect for today's meet. It's also well-covered by the team, making me feel safe and secure. At least as much as I can be under the circumstances.

I meet Ronan's eyes and grin. "I'm surprised you don't have someone in a plane above," I say.

"I was going to," Ronan admits. "But considering that would stand out, we decided against it."

"Right. So, what now?" I ask.

"Now we wait."

I sigh. I know we came early in order to get ready, but this is the part that I've dreaded the most. The sitting and waiting until Mr. White shows up. And because we anticipate that he'll also come early to scope the situation out, we can't even talk or move about. Nobody except for Derek and Arnold, who are frolicking on the beach.

By the time Mr. White gets here, I expect they'll be exhausted.

"Let's get you miked," Ronan says. "Then I'm going to get in place." He hands me a little plastic box and tells me to open it. I do and find a small pin, like a tiepin, and also a little black circle of plastic.

"That's the earphone," he says, pointing to the black circle. I nod, then slip it into my ear, immediately hearing the chatter between Nova and Derek as they discuss their lines of sight.

"And this must be the mic," I say, tuning them out as I hold up the tiepin.

He nods, then takes it from me. It's in the shape of a B, as if it's a monogrammed piece of jewelry. He puts it on the dress, just on the collar, and his finger brushes my skin. I put my hand over his, forcing him to stop, the pressure of the pin's backing digging into my chest.

I meet his eyes. "Tell me it's going to be okay." I know that everyone can hear me now; the mic is on, and I have my headset in, but I don't care. I need to hear this.

"You're going to be fine. This is what we do."

"Damn right it is," Nova says, and I can't help but grin.

"We've got your back, Brandy," Shane says. "Now the rest of you shut up. We've got a job to do."

"I think that's my line," Ronan says with a grin. "But he's right, everybody quiet. It's game time."

At the words *it's game time*, my heart starts to jump. But two hours later, I'm bored out of my mind. I've been sitting at this table, my back to Nova and Ronan to my left under his tarps, scrolling through my phone as if I have nothing better to do and no cares in the world.

I'm starting to think Mr. White won't come, and I'm so bored that I've almost forgotten why I'm here in the first place.

Not really, of course, but my mind is definitely wandering, which is probably why I jump a mile when I hear Derek's voice in my ear. "Someone approaching on the beach from the north," he says, and I realize that he must have one hell of a powerful telescope with him on that little boat.

I wait, my heart pounding again, and I hear Ronan's soft voice, "It's okay. Just take a few deep breaths."

I close my eyes, mortified to realize they can all hear my heartbeat. "I'm fine," I say. "It's just nerves. No big deal."

Nobody answers, but that's okay. Derek's voice is in my ear again, noting Mr. White's progress. "Coming up the stairs," he says, his voice a whisper now. Less than two minutes later, Mr. White is seated across from me.

"Ms. Bradshaw. It's so good to see you again." Mr. White pulls out the chair and sits. His hands are on the table, and he fidgets with his thumbs. "Thank you for meeting me. I... I appreciate you being willing to consider my proposal."

"You didn't give me much in the email. I'd asked you to send me general information." I try to sound politely irritated. Like a woman who doesn't like her procedures messed with.

He laughs. "Yes. An abundance of caution, should I say? Even being vague, one hates to leave a paper trail."

"I don't appreciate you ignoring my instructions." The plan is for me to try and get as much information out of him as possible about his job for my double and also about how he met me. "It makes me question your motives for meeting at all, especially since I don't specifically remember meeting you. I have a policy against doing business with people I don't recall."

"Good job," Nova says, her voice soft in my ear.

I force myself not to preen as he says, "We met in Geneva about eighteen months ago. A party, not a trade show. I was being overly cryptic."

"I see." I don't, but I hope he goes on.

"You were with your partner. And he, ah, mentioned that you were expanding your repertoire. Taking new clients for, um, wet work." At the last, he lowers his voice.

"I suppose he must have trusted you to mention that little fact." I wonder who he's talking about. Mr. Big? Someone else?

"Oh, yes." He sits back, as if waiting for me to pick up the thread of the conversation, but I'm having a hell of a time concentrating, as all hell is breaking loose in my ear.

"—parked on the overlook. Could be a tourist."

"I'm not taking the chance," Ronan says, his voice barely audible.

"Rifle!" And before I can even get my mind around what they are talking about, Ronan has burst up off the bench like some giant monster, his tarps flying everywhere.

He throws himself toward me, and the next instant, we're tumbling to the ground, my ears ringing from the sound of a shot. I'm breathing hard, Ronan's weight crushing me. After what feels like an eternity, he pushes himself up and looks at my face, his voice frantic as he asks, "Are you okay?"

I nod, taking stock. I'm a little bruised, but I'm fine. "What's going on?"

Ronan has crawled to the far side of the table, and I hear his sharp curse. "Subject down. Repeat, subject down!"

I look over to see Mr. White's body sprawled on the ground, the chair tipped over from where he's fallen backwards—his chest blown open from the force of a bullet.

I gag, barely able to keep from vomiting. "That—was that meant for me?"

"Yeah," Ronan says grimly. "Yeah, it was."

At that, I really do throw up, and as I'm retching, I hear Nova's voice in my ear. "I got a shot off. Shattered the windshield, but the shooter's gone. And fuck me, it was Brandy."

I fight a fresh wave of nausea as I meet Ronan's eyes. "This isn't just about framing me for Mr. Big's murder," I say. "This is about getting me out of the picture altogether."

"You're right," Ronan says, pulling me into his lap and wrapping me in his arms. "But I'm not going to let that happen."

"I'm not going to let that happen," Ronan repeated. He heard the tremor in his voice and tried to dial it back. God, he could have lost her just now. He could have fucking lost her. "I swear to God, Brandy, I'm going to keep you safe."

"Okay, okay. I'm okay." She was breathing hard, looking more than a little shell-shocked.

"Come on, angel." He hooked an arm around her, helping her stand. "Let's get you back to the hotel."

"Yes. Yes, please."

"Wrap this up," Ronan said to the team. "Clear the scene."

"I got the license plate," Nova said. "We'll work on tracking. You just worry about Brandy."

He lifted his hand in acknowledgement, then took out his earpiece. Brandy's too. She needed to be away from this right now. As far away as he could get her.

She could have died.

But she didn't. That was why he had the team.

She could have fucking died. Just like Michelle. He could have fucking failed her.

Stop it! Just stop it!

They drove in silence, and it broke his heart the way she curled up in the seat hugging herself, looking small and fragile. She barely moved except to sip from a water bottle, and she said nothing. Just sucked on the breath mint she'd found in her purse. Quiet, a little lost. And all he wanted to do was hold her.

That's exactly what he intended to do once they stepped through the door to their suite. Hold her. Soothe her.

He didn't expect Brandy to make the first move, and he gasped when she pulled him to her and kissed him, clinging so tight it was if she was soaking up his strength.

When she finally stepped back, her expression was full of admiration. "Thank you," she said. "You and the whole team."

He felt the growl rising in his throat, and he shook his head, suddenly furious with her for not seeing the fuck-up. For trusting him when he damn well didn't deserve it. "You're *thanking* me? Are you insane? I could have lost you. I could have fucking lost you today."

"No." Her eyes went wide. "You took care of—"

But he didn't let her finish. He pushed her back, slamming her against the wall, his mouth closing hard on hers, claiming her in a hard, bruising kiss. Wanting her, needing her.

Terrified that she could be taken from him again—

Again?

He roughly pushed away, leaving her breathless. Her

hand went to her mouth, and he saw that it was red, stained from the harshness of his kisses.

"I'm sorry."

She shook her head. "No. I told you. You don't have to be sorry."

"I promised I would protect you. I almost failed."

"You didn't fail." She grabbed his hands. "Ronan, stop it."

"How? How can you trust me after what I did? After everything I screwed up?"

"You didn't screw up. I'm alive. You planned for the worst, just like you said, and you saved me."

He just shook his head, then slumped down on the sofa. After a moment, he held out his hand for her, needing her touch, though he damn well didn't deserve it. She took it, then sat beside him.

"Ronan. Are you okay?"

His laugh was harsh. "No. I'm really not."

"Talk to me. Please? I—I know it would be better if no one took a shot at me, but I don't understand why you're upset. You're the one that saved me. You and the team."

He shook his head. How could he tell her? How could he open that door? Reveal his foibles and failures? The giant gash in his soul.

"Ronan," she said, reaching for his hands. "Please. Please talk to me."

He closed his eyes, surprised by his need to do exactly that. To tell this woman the secrets he'd never even told Devlin, his closest friend.

"Ronan?" Her hand was on his face, and she shifted him gently until he was forced to meet her eyes. "You don't have to tell me anything if you don't want to. But I think it might help. Or if you want, I can just sit here with you."

He drew in a breath, then cupped her head, feeling the softness of her hair. "You're an amazing woman, Brandy Bradshaw." He meant it, too. So many other women had tried to pry his pain out of him, as if they were mining ore, about to tap the motherlode. As if it was all about them.

With Brandy, his pain was his own, and she was offering him nothing more than solace, if and when he wanted it.

What surprised him was that he did want it. For the first time ever, he wanted to tell someone. *No.* Not some-one. *Her.*

He took her hands in his, then held them in his lap, fixating on their joined fingers rather than her beautiful face. "There was a woman," he said, the words bitter in his mouth. He drew a ragged breath, his eyes filling with tears. "And I loved her."

Her grip on his hand tightened, but she said nothing. Just silently urged him to continue talking.

"A long time ago," he began, the words coming slowly at first. "It all happened so long ago. I was young. Eigh-teen, with the world in front of me. I'd been accepted into Harvard. My dad was so proud. He was my world back then."

He shifted on the sofa to face her more directly as she leaned toward him, all her attention on what he was saying, as if he was the only thing that existed in the world right then.

"My mother died when I was six, and I'd grown up

with my dad as my best friend. He was my biggest fan, telling me that one day, I'd take over his business, and I'd blow all his success out of the water. And my dad was very, very successful."

She said nothing, but her eyes said that he mattered. That his pain mattered.

"There was a girl. Michelle. Senior year of high school, and we were in love. Not a teenage love. This was the real thing. She got accepted to Harvard, too, and the plan was that we'd get married after we graduated." He closed his eyes, then drew in a breath. "Then we found out she was pregnant."

He felt Brandy's hand tighten around his, but she didn't interrupt.

"We were thrilled. We loved each other. We'd get married sooner. I'd get a job, switch to another school where I could go part-time. I'd still end up with a degree in finance, and I'd get work experience at the same time. We were excited. It was all going to be a great adventure, and so long as we had each other, nothing could go wrong."

"Your father." Her voice was barely a whisper.

"Yes. My father."

"What happened?" she asked when the silence lingered.

"I made the mistake of telling him everything. He loved me. I thought he'd understand. He didn't."

He tugged his hand free, then pressed his fingers to his temples, trying to rub away the headache that was forming. "My father lost it. Completely. He said he knew I'd been screwing the little tramp—his words—but he couldn't believe that I'd knocked her up. He told me that he wouldn't have it. He said that he would make sure I didn't ruin my life."

He drew a breath, then held it until he was certain the tears were at bay.

"I didn't ruin my life," he continued. "My father ruined it for me. He told me that if we didn't break up, I would regret it, and so would Michelle. That he would make sure she went away. That he'd do whatever it took to make sure of it."

"How?"

"He didn't elaborate. I'd never realized how ruthless a man my father was. To me, he'd always been a hero. A loving father. A respected member of the community. But that conversation scared me. I told Michelle about him. That my father was angry. That he wanted her to just disappear. But I told her it didn't matter. That I had her back, and I always would, and once we were a happy family, I knew he'd love her just as I did."

"But that's not what happened."

"No," he said. "It's not. I never expected it. I was afraid he'd talk with her parents. Try to pressure her to put the baby up for adoption."

He felt Brandy squeeze his hand, and he remembered that was exactly what had happened to her child. Not one born of love, but still a baby that was taken from her.

"Brandy—"

"No. I'm fine. Go on."

He studied her face, then drew in a breath as he nodded. "I didn't know what my dad would do, but my best guess was that he'd to drive a wedge between us so that we'd break up. I didn't care. I knew we wouldn't. We were young, but what was between us was real."

"But that wasn't what he did."

He drew a breath, then closed his eyes. "No. It wasn't. Instead, he killed her. Or rather he hid behind his money and hired someone else to do what he didn't have the balls to do himself."

"Oh, God." Her hand tightened around his, and when he looked at her, he saw his own pain reflected on her face.

"I saw my real father that day. And I hated him." He drew a breath. "I learned a lesson, too. A lesson in trust. And a lesson about the fragility of what you believe. What you can have. What is real. I loved my father, and he betrayed me. I loved Michelle, and she was gone in a heartbeat."

"And so you don't get close anymore."

He lifted his shoulders, acknowledging her words.

"You're close to Devlin."

"We work together. He understands the risk. All my friends understand the risks. And as for women—" He cut himself off, shaking his head. "Well, I already told you I don't do relationships. This is why."

"Ronan—"

He lifted a hand, cutting her off. "I'm telling you this so you understand. You deserve that. Sheldon Cartwright's bullet killed me, too. Or at least it killed the naïve boy I'd once been. He changed the way I look at the world. Him, and my father. My life, my relationships, everything."

"Sheldon Cartwright?"

"The man my father hired. He's a fixer. Still alive, still working."

"A fixer? Like an assassin?"

"Sometimes. Someone who will do whatever it takes to get a job done." At Brandy's nod, he continued. "That was how my dad saw the situation. He had a problem. He needed someone to fix it. And Sheldon did. He blew out the tires on Michelle's car when she was on Mulholland Drive. The car flipped. She went over. She and the baby were killed instantly. If they hadn't been, I'm sure Sheldon would've arranged for the car to blow up. Sent a flare into the gas tank or something. The man is thorough. I've researched him since then. I've spent a lot of time researching him since then."

"Cartwright," Brandy said. "Isn't that the name that Jacey—"

"Yes."

Brandy leaned back, her eyes wide. "You know where he is."

He nodded. But he didn't elaborate. Instead, he said, "I joined the military after that. My father kept trying to pull me back, but I wouldn't come. It took all my strength not to kill that fucker. But I wanted him to know that he'd lost. He played the wrong hand, and he lost me forever. I let him live not because of love or the thought that I didn't have the right. I did it to punish him. He's dead now. A heart attack. As far as I'm concerned, the bastard got off easy."

He hesitated before continuing, his hand tight around hers, drawing comfort from her steady presence beside him.

"He never changed his will. That son-of-a-bitch left me almost $1 billion in securities, cash, and properties."

He saw her eyes widen, but she didn't interrupt.

"A lot of that goes to charities now, including the Devlin Saint Foundation and Saint's Angels. Anonymous, of course. Even Devlin doesn't know how much I contribute. Tamra has an idea—she's helped me get it into the organization without it being known. Although, considering this is Devlin we're talking about, he may know. That man seems to know everything. But at least he's respecting my anonymity."

He turned on the sofa, looking into her face then reaching out to stroke her hair, twisting that tiny bit of pink between two fingers. *She was so beautiful. So trusting. She'd put her life in his hands today, and he'd almost lost it.*

He swallowed, and his voice sounded ragged when he said, "I failed Michelle, and I should have known that I couldn't swear to keep you safe."

"I am safe, Ronan. You did protect me."

"Maybe, but I lost something today too."

"What?"

"Her."

She shook her head, her brow furrowed. "I don't know what you mean."

He drew in a breath, then released it slowly, trying to organize his thoughts. "I loved her. Losing her broke me, and I was broken for a long time. I think I still am."

"No—"

"I didn't mean to fall for you." He watched her mouth open. The light flicker in her eyes. The light he had to kill. "God, Brandy, I didn't want to. I'm not entirely sure what happened, other than it's you, and you're one of the most incredible women I have ever met."

"Ronan, I—"

He held up a hand. "No. I need to finish. Because I can't stand the thought of losing you either. I meant what I said before. I fuck. I don't do relationships. I can't. I about died when I lost Michelle. I can't go through that again. For a moment, that first night with you, I thought maybe I could. Because, dammit, I'm falling in love with you. But I can't. Not even with you."

He saw the way her eyes widened. The shock of understanding. The hint of joy that he loved her, then the dark sadness when she realized that it didn't matter. That he wouldn't take those next steps. Not ever. He had to protect his heart.

And that was why, even though he was longing to touch her, he couldn't. He wanted to tell her that he wished he could be a different man, but he knew himself. He knew what he was capable of. And he knew that she would be his breaking point.

"I—I'm not Michelle," she said. "I'm right here. No one is trying to punish you by hurting me."

"But they're still trying to hurt you."

"That's not because of you. That's because of my face."

"But it could be. Someday it will be because that's the world I live in. My enemies will find me, and they'll find my weakness. And that's you."

"But you'll do whatever you can to keep them from hurting me."

"How the fuck can you believe that? Didn't I just tell you how I failed Michelle?"

"That wasn't your fault. And you *did* save me. The kidnapping. And today. God, Ronan, you're my hero. Don't you know that? But I don't expect anything other than that you try. I don't believe that you're some mythical hero who never misses. That's not the man you are. That's not the man anybody is, and no one expects you to be."

Nobody but himself.

He wanted to answer her, but he didn't know what to say. At the end of the day, he was a flawed man. A coward. But he knew his limits; he knew the pain that he could endure.

Torture at the hands of a bad guy? That he could handle.

Having his heart ripped out again by the loss of a woman he loved? No. He couldn't endure that. And if he had to, he'd walk away just to keep her and his heart safe.

"Ronan? Please, talk to me."

He looked at her, not sure what to say, and was saved by the ringing of his phone. He glanced down, saw the caller ID, then looked back at her eyes. "I'm sorry, Brandy," he said. "I have to take this."

"What's going on?" Ronan asked, answering the call from Colonel Seagrave.

"We know why Cartwright came to the LA area." The man's gruff voice was sharp, his tone indicating the urgency of the conversation. "Have you engaged?"

"No. I've got a crisis brewing here."

"You may miss your opportunity, Ronan. The rumor is he's here to personally take out one of his operatives. Apparently one of his assassins went on an ordered hit, then betrayed him."

"So now he's here, tracking down his underling, with an intent to take him out? How did he betray him?"

"Word is he pulled an Alan Rickman," Seagrave said.

"Explain."

Seagrave chuckled. "That movie. *Die Hard.* Apparently, the underling realized that the target had an attaché case full of negotiable bearer bonds. Decided to quit working for his boss, pulled up stakes, and ran."

"That's risky," Ronan said, letting out a low whistle. "Sheldon Cartwright's not a man to cross." He'd been paying attention to Cartwright ever since he'd learned the identity of the man his father had hired to kill Michelle. Not that he'd learned it directly from his father, but Ronan had picked up a few skills of his own along the way. He'd broken into his father's office one evening, then gone through his files. Since then—for almost two decades—he'd been trying to track the man down. It was a chore. Even with all the resources he had available to him through Saint's Angels, this was the first time he'd had a solid lead.

"I don't understand why you're not in LA," Seagrave said. "I don't know why you want this man so badly, but I know that you do. Hell, you've had me looking for him for as long as I've known you."

"You asked me what would incentivize me to do work for you. This was it."

"Which is why, again, I'm asking why you aren't in

Los Angeles. This is not a man who lingers. Honestly, I'm surprised he's doing the job himself, but I think he's a man who doesn't stand for being double-crossed. My guess is that the traitor's holed up somewhere in LA County, is going to be dead by the end of the day, and that Sheldon Cartwright will be on a jet heading back to Europe by noon tomorrow. Your clock is ticking, boy."

"I understand. Do we have any details on the traitor? It might help me locate Cartwright when I wrap up here."

"Nothing. But one of our operatives was able to hack into a server. Downloaded a few files before a self-destruct kicked in. We're working on getting around the encryption."

"And you're sure it's Cartwright? You're positive he didn't send a flunky?"

"I told you. I'm positive."

"Okay. Thank you for the information. I'll let you know when I get up there. I've got something I have to deal with here first."

He waited for Seagrave to end the call. But his friend didn't. "I'm worried about you, son."

Ronan closed his eyes, the word meaning more than Seagrave could know. The older man had been like a father to him for years. Ronan had worked for him after he left the military, taking contract work across the globe until he'd quit to form his own security consulting company, a job that was mostly for show. He didn't need the money, but it served as a solid cover for the work he did for Saint's Angels.

Even when Ronan left the SOC, Seagrave had been nothing but supportive. Which said a hell of a lot about the man and only emphasized what a shit Ronan's father had been.

He drew a breath. He trusted Seagrave, and honestly, he was tempted to tell him everything. But he didn't fully trust the others in the department. Not for any specific reason. Simply because that's the kind of person he was; the only people he fully trusted were Saint's Angels.

And Brandy.

As the silence lingered, Seagrave cleared his throat. "If you need support, you let me know."

He thought about the afternoon. About the killer who had almost taken out Brandy. About the woman who was walking around with her face.

"Actually, there is something. I need a safe house. And I need your word that no one else will know you've told me about it."

"Done."

CHAPTER TWENTY-FOUR

"So this is a safe house," I say, looking around the plain little two-bedroom, two-bath home in the inland part of Laguna Cortez. "What's the plan?" I ask, pulling out a chair at the kitchen table and sitting down.

In truth, I don't care about the plan. I want to get back to the conversation we had before we left the hotel. The one where he said he could fall in love with me. The one where he said that didn't matter.

But I can't seem to conjure the words because I don't know how to tell him that it matters. That I understand why he's scared. That I'm scared, too. But isn't it better for us to be scared together?

Ronan is looking in the refrigerator, which is well-stocked. I guess they don't want people who stay in safe houses to go grocery shopping. He grabs a beer and offers me one. It's not my favorite, but I take it.

"We hole up here," he says. "We'll dig in with the research, try to track her down."

"What kind of research?"

"When I talked to Colonel Seagrave, he didn't have a report on the status of the security tape review from your house. I'll give the team a call directly and see if they've heard anything. Beyond that, you're right. There's not a lot we can do. We did get the license number of the car as she pulled away from the resort, but I have a feeling it's going to turn out to be stolen."

I nod again, disappointed, but I also understand that we're not living in a movie. Things are going to be slow. And we may never get the answers we want. I frown at the thought. "So how long are we here? Nothing personal, but I'd like to go back home to Jake at some point. And when I do go home, I want to know that people aren't going to shoot at me."

He comes over and sits in the chair next to me, then he reaches out and takes my hands. "I know. We're working on it."

I stand up and start pacing. "I don't mean to sound ungrateful. I'm not. I like knowing you've got my back, and I definitely like being taken care of. It's just … *safe house*. I mean, when did safe houses and almost getting shot in the back enter into my life picture?"

I'm trying to sound light and airy, as if this is all just something to ponder, but I fail. Even I can hear the fear I'm trying to disguise, and soon enough, Ronan is standing, too, and pulling me into his arms.

"We're going to figure this out."

I nod, not looking in his eyes. I want it figured out—I do. But the downside of that success is I lose Ronan. Because that is one thing he's made perfectly clear.

I draw a breath. "Listen, Ronan…"

He looks at me. "What is it, angel?"

I shake my head, feeling like a fool, but we're trapped in a tiny safe house. Do I really want to start an uncomfortable conversation about a future he swears he doesn't want?

No, I don't. Because as much as I want that conversation to end with him pulling me close and promising never to leave me, I've seen the damage that the past has done to this man.

So instead, I shake my head again, then move out of his embrace. "Nothing," I say, then shove my hands into the pockets of the sweatpants I'm wearing.

"Just, um, that I should probably see if there's anything in that refrigerator to cook for dinner."

He reaches out, brushing my elbow. "You don't have to cook. I'll do that."

I shake my head. "No. This is the way it works. You save my life, and I feed you."

"Well, that sounds like a fair deal."

I open the refrigerator door and frown at the contents. Then I open the freezer. It's a little better there. There's a roast, which I don't have time to defrost, but there's also some frozen hamburger patties. I go check the pantry and find a package of hamburger buns that are only a few days old. Either the turnaround in a safe house is frequent, or someone added to this stock before we arrived.

"So the guy you were talking to," I say as I begin prepping the meal, "he's that Colonel from the place you and Tamra told me about? That covert branch?"

"Yes. Anderson Seagrave. Good guy. I've known him for years."

"And he's helping you track Sheldon Cartwright? The guy who killed Michelle?"

"My father killed her." His voice is harsh. No nonsense. "But yes. According to Seagrave, he's in LA on a revenge mission. Payback for an operative who betrayed him."

"Which means you still have time. That night you stayed with me instead of going on your trip didn't screw you over. You can go up to LA right now. You can get your revenge."

His jawline tightens. "I'm not leaving you."

"It's a safe house, Ronan. Aren't they named that for a reason?"

"I'm not leaving you."

I shake my head, turning away from the burgers now sizzling on the grill. "You can't put this on protecting me," I say. "Reggie is here. That whole team that surrounded us at the restaurant is here. You should go. I'll be fine."

"No."

I gape at him.

"End of subject, okay?" His voice is gentle. "You're just going to have to live with the fact that I'm not leaving you. Do you really think I'd trust your safety to someone else?"

"You trust Saint's Angels."

"Not for this," he says. "Not for you."

My heart squeezes, and I nod. "Okay. But, Ronan, is this ever going to be over?"

"It will. I promise you."

I look away, purportedly to continue working on the burgers. He puts his hand on my shoulder. "You okay?"

I turn to look at him. "Once it's over, whatever this is

between us will be over, too. You've made that pretty darn clear."

"Brandy..."

"I don't want it to be," I blurt. "I like the way I am with you. I'm bolder. I'm more daring." I put down the spatula and slide my arms around his neck. Then, without analyzing what I'm doing, I rise up on my toes and kiss him. And the glory of it is, he kisses me back. It's long and lingering, and it's the kind of kiss that could lead somewhere. And I really, really want it to.

"Brandy," he says, breathing hard as he pulls back.

I shake my head, then twist around to turn off the grill. "Quiet. No arguments. I know the score. I know you don't want a relationship. I don't have any illusions about that. But right now, this is what I want. Please, Ronan. Please let me have what I want."

"Brandy, we can't," he says, but even as he speaks, his hands are stroking my back.

"We can," I say. "You do sex with no strings all the time. Isn't that what you've told me? This time, I want you to do it with me." I bite my lower lip, gathering courage as I slide my hand down to cup him. He's wearing jeans, and I can feel his cock straining against the denim, hard and huge.

He groans, and it's like the sound flips a switch inside me. I feel an electric tingle coursing through my body, then culminating in a wild heat between my thighs. My fingers fumble at the button of his jeans, then tug down his zipper. I'm breathing hard as I tilt my head back. "If you want me to stop, I will. But you have to say so now."

For a second, I'm afraid he'll say exactly that. Then his hands go to my waist, sliding down the back of the sweatpants I pulled on. I'm not wearing underwear, and I moan when his hand slips between my legs, his fingertips finding me already wet. This isn't something I ever thought I could do—sex even though I know it won't go anywhere because he doesn't want it to—but with Ronan, I don't care. It's safe with him. I know he won't hurt me. I can be with him, and I can *feel*. And any hurt that comes at the end is because I want something I can't have, but there are no illusions. No fake promises. No surprises.

These moments are just for us, and there's a freedom in that.

I want more, yes. But right now, I'm willing to take whatever he can give. Or, I think, as I see the heat in his eyes, I'm willing to give whatever he wants to take.

CHAPTER TWENTY-FIVE

"**O**ff," he demanded, tugging down her sweatpants. He wanted to see her. Wanted to feel her. His thoughts were a frenzy of lust and need, and right then, Ronan felt as though he couldn't survive the night if his cock wasn't buried deep inside this woman. *Brandy.* A woman whose heart he admired, whose laughter thrilled him, whose body enticed him. He wanted to make love to her, slow and easy. And he wanted to pin her down and fuck her hard until she screamed his name.

Everything. With Brandy, dammit, he wanted everything.

To his delight, she followed his orders, tugging off her sweatpants and standing before him in only her thin, white tee. She was so lovely, her skin glowing in the light from the kitchen's single bulb.

"Now, angel," he said, but she shook her head, her teeth grating her lower lip in a way that only made him harder. She glanced down, her eyes going to his cock, and he realized that he was stroking himself, his hand inside his briefs. She met his eyes, then slid her own hand between her legs, mimicking his motions as she played with her pussy.

"Christ, angel, you're going to drive me insane."

"Maybe that's the plan," she said, taking the hem of her tee and pulling it over her head, leaving her completely naked in front of him. He slowed the way he was palming himself, certain that he was going to push himself over, and he didn't want to explode until his cock was buried deep inside her.

"Now, angel," he said, and she took a step toward him.

"Giving orders?"

"I am," he said, not sure what game they were playing but liking it. She knew his rules. His parameters. She knew he didn't do relationships. But dear God, he didn't want to lose her. If they could share a bed—if they could play these games—then at least she could stay in his life.

With a slow grin, he freed his cock, then sat in one of the kitchen chairs. "Come here, angel."

She obeyed, then put her hands on his shoulders before leaning in, whispering so that her breath tickled his ear. "Tell me what to do."

"I want a lap dance, angel. I want to see you ride my cock."

Her tongue stoked the curve of his ear, and he reached out, his hands cupping her ass as she whispered, "I like this. I like being a bad girl. But only for you, Ronan," she added, her hands tightening on his shoulders as she straddled him, then slowly lowered herself until her soaked pussy teased the head of his cock.

"And I really, really, really like fucking you," she

added at the same time that she lowered her body, impaling herself on him in one bold stroke.

His hands were still on the mounds of her ass, and he helped her ride him, working their rhythm until she was rising and falling all on her own, her breath coming hard and fast, then her pussy clenching around him as she came, milking him until he exploded inside her and they both gasped, lost in the haze of passion.

She leaned forward, her head on his shoulder, her arms around his neck. He held her close, wishing they could stay like that all night, their bodies connected. For a few minutes, he simply held her, enjoying their closeness. Then he shifted her so that he could stand, hushing her soft protests as he lifted her, cradling her body as he carried her to the bed.

He slipped in beside her, and she murmured his name as she snuggled close, drifting off into sleep.

He was falling in love with this woman, that much was certain, and it scared him to death. Here she was, trusting him, sleeping so peacefully in his arms even though the threat still surrounded them.

It didn't matter. He'd do whatever he had to do to keep her safe, but he knew better than anyone that even his best might not be enough.

And his best? Really?

He was hiding in a damn safe house. Hiding and claiming her like he had a right to her, when they both knew that in the end, he was just going to push her away.

He groaned, bending his head so that his forehead pressed up against her hair. What the fuck was wrong with him?

He sat up, intending to go into the living room for his

phone. He needed to check in with the team. Start from scratch. Figure a new way to find the bitch because Brandy deserved more than hiding. She deserved answers. Closure. And he needed to do that for her.

He swung his legs over the side of the bed and was about to stand when he heard a creak. He froze, listening. Another one. Soft, barely noticeable. But he noticed.

Her eyes widened, and he pressed a finger to her lips then shook his head. Now the eyes were wide with fear.

"Moan," he whispered.

Her brows formed a V, a silent question mark.

He leaned in, his lips brushing her ear. "Moan like I'm deep inside you. Three, four times. Make it sound good. Hell, make the bed squeak. Then hide. Get under the bed."

Ronan. The word wasn't even a whisper, but he pressed his fingers to her lips, quieting her, then shook his head. He mouthed a single word. *Now.*

She nodded, her eyes wide with fear, but she did as he asked, throwing her head back and moaning as if they were making love. Dear God, he wished they were.

He used the sound for cover as he grabbed his gun off the bedside table and moved to the door. He listened, cracked it open, then moved into the living room as Brandy cried out, "Yes, oh, God, Ronan, yes."

He moved around the perimeter, still naked but not willing to take the time to put anything on.

Slowly—carefully—he moved through the house, checking everywhere even after Brandy's moans stopped. He hoped she'd slid under the bed as he'd instructed, though he was beginning to think it wasn't necessary. He'd seen no evidence of anyone else in the house.

Perhaps it was just the creaking of the building's bones. A natural settling of the foundation.

He was about to turn on the lights and tell her she could come out when he heard the low whisper of his name.

He whipped around. She was there. Standing in the living room in front of the couch in the bathrobe she'd brought from the hotel. There was a mirror behind her mounted on the wall, and he saw his own expression of surprise because standing there behind him and reflected in the mirror was Brandy again, this Brandy wearing the familiar sweats and T-shirt.

The Brandy in front of him screamed, one hand flying to her mouth and the other staying in her pocket as she cried, "Behind you!"

The Brandy in the mirror took a step back, her hand rising, holding a gun. For a millisecond, fear cut through him. The double was going to shoot him in the back, then shoot Brandy, who stood in front of him, trembling in the robe.

He began to whirl toward the woman behind him, noting the way she took a step back. Then, with no warning, he spun back to the Brandy in the robe. Fired once and dropped her.

For a moment, cold fear rushed through him. *What if he'd gotten it wrong?*

He ran toward her, his heart pounding with fear, only relaxing when he'd ripped the mask off, revealing a woman he didn't know. A woman with dark hair and wide, surprised eyes. Dead, one hand still in her pocket holding a gun. He turned and ran behind him, finding his Brandy on the floor, hugging her knees. She looked up at him, her eyes wild and terrified. "How did you know? How did you know which one was the real me?"

"You were holding a Ruger," he said. "A woman like that would never carry a .22. Plus, her fingernails," he added. "And baby, she's nowhere near as pretty as you."

He bent in front of her and pulled her close, holding her as she sobbed against him. "Why did you leave the bedroom? I told you to stay."

"You texted me. You told me to come out."

He almost kicked himself. He'd left his phone in the living room. How the hell the double had managed to unlock it, he didn't know, but she'd texted Brandy, using him as bait.

"Fucking bitch."

"Is it over?"

"Yeah, angel. It's done. She wanted to set you up for Mr. Big's murder. But you're in the clear now."

CHAPTER TWENTY-SIX

B lue and red lights flash throughout the neighborhood, illuminating the homes that surround this little safe house. I stand next to Ronan, holding his hand as uniformed cops and detectives work the area. Inside, they're dealing with the body.

The body.

"Apparently she managed to get a tracking device on your car," Lamar tells Ronan.

Ronan curses softly, and I look at him. "She must have managed it when we were at the resort. Realized which car was mine. Approached it once we were all set up."

"It doesn't matter," Lamar said. "She's dead now. No longer a problem."

"She's very dead," Chief Randall says as he walks up. He looks at me. "How are you doing, sugar?"

"I'm doing fine, sir." I've known Chief Randall almost my whole life. Ellie's father used to be the chief of police in Laguna Cortez, but Chief Randall took over after he was killed. He ended up being something of a surrogate father to Ellie. And to me he's like an uncle.

"I wish you'd told me what was going on," he says. "It's the freakiest damn thing I've ever seen."

"I'm sorry, sir," I say.

"I take responsibility," Ronan said.

The chief turns to Lamar. "And you knew nothing?"

"No, sir. Not a thing."

I watch the chief's face. I don't think he believes Lamar.

"This was a classified matter," Ronan says. He nods across the street to where Colonel Anderson Seagrave sits in his wheelchair talking to one of the lieutenants. "As you know, I have a Special Forces background," Ronan continues. "Now I do some work for the military. Classified. We had reason to believe that this woman was connected to an active operation, so we stepped in."

"Well, I wish I'd known," Chief Randall says as Colonel Seagrave crosses the street toward us.

"I do apologize for not calling you personally," the colonel says. "I hope that there are no hard feelings and that you'll process this discreetly."

Chief Randall studies the colonel, then nods. "There are times when our small police department doesn't have the resources we need."

Anderson nods slowly. "Well, we're always happy to oblige if you need interagency assistance."

"Appreciate that," Chief Randall says.

I look to Ronan, who's fighting a smile. Apparently, this is the way things are done and secrets are kept.

Chief Randall's attention goes to me and Ronan. "I

think you two are done here. Detective, do you have any follow-up questions for them?" he asks Lamar.

Lamar shakes his head. "No, sir. I think we're wrapped." He looks at me. "I'll call you later. And I'll be here on scene for another half hour or so if you need me. Right over there." He points to where a group of officers are talking to the coroner. I nod. "Thank you."

Chief Randall gives me a hug, then moves away. Once I'm alone with Ronan, I relax a little bit.

"You okay?"

I look up at him and nod. But I'm not. I'm really not. All of this drama, that terrifying fear. Seeing that crazy bitch wearing my face. All of that I could deal with. It shocked the hell out of me, but it was something that could be handled. Something that would either turn out good or bad. And thankfully, it ended okay. I'm alive, and my double is dead. So at the end of the day, it's all good.

Or, at least, it's good compared to what has to come next. Because this is the part that's going to break me.

"Let's go inside and get our things," Ronan says. "I'll take you home. Are you ready to go back there?"

I know that the house has been completely cleaned, the carpet in the living room replaced, the entire property swept for bugs, cameras, and listening devices. It will be weird to be back there again, but it's my home.

I don't know what's going to happen now that my landlord is dead, but until they kick me out, I'm considering it my place.

"Brandy?" he prompts.

I manage a smile. "Yes. I want to go home. I think it's time to shift back to normal."

We're silent on the drive home, me thinking about

what I have to say and Ronan probably lost in reliving what happened tonight. He reaches over and takes my hand as we drive up the canyon road toward my street. A moment later, he pulls into my driveway, then kills the engine.

"Should I come in?"

I draw a breath, then shake my head. "I can't believe I'm saying this, but I think you'd better not."

It's obviously not the answer he expected.

"Oh."

"It's just that—I know what I said last night. And I meant it. I wanted comfort from you, and I didn't care about strings. But the thing is, I still want you. And I know you don't want the same thing. But I do. I want a relationship. I always have. If I let you in, I'm just going to keep getting closer to you. I'm already in love with you, and that means that when you end it, when you say it's too close, you'll pull away, and you'll break my heart. And honestly, it's about to break anyway."

I feel the tears streaming down my cheeks, and I wipe them away. He reaches for me, but I shake my head. I can't stay strong with him touching me. And I know that I need to be strong.

"I just don't think I could survive it. If I get any deeper ... I'm just. I'm just really sorry."

"Angel, you know how I feel about you. But you know why I can't. I thought I explained it to you."

"You did, and I get it. It all ties back to Michelle. And Ronan, I'm so sorry that that happened. I'm so sorry she's dead, and I'm even more sorry that you blame yourself. It's not your fault. But you're letting it eat away at you. You didn't kill her. Sheldon Cartwright did. Your father did. And you let them kill you, too. I hope you find Cartwright someday, I really do. But it won't bring her back."

I sniff, fighting tears, still not quite believing I'm truly ending this. "You think you can avoid a relationship. That you can just walk away if you don't get too close. But you can't. You're already close, and now you're refusing to go all in because you're terrified."

I see him cringe and wish I could call back the words, but they're true. This is a man who's not scared of anything, and yet he's a coward about love.

I draw a breath and continue. "I thought I was okay with casual, but I'm not. We can call it casual and say there's no commitment, but it's not true. Not to me. And I don't think to you either. But I don't care about what it is you really feel inside. I don't want to console myself by telling myself that you really feel the same way about me that I feel about you, even if you won't say it. Even if you won't look toward marriage or a relationship. Even if you just call it casual sex."

I know I should just stop, but I have to get this out, as much for me as for him. Because I don't want to end it either, but for all these reasons, I know that it's right.

"Brandy—"

I shake my head; I'm not done yet. "There's nothing casual between us, Ronan. I know it, and I think you know it. But you won't acknowledge it. Because you think you're protecting your heart. But I don't want to live that way. I can't. I want all of you. Or none. And I want to live the truth, not a lie. I deserve that. And I think that you do too."

"That's what you need?"

"It is."

For a moment, he actually looks scared, and I don't think that I have ever seen him look scared in all the time that I've known him. Except for that one moment just a few hours ago, when he wasn't sure if he'd made the right choice when he'd fired that gun.

"Well, then I guess you should go."

My tears run freely now. I open the door and get out of the car. I hold it open as I look back at him. "I'm not angry with you," I say. "But I do feel desperately sorry for you."

CHAPTER TWENTY-SEVEN

"You look pretty glum, man."

Ronan looked up to see Devlin standing beside him. Ronan was in the back of the bar at the Cask and Barrel, a favorite haunt in the Laguna Cortez Arts District. He reached for his drink, tossed the rest of it back, and put the glass down. "What are you doing here?"

The corner of Devlin's mouth twitched, but he didn't say anything, not about Ronan's harsh response, not about the fact that Ronan had just downed his third drink, and not about the fact that Ronan obviously wanted to be alone. Thus, the dark corner and the small table with only one chair.

"I'm really not in the mood for company."

Devlin took two strides away, and for a moment Ronan felt a pang of regret that his friend was leaving. Then Devlin grabbed the back of a chair, dragged it over, and sat down, and that pang turned to irritation.

Devlin raised his hand, signaling for the bartender to

bring over another round. "Brandy told Ellie what happened with Michelle. Ellie told me."

Ronan closed his eyes, his hands fisting on the edge of the table as he fought the urge to tumble the entire thing over and send the drinks and snacks scattering across the floor. Instead, he drew a breath, lifted his head, and looked his friend in the eye. "That was supposed to be between me and Brandy."

"I know. She knows, too. And I understand why you've never told me, although I wish you had. It probably would've helped to talk about it."

Ronan shook his head. "All it does is make it hurt more."

"Is that what hurts?" Devlin asked. "Is it the loss of Michelle, your first love? Or is it the fact that you can't get past it and see what you have right in front of you?"

"Don't start with me."

"I'm not starting anything. I'm just asking questions. Because it seems to me that you've been picking at a wound for years, not letting it heal."

"You know all of that from what you've learned in the last ten minutes?"

"It's been closer to twenty-four hours, actually, but let's not bother with specifics."

"Damn it. I don't want to talk about this. And honestly, I can't believe Brandy talked about it either."

"Yeah. I'm sure she told Ellie so that she could get back at you for being such a distant motherfucker. What a bitch."

"Don't you dare call her—" Ronan realized he'd gotten to his feet. He sat back down. "Fuck."

"Don't be an ass, buddy. She told El because her

heart's broken and she needed to talk to somebody. And guess what? You weren't there."

"She's the one who walked," Ronan said, irritated when Devlin laughed.

"You can tell yourself that story, but that doesn't make it true."

"Fuck." Ronan's heart twisted, and he lifted his glass. It was empty, but he took a sip anyway, as if that would manufacture a few dregs and he could get lost in the haze of alcohol once again.

He slammed the glass down—it was futile—then snatched the new drink off the waiter's tray as he brought it over. Devlin watched as he tossed it back, ignoring his own drink. He pushed his glass toward Ronan. "Need another? Need to be just a little more numb?"

"You're a goddamn asshole," Ronan said.

"I've been called worse. Sometimes by you."

At that, Ronan had to fight a laugh. He didn't want to laugh. He didn't want anything to chip away at the emptiness in his heart. Sometimes it was better to just be alone. Friends. Love. All it did was get messy. And Devlin just sitting there looking so smug in the life that he'd built. A marriage to a woman he loved. Eventually children. And yet he must know that it could all be ripped away. As strong as Ellie was, someone could take her. And Devlin couldn't protect her, not every minute of every day.

And if there were children...

Oh, God, how would he live with the trauma if something happened to one of them?

He looked down, feeling the tears sting his eyes.

"Would you please just leave?" He didn't look at his friend. He couldn't. If he looked, he'd lose it.

"Why are you still punishing yourself?" The words were soft but earnest. It wasn't a real question. It was more of a statement. Devlin was stating the obvious, telling Ronan that he was being a fool. That he had to move forward. But it wasn't Ronan who was the fool. It was Devlin. Because Devlin could lose everything, and then where would he be?

This way was better, Ronan thought. This way, he had nothing to lose.

"If you're not going to go, I will. I made a reservation at Masque."

Devlin leaned back, studying him. "Oh?"

It was the truth, but it was also a lie. Ronan had made a reservation at the sex club, true. He'd booked a private room and asked the staff to find him two women who would be willing to spend the full night with him. A wild night. The kind of night that could make him forget. Lost in pain and pleasure, sensory overload to fry his mind. To substitute for love and trust and affection. He wanted that. He wanted to get back to the place where that was enough.

But goddamn it, it wouldn't be. And he didn't know what the hell to do. He'd wanted to blame Brandy for walking. They had been doing just fine, enjoying each other. And then she had to go and end it.

Prick, he'd thought. He knew perfectly well why she'd ended it, and running to Masque wasn't the solution.

But if not, how did he move forward now? He didn't know, but he'd called back and canceled the reservation.

Devlin, however, didn't need to know that.

He looked up, realizing he'd been staring at the inside of his glass. Devlin was staring at him.

"Just stop it already," Ronan snapped. "Seriously, you're getting on my nerves, and we're going to have issues."

"Then that's what we'll have. You're my best friend, my closest friend. I'm worried about you, buddy. I'd also be happy to knock some sense into you right now. I'm starting to think that may be the only way. So if you want to step out in the alley, let's go for it."

"God, you're an asshole."

"This isn't about you being scared to love her because you might lose her."

"What the hell do you know about it?"

"I know that you already love her. And if anything happens to her, you'll be ripped to shreds whether you're in a relationship or not. Whether she's your wife, whether she's your girlfriend, whether she's a friend who lives a thousand miles away who you see only once a year. You're in love with Brandy. Anything happens to her, and you will be devastated. You say you don't want a relationship, and that's fine. But do you really think that's going to save your heart?"

"I did not ask you to come in here and psychoanalyze me."

Devin took a sip of his drink. "No, you didn't. But that's what I'm doing."

"Really. You? Do we really want to have this conversation? Seems to me you're the one who ran far and fast. Hell, you want to talk about climbing under rocks? You climbed under the biggest rock of all, hid away from the whole goddamn world, not just Ellie."

"I did. And I got the fuck over it. And you know what? My life is better for it. You've been carrying the wrong baggage. You're not afraid to love her. You're not even afraid to lose her."

Ronan leaned back, the words like daggers.

"At least not so much that it scares you away. You're not afraid of love. You love me. You love Ellie. You love Reggie. You haven't backed away from Saint's Angels or asked any of us to. And you love Brandy. Deeply. And that's not going to change."

Ronan felt his spine tingling. He wanted to get up. He wanted to walk the hell away. He didn't want to hear this. Devlin was edging around something—he didn't know what, but it felt dangerous. And yet he couldn't help but say, "What the fuck is your point?"

"You're not protecting your heart from falling in love and having it broken. You're already in love. You're punishing yourself for Michelle's death by staying away despite love, thinking that will hurt less. But you know it won't."

Ronan said nothing.

"It wasn't your fault, Ronan. You were a kid. You didn't know what your father would do."

"He told me that he would take care of it. He told me he'd get rid of her, but I didn't believe him."

"And why would you have? Why would you have thought that your father would actually kill the girl you loved? Get rid of her? That sounds like he'd try to pay her off, make her go away. You couldn't have known. You couldn't have even suspected. In hindsight, you've got perfect vision. But back then, you couldn't see a thing."

"Don't," Ronan said. "Just don't."

"It's not me that shouldn't. It's you. Don't do this, man. Don't second-guess choices you made when you were younger, when you had no reason to believe that your father would do anything and when you didn't have the ability to fight back to stop him anyway. It's not your fault. Quit punishing yourself. Because guess what, by punishing yourself, you're punishing Brandy too, and she sure as hell doesn't deserve that."

"Shut the fuck up," Ronan said, pushing back from the table, the scrape from his chair so loud that the other patrons turned to stare. He stood up.

"Where are you going?"

"Home. Going to go drown my misery in a whiskey by myself. Thanks so much for this talk. I didn't ask for it. And you're wrong. I'm not punishing myself."

"Whatever you say, man," Devlin said. He lifted his drink, swallowed the rest of it, then stood as well. "Call me if you need to talk. If not, I hope you find your answers. We're all rooting for you. But you've got to walk this path alone."

And then his friend turned and walked out of the bar, leaving Ronan standing there feeling lost and hollow. He glanced around and saw everyone staring at him. His hand went to his temples, and he rubbed.

Then he turned and went out the back door to the alley. He started walking, leaving his car behind as he walked the four miles to his house. And all the way, he tried to remember what Michelle looked like. But he couldn't do it. He had photographs of her. God knew he saw her in his dreams, but trying to conjure the real her in his mind, the way her face lit up when she talked, the animation of it? He couldn't do it.

She wasn't real to him anymore. She was a portrait of a girl. A snapshot in time. He'd loved her, and he'd failed her. Her and their child. And as he walked toward his home and the life he lived alone, he brushed away a tear and told himself that he was doing the right thing.

The only problem was, he wasn't sure he still believed that.

CHAPTER TWENTY-EIGHT

R onan woke to the feel of Brandy under his fingers. That was all that lingered of the dream, a sensual dream that he couldn't recall but craved the memory of.

The memory? Hell, he craved the woman. It had been less than two days since she'd walked away, but it felt like a lifetime.

He pushed himself up and sat on the edge of the bed, then told himself this feeling would go away. This craving for her, and not just sexually. He missed her smile. Her laugh. He missed talking to her. Hell, he missed *not* talking to her and simply *being*.

She was a light in his dark world, and he'd intentionally snuffed it.

For the best. Walking away was for the best.

The words slammed through his mind, bold in their blatant truth. A truth he'd told himself for years, ever since he lost Michelle.

It was easier—better—to be alone.

But more and more, he was doubting that axiom. He

loved her, after all. More important, she loved him. And instead of honoring that, he was running from it.

You have to.

The dark, familiar voice filled him.

You have to in order to keep her safe.

But did he?

Maybe Devlin was right. Maybe the best way to keep her safe was to keep her close.

More important, maybe it wasn't about keeping her safe at all. He would, of course. He'd do whatever it took to keep the dark parts of the world from finding and hurting her. But maybe that wasn't the most important thing. Maybe the most important thing was being with her. Loving her. And letting her love him back.

"I'm sorry," he whispered, realizing he was speaking to Michelle. For all these years, he'd focused on his guilt when he should have been cherishing the time they'd had. Cherishing it—and letting her go. Letting them both move on. Not acceptance so much as peace.

He pushed up off the bed, wired and edgy. He was about to head into the shower when his security system announced that someone was opening the gate.

Brandy?

Immediately, he called himself a fool. She didn't have the gate code, and when he looked at the monitor app on his phone, he saw Tamra parking his Range Rover and walking to the front door.

Five minutes later they were at his kitchen table, him in sweats and a tee, her looking as professional as always. Which made sense, of course, as it was already past noon.

"Thanks for bringing my car."

"Not a problem. You can drive me back to the foundation or I'll call for a rideshare." She smiled, then reached out to put her hand over his. "Mostly, I was glad for the excuse to see how you're doing. Devlin's worried about you."

"What did he say?"

"Nothing specific. But I know that you and Brandy broke up."

"We weren't ever together."

"Weren't you?" she said as if he was the one who was wrong. Hell, maybe he was.

She cleared her throat. "I have some news. The team was finally able to decrypt more of the recovered footage from Mr. Matheson's phone."

"Anything interesting?"

"Nothing helpful at this juncture. Just images of Matheson with the woman under the mask. And with her wearing the mask. A few of the two of them looking at blueprints. Specs, I assume, for a job. And we've scoured the place again, ensuring that all the cameras are gone. The odds are no one else had access to the feed, but I don't like the idea of Brandy living in the eye of hidden cameras."

"Neither do I."

"I considered suggesting that she rent Ellie's property. It's smaller, but workable."

"That's a good idea," he agreed. "Or—"

"Or?"

He shook his head. He'd been about to point out that there was plenty of room in the lighthouse. Two floors that were used primarily for storage. They'd make an excellent space for her. But that wasn't a road he was going to walk down.

"So how are you feeling?" she asked, not pressing him for details. Probably because she knew exactly what he'd been thinking. Tamra had a knack of knowing what "her boys"—as she often called Devlin and Ronan—were thinking. Most of the time, he appreciated it, especially having grown up without a mother.

Today, it just put him on edge.

Still, he couldn't lie to her. "Honestly," he said, "I'm feeling a little like a fool. A melancholy fool."

She reached over and patted his hand. "I'm here to listen if you want to talk about it."

He didn't, but his mouth started moving anyway. "I can't even remember what she looked like."

"Michelle?"

He nodded. Tamra was the one person he'd told. Tamra, who was a stand-in for everyone's mother.

"She stopped being the woman I loved years ago. She became someone I had to avenge. I held on to my guilt for so long that I've lost the only other woman in my life I ever loved."

"She's not lost, Ronan. You can get her back."

The words hit him with the force of a train. He'd screwed up with Brandy—screwed up bigtime. But unlike Michelle, he really could get Brandy back.

He could. And, dammit, he would.

He pushed back from the table to stand. "I need to go. Can I drop you somewhere?"

"She's not home," Tamra said, obviously understanding the thread of his thoughts. "She's at the expo center this morning, setting up for tonight's grand opening. But I bet she'd like to see that gorgeous face of yours there."

"I'll need a ticket."

Tamra smiled. "I think I can manage that." She pulled out her phone and dialed. "Cara, it's Tamra. Listen, can you get me a pass for the Expo this morning? Yes, I know it's closed to the public. The foundation has a client who is hoping to get a behind the scenes peek. Just set it up as someone on BB Bags' payroll. Yes, thank you. Just leave it in my name. You're the best."

She ended the call and flashed Ronan a conspiratorial smile. "Easy as pie."

FIFTEEN MINUTES LATER, Ronan was dressed and cruising down Sunset Canyon toward Costa Mesa, having already dropped Tamra at the foundation. He was about to merge onto the freeway when his phone rang, the in-dash system identifying the caller as Colonel Seagrave.

"Colonel, what can I do for you?"

"You need to hurry," Seagrave said, his voice as hard as stone. "Brandy's still in danger."

Ronan's entire body went cold. "Tell me," he said as he hit the accelerator, his attention now divided between getting safely to the expo center and hearing every detail of what Seagrave had to say.

"We recovered the fake Brandy's phone. Her name is Tiffany Shein, and she's been on Interpol's radar for awhile. As herself, not Brandy. Apparently she and Matheson worked as a team. Some small cons, a few larger heists. They've done a few jobs directly—your Mr.

White was evidence of that—but mostly they're guns for hire."

"And she used Brandy's face when making a hit."

"We've scoured footage. From what we can tell that was a relatively new alias. But she did come up on footage in a hotel in London. An industrialist—one we know was dirty—was assassinated. Brandy—or her double—was in the elevator not long before the hit. London police never identified her. Apparently Brandy doesn't have a passport."

"We'll need to fill them in at some point. I don't want this blowing back on her. But this hardly puts her in danger. Especially now that we know the scam."

"Son," Seagrave said gravely, "the London hit was authorized by someone else."

"Who?" Ronan said, his body going cold with dread.

"Sheldon Cartwright."

"Oh God," Ronan said. "This is the job with the bearer bonds. This Tiffany woman—this fake Brandy— stole from Sheldon Cartwright."

"It looks that way." Seagrave sighed. "My guess is that Cartwright doesn't know what she really looks like. My guess is also that he's seen the security footage, too. As far as Sheldon Cartwright is concerned, Brandy stole his money."

"She deliberately put Brandy in the line of fire," Ronan said, his voice harsh with fury.

"And he has no way of knowing that the real thief is dead and that our Brandy has no information about those stolen bonds. And son, as one of the new designers at the Expo, her face has been in the newspapers, local magazines, and even on advertisements during local morning shows. Her face and her name."

"That's why he came to LA," he said, then cursed when he realized he'd almost missed his exit. He crossed over three lanes of traffic, endured the horns and brakes, then careened down the ramp to the street. "He's been waiting for today. For the Expo to open."

"Or not open. The event doesn't start until this evening. My guess is there are only a few exhibitors there. I have a team on the way with orders to answer to you." He gave Ronan the details of where to meet the three operatives, all that Seagrave had in the area.

Ronan thanked his friend, ended the call, then floored it, blowing through intersections as he sped to the expo center even as he issued the voice command to call Brandy.

Her voice mail answered, and he cursed. "Get out of the center," he said. "Don't argue, just go. Head to my place and call me when you get this message. Avoid the main exits and—*shit*," he said as the call went dead.

He cursed again, unsure if she'd even get the message. Cell service was terrible in the center, and she may not have bothered to hook into Wi-Fi.

Fuck, fuck, fuck.

He needed a plan. He needed a surefire way to ensure Brandy's safety. If he had the damn briefcase, he could bargain, but he didn't have a clue where that was. How could he—

He knew.

It wasn't a perfect plan, but it was the only shot he had.

CHAPTER TWENTY-NINE

"Are you using this cart?" I smile politely, but I'm silently seething. Cara and I have been moving boxes, display cases, banners, and posters from the rented van to my little corner of the Expo for last two hours. We'd both gone over to the vending station to get a snack, and when we came back, the cart that we'd been using was gone. Unfortunately, the van is still half-full.

Now Cara is at the booth, and I'm in search of a replacement cart.

"Yes, I am," the man in the dapper suit says. He looks me up and down, then sniffs. "I'm sure if you continue to look around, you could find a grocery cart or something." He turns on his heel and walks away.

I roll my eyes. Apparently, fashion really is a dog-eat-dog business.

I have a small grocery cart that I keep in my car, but I forgot to put it in the van. Which means that unless I find a cart, I'm stuck carrying one box at a time. I'm not excited about the prospect—especially since the repetitive walk leave too much time for my mind to wander to Ronan—but I don't see that I have a choice.

I'm resigned to that plan and heading for my car when my phone rings. I see that it's Cara and answer it right away. "Tell me that you found a cart," I say.

The fact is, it's lunch hour now, and the expo center has pretty much cleared out, so there should be carts galore. I'm assuming everyone is desperate to keep theirs for when they return and finish unpacking. Honestly, it's terribly unfair.

"No carts," she says, her voice tight and strained.

"Cara? What's wrong?"

"I—Brandy, he says he's going to kill me."

Her words—and the tangible fear in her voice—turn my blood to ice.

"Who?" My hands are shaking, and I force them to hold still so that I don't drop my phone. At the same time, I hurry back toward the main hall. I need to see what's going on. I need to see who has her.

"Who?" The voice at the other end of the line is low, smarmy, and male. With just the hint of an unplaceable foreign accent. "Why, me, my dear."

I don't know this voice, but it scares me. It scares me a lot. "Who are you?"

"You should know. You're the one who betrayed me."

My knees go weak, and I sink against the wall and slowly sag to the floor. "I—I'm not who you think I am."

"No. I suppose you are not. I thought I could trust you. I want my money, you little bitch. I want it now."

Ronan. His name echoes in my mind, and I want him beside me. I don't know how to handle this. I don't know what to do.

I hurry, walking faster toward the center. Then I stop. I'm in the one hallway that actually gets phone reception. If I go too fast, I could lose him. I need to know what he needs me to do, because otherwise Cara is screwed. "What do you want?"

"I told you. I want the money."

"I—I don't have it. I told you."

"Oh, but you can get it. If you don't, it's your life. Your little friend's, too. She'll go first. So that you'll know exactly what to expect if you don't cooperate."

"No! I'll cooperate. I'll—"

"Brandy?"

"Cara! Hang on, okay. I'm going to—"

"He says he's going to kill me right here if you don't come. There's nobody else around. No one to help me."

I hear someone whisper, then Cara's soft whimper.

"He says to tell you there are two security guards on the far side of the room, but if I scream—and if you do anything—he'll blow my head off then kill the guards. Brandy," she adds, her voice trembling, "I believe him."

"I understand." I'm so terrified I'm shaking, but I tell myself to get a grip. Falling apart won't help her. I need to do something, but I don't know what.

All I do know is that I need Ronan, and he's not here.

"I expect you here within five minutes. No, within three minutes," he says. "Otherwise, she's dead. And trust me when I say you'll be next."

"I believe you. I'll be there."

I'm all the way on the other side of the center. If I run, I can get there in three minutes.

Maybe.

I take off, using the voice activation on my phone to

dial Ronan. I'm wearing my headset, and I hear it ringing as I sprint, forcing myself to move faster, thankful I haven't changed for tonight and am wearing jeans and sneakers.

I'm pounding through the hallways, ignoring the stares from people who are looking at me. I don't even have time to ask for help, and Ronan's phone just keeps ringing and ringing and ringing, and I'm terrified he won't answer.

I can see the door at the far end of the hall. It's open, and I can just make out a man in a black suit standing by Cara. My stomach twists, and I try to force myself to run faster.

Then the ringing in my ear stops, and I hear Ronan's voice. "Brandy?"

"Ronan!" I'm breathless and terrified, and my voice is a squeak. And I can't stop moving, because the clock is ticking, and it's been almost two minutes already.

"Please," I say, trying to speak and breathe. "Please, you have to come, you have to help."

"Bran—"

And that's it. The line is dead. Reception lost. Reception, I think, and me too. Because I don't know what to do now. I don't know how to save Cara or myself.

So I do the only thing I can. I go to my booth, look the black-clad man in the face, and say very simply. "I'm here."

∽

"Where are you taking me?" I ask as the man clutches my arm. He's steering me through the expo center to an exit in the back. "I'm taking you away, my dear. And we're going to have a little discussion about what you did with my money."

"I told you. It's not me. You have the wrong woman. She copied me. She pretended to be me. But I don't know her."

"I always knew you were a clever one. That's why I hired you. But too clever by half, I think. Now come on."

We're followed by six other men who had, when he'd released Cara and taken me instead, slipped out of the shadows from neighboring booths. They fell in step behind him, and he walked me out of the Expo center just as easy as you please. I don't know what's going to happen. I don't know if he's going to kill me. I don't know if he's going to torture me.

If this were a movie, I'd say that Ronan will come to my rescue at just the right time. Only seconds before this man tries to kill me.

But this isn't a movie, and I don't know if Ronan was even able to hear me, much less if he knows where to find me. Because even I don't know where this man is taking me.

We follow the outer hall of the circular building, and then, to my relief, I hear an alarm start to ring. It's a fire alarm, and an automated voice comes on asking that all patrons please exit the building. That there is a fire in the expo hall.

I breathe a sigh of relief. *Cara*, I think.

The dark man's hand on my arm tightens, and he tugs me to the side, leading me to a door labeled *Emergency Exit*.

"They can't possibly think it's that easy," my captor

says. "But this is no problem." He leads me down a set of stairs, and I realize he's taking me into the parking garage. I feel a glimmer of hope. Surely by now Cara has told someone, and they're guarding the exits. Every car that passes through must either pay or have a key card. Surely there's no way we'll get out.

The man holding me doesn't seem to be perturbed, though. Instead, he leads me toward three Lincoln Town Cars parked in a line right across from the elevator. I note with horror that they all have diplomatic plates. Fake, I'm sure, but that's not going to matter.

I start to sag, losing hope. I don't know for certain, but my guess is that they'll have no trouble getting out. What guard would argue with a diplomat rushing to safety?

I expect to be shoved into one of the cars right away, but instead, the dark man comes to a stop only inches from me.

The six men fall in behind him in two rows of three. The man himself doesn't pay them any heed, as if he's the type of man who goes everywhere with an entourage.

"Where is my money?" he says, his voice as smooth as silk.

"Please. I swear to you. I don't know."

"Because you aren't the bitch who stole it. Because someone is pretending to be you. What a clever story."

"It's true. I swear."

He lifts a shoulder. "Then you're useless to me. And I don't keep things that are useless."

For a moment, relief floods through me. *He's going to let me go.* Then I see him nod to one of the six.

"Mr. Jones, if you please."

A gaunt man with pasty skin steps forward, brandishing a knife big enough to cut a whale.

"I—" I take a step back.

"What? Have you remembered who you are? Funny how one's memory can be jogged so easily."

"I don't have the money," I say. "I swear."

Mr. Jones is right beside me now, his hand clutching my upper arm, the tip of his knife under my chin. I hear myself whimper, my body cold with fear. "Please," I cry. "I don't have it. Truly. But I know where it is. I—I can take you there."

Lies, of course. And I have no plan. Nothing but to try and buy time, hoping Ronan will find me. My phone is in my pocket. And Ellie and I use the location feature all the time to find each other when we go shopping.

Ronan will call Devlin. Ellie will check her phone. He'll find me.

If I can just stay alive long enough, I know that he will find me.

"Mr. Cartwright?" Mr. Jones is looking at his boss for instructions, but I'm barely paying attention. The garage is swimming now, my mind spiraling not just from fear but from the realization of who my captor is—*Cartwright*.

This man is Sheldon Cartwright.

It takes all my effort not to burst forward, kicking and screaming. I want to hurt this man who hurt Ronan. Hell, I want to kill him.

But I want to survive even more. So all I do is stand there, helpless, and hope that he'll let me take him on this wild goose chase, praying all the while that Ronan will catch up and save me before it's too late.

CHAPTER THIRTY

The sight of Cara curled up in a corner, huddled and shivering and terrified, stuck with Ronan as he and Seagrave's three men hurried through the expo hall. The poor girl had only been able to point in the direction that they'd taken Brandy.

He wished there was time to wait for a team from Saint's Angels to arrive, but there wasn't. They were coming, sure, but he was certain they'd arrive too late.

He had only one shot, and thank God Seagrave's most sacred rule was that his men and their vehicles always be fully equipped.

Now, Ronan clutched the briefcase they'd provided him. A bluff, yes, but maybe it would be enough. It had to be, because there was no way he was going to lose Brandy. No way in hell.

He raced down the hall, the SOC men right at his heels. They pounded down the stairs to the parking structure, slamming through the doors at every level, hoping to see a sign of where Cartwright and his men had gone with Brandy. Hoping that they would find her alive.

Of course she was alive, he told himself. Cartwright wouldn't kill her. Not yet. Not until he was sure that she didn't know where the money was.

God, he hoped he was right.

When they reached sub-level four, he jolted to a stop right before slamming through the door. *Brandy!*

He held his breath, listening. "Please," she said, her voice heavy with fear as it filtered through the door. "Please, it's not me you want."

He winced, hoping Cartwright didn't believe her. If he did, Brandy was dead, because what possible use would the prick have for her then?

Squaring his shoulders, he looked at the men. "Stay here unless I give the signal." And then, without waiting for acknowledgment, he clutched the handle of the brief-case, pushed open the parking garage door, and said, "Cartwright. I have what you want."

As he'd hoped, the man turned around to face him. He'd never seen Sheldon Cartwright in person before, and the pictures that he'd managed to wrangle throughout his years of chasing this ghost were always too dark to distinguish features. There was a reason that the man had survived so long in the underworld. He knew how to hide.

But ghost or not, somehow, Ronan was going to kill him.

"Who the hell are you?" Cartwright said.

"I'm the man with your money." He lifted the brief-case and saw Cartwright's eyes dip quickly before lifting his face back to his enemy.

In his peripheral vision, Ronan saw Brandy. Her eyes were wide, full of shock and confusion. And hope.

He forced himself not to look directly at her. Cartwright couldn't know that she meant something to him. Once he knew that, the prick would have even more leverage than he already did.

Instead, he looked directly at the man, noting the six others behind him. A quick glance around suggested that there was nobody else. He hoped he was right about that.

"Bearer bonds," he said. "All of them. All I want is the girl."

"Well, isn't that sweet?"

The situation was fucked, and he knew it. One against seven. Doable, but the odds were terrible.

Worst of all, Brandy stood beside Cartwright, her body rigid with fear. He couldn't risk accidentally shooting her. Cartwright might use her as a shield. There might be a moment before he fell when he'd take Brandy down with him.

But Ronan didn't have another choice. He had to try. Because the next thing that would happen was that Cartwright's men would shoot him or Brandy.

Not acceptable. He stepped forward, holding out the case. "Take it," he said "Take it. Check it, then give me the girl. On your honor."

Cartwright's brows rose. "My honor?"

"Surely you have some?"

The man cocked his head to the side, and Ronan wanted to smash his face in. *Honor*. The hell he did. But if playing games was what it took, then Ronan would play them. "Three steps forward," Cartwright said. "Put the case down, three steps back."

Ronan nodded, then did as he was told, setting the case down, then backing up. Cartwright nodded at one of the men behind him. "You. Go check the case. Make sure it's not rigged."

The man moved forward, looking at the case, carefully examining it from all sides. "Nothing that suggests it's armed. No trigger on the latch. Could be something inside."

Cartwright narrowed his eyes as he stared at Ronan. Ronan knew what he was thinking. He could have Ronan open the case, but if it was a bomb, then he'd just lost the chance of finding out where the money was. Assuming Ronan even knew.

But Ronan did know about the bearer bonds. Why would he if he didn't know their location?

Tricky, tricky, and Ronan watched as all that pondering played across Cartwright's face.

He saw the moment Cartwright reached his decision.

"Open it," Cartwright told the flunky. The man licked his lips nervously but didn't object. Objecting would mean a bullet in his head. Ronan knew that as well as the flunky did. He squatted in front of the case, then clicked the locks. Nothing happened. He breathed a sigh of relief then opened the lid.

Immediately, the tubes rigged inside exploded. Not bombs, not bearer bonds, just tear gas, courtesy of the well-prepared SOC operatives. In the same moment that the canisters blew, Ronan yanked up the mask he'd hidden in his shirt. Then he leaped forward, knocking a howling Cartwright out of the way as he grabbed Brandy's arm and hauled her toward him.

She was coughing, her face streaked and red. But she was alive and free.

He had a mask for her as well, and he put it on her, then let her fumble for the straps. "Take her," he yelled to one of the operatives, who'd burst from the stairwell at the sound of the explosion, his mask already in place. The operative took Brandy's arm and pulled her to safety as Ronan and the other two took out the remaining five flunkies with tranquilizer guns ... a promise to Seagrave so that any of Cartwright's subordinates could be interrogated about the breadth and scope of Cartwright's enterprise.

Not that it would be Cartwright's for long. Because as the bastard's eyes swelled and his face burned, Ronan lifted his gun, looked straight at the man who had killed Michelle and kidnapped Brandy, then put a bullet through his brain.

Ten minutes later, the air was clear, and he was giving a statement to a local police officer. Explaining how they'd used the gas in the mission, that Cartwright had pulled his own weapon, not as affected by the gas as the others, and that Ronan had fired in self-defense.

The others, of course, were under arrest, cuffed and being escorted into transport vans.

Colonel Seagrave was there too, and he added his weight to the statement, saying that the man was a notorious killer who was on the military and Interpol's radar.

It was all perfunctory. All just going through the motions. Cartwright was dead, and Ronan knew there would be no blowback.

It was, he thought, some bit of justice. He sighed, the weight finally lifted from his shoulders.

It was time to move on. Time to let it go.

Hope filled him as he walked to the stairwell and Brandy threw herself into his arms. He held her close, then kissed her. "I love you," he whispered as she held him tight. "Oh, God, Brandy, I love you."

"Y ou're serious?" Brandy asked as she spun in the round room high in the lighthouse. "I can really live here?"

Ronan cleared his throat. "Ah, actually, I was hoping you'd use these two floors as your office. Now that your bags are selling all over the country, you deserve a special office space, after all. And I thought you could live in the house with me."

Her sweet smile warmed his heart. "You're asking me to move in with you?"

"Sort of. Not exactly."

Her brow furrowed. "What does that mean?"

He dragged his fingers through his hair, then swallowed. His mouth was dry from nerves, damn him. Not because of what he was about to do—he had no doubts at all. And not because he was afraid she'd say no—he was confident that she loved him.

No, he was nervous because this was one of those

moments in life to be treasured. And damned if he didn't want it to be perfect.

Slowly, he got down on one knee, hiding his smile as her eyes went wide and her hand went to her mouth. He took her free hand in his, his heart pounding. Not with fear, but with joy. That sense of certainty that this was perfect.

"It means that I love you, Brandy," he said. "You've brightened my world. You've made me forget my sorrow and find my joy. You've brought me love, angel, and with you in my arms, I'm looking to the future and not to the past. I want to go there—to the future—with you."

He drew a breath. "Brandy Bradshaw, angel, will you marry me?"

Her smile illuminated her face. "If you don't already know the answer," she said, dropping to her knees in front of him, "then you're asking the wrong question."

He laughed. "God, I love you."

"That's good," she said. "Because I'm going to marry you. I love you, Ronan," she added, her lashes wet with tears. "You make me so happy."

"Angel," he said, "that makes us even."

Then, as the pink-orange glow from the sunset outside the lighthouse window filled the room, he took his fiancée into his arms and kissed her.

THE END

"J. Kenner knows how to deliver a tortured alpha that everyone will fall for hard. Saint is exactly the sinner I want in my bed." *- Laurelin Paige, NYT bestselling author*

The Fallen Saint Trilogy
By J. Kenner
My Fallen Saint
My Beautiful Sin
My Cruel Salvation

MY FALLEN SAINT
CHAPTER ONE

The wind stings my face and the glare from the afternoon sun obscures my vision as I fly down the long stretch of Sunset Canyon Road at well over a hundred miles per hour.

My heart pounds and my palms are sweaty, but not because of my speed. On the contrary, this is what I need. The rush. The thrill. I crave it like a junkie, and it affects me like a toddler on a sugar high.

Honestly, it's taking every ounce of my willpower not to put my 1965 Shelby Cobra through her paces and kick her powerful engine up even more.

I can't, though. Not today. Not here.

Not when I'm back, and certainly not when my homecoming has roused a swarm of butterflies in my stomach. When every curve in this road brings back memories that have tears clogging my throat and my bowels rumbling with nerves.

Dammit.

I pound down the clutch, then slam my foot onto the

brake, shifting into neutral as I simultaneously yank the wheel sharply to the left. The tires squeal in protest as I make a U-turn across the oncoming lane, the car's ass fishtailing before skidding to a stop in the turnout. I'm breathing hard, and honestly, I think Shelby is, too. She's more than a car to me; she's a lifelong best friend, and I don't usually fuck with her like this.

Now, though...

Well, now she's dangerously close to the cliff's edge, her entire passenger side resting parallel to a void that boasts a view of the distant coastline. Not to mention a seriously stunning glimpse of the small downtown below.

I ratchet up the emergency brake as my heartbeat pounds in my throat. And only when I'm certain we won't go skidding down the side of the cliff do I kill Shelby's engine, wipe my sweaty palms on my jeans, and let my body relax.

Well, hello to you, too, Laguna Cortez.

With a sigh, I take off my ball cap, allowing my dark curls to bounce free around my face and graze my shoulders.

"Get a grip, Ellie," I murmur, then suck in a deep breath. Not so much for courage—I'm not afraid of this town—but for fortitude. Because Laguna Cortez beat me down before, and it's going to take all of my strength to walk those streets again.

One more breath, and then I step out of the car. I walk to the edge of the turnout. There's no barrier, and loose dirt and small stones clatter down the hill as I balance on the very edge.

Below me, jagged rocks protrude from the canyon walls. Further down, the harsh angles smooth to gentle slopes with homes of all shapes and sizes nestled among the rocks and scrubby plants. The tiled roofs follow the tightly winding road that leads down to the Arts District. Tucked neatly in the valley formed by a U of hills and canyons, the area opens onto the town's largest beach and draws a steady stream of tourists and locals.

As far as the public is concerned, Laguna Cortez is one of the gems of the Pacific Coast. A laid-back town with just under sixty-thousand people and miles of sandy and rocky beaches.

Most people would give their right arm to live here.

As far as I'm concerned, it's hell.

It's the place where I lost my heart and my virginity. Not to mention everybody close to me. My parents. My uncle.

And Alex.

The boy I'd loved. The man who broke me.

Not a single one of them is here anymore. My family, all dead. And Alex, long gone.

I ran, too, desperate to escape the weight of my losses and the sting of betrayal. I swore to myself that I'd never return.

As far as I was concerned, nothing would get me back.

But now it's ten years later, and here am I again, drawn back down to hell by the ghosts of my past.

MY FALLEN SAINT
CHAPTER TWO

I met Alex Leto on my sixteenth birthday, and the first time I saw him, something inside me turned on. Something like happiness, yet so much more complicated. Optimism, maybe, but mixed with rainbows and unicorns.

The day started gray and dismal, with storms rolling in at dawn. They parked themselves over my house, spread their dark gray arms, and stirred up wind and rain from daybreak all the way into the evening. Six of my ten invited guests called to cancel, but even before the party started, I'd known that it was ruined.

I should have seen it coming. Maybe not a gale, but something. After all, I was not the most blessed of kids. For starters, I was an orphan.

I'd turned four the day after my mother died, and though I used to tell my dad that I remembered her, by the time I was ten, that was a lie.

Her brother, my Uncle Peter, moved his commercial real estate business to Laguna Cortez after she died. My dad couldn't afford to hire help, and as Chief of Police he had an erratic schedule. Daddy and I lived in the hills, but I'd go to Uncle Peter's huge, light-filled beach house most days after school.

It was a stunning home, but I hated every moment away from my dad. Maybe some part of me knew what was coming. I don't know. All I know is that I wanted him beside me and safe.

But wanting doesn't matter. It never does. Wants are just so much fluff, and Fate is a goddamn bitch. The summer I turned thirteen, I learned that lesson well.

That's when a gunman murdered my father, then killed himself. People tried to comfort me by pointing out that my father died on duty in the job he loved. But it didn't help. He was still horribly, painfully dead.

After that, my life spiraled even more. I moved in with Uncle Peter, and all my friends thought that I was so lucky, because there aren't that many beachfront homes in Laguna Cortez.

But I wasn't. I wasn't lucky at all.

Eventually, I grew accustomed to my new normal. I'd find myself going entire days feeling happy, only to hate myself at night, because how could I experience joy when my parents had both died so horribly?

Which was why I wasn't surprised when the storms rolled in on my birthday, because life will always sneak up and bite you.

Still, even with only a few kids showing up, we'd had fun. Instead of the beach, we settled into the media room to watch movies. And when Brandy and I went downstairs to ask Uncle Peter if my favorite pizza place was delivering in the storm, there *he* was.

A few years older than me, Alex was tall and lean, with close-cropped blond hair, a clean-shaven face that still had a boyish roundness, but an expression that was fully adult. His sandy brown eyes held me in place when he turned to look at me. And when his wide mouth curved into a friendly smile, a low, thrum teased between my thighs.

I'd had a crush or two by then, but I'd never reacted that viscerally to a guy. But Alex ... well, a mere glimpse gave me more understanding of what all the fuss was about than any of the late-night gossip sessions at Brandy's frequent slumber parties.

When he came over to shake my hand and wish me a happy birthday, I almost passed out. I was so flustered that I could only stand there, my hand in his, as I tried to play back the conversation of the last few seconds.

Alex Leto. That's how he'd introduced himself. And he was working for Uncle Peter during his gap year while he decided on a college.

"Hi," I'd squeaked, then kicked myself for being utterly uninteresting.

"Trouble with the movie?" Uncle Peter had asked, and I'd squinted at him, not understanding a word. "The projector," he clarified. "Did you come down because I need to fix something?"

"Oh! Right. Pizza. We want to order pizza. Will they deliver in this weather?"

"If not, I can go get it for you," Alex said, and if I hadn't already fallen hard, that would have sealed the deal. A real live Prince Charming right in my kitchen.

Once Uncle Peter agreed, there'd been no more reason to hang out in the kitchen, and Brandy and I reluctantly went back to the media room. "Oh. My. God," she whisper-squealed as we climbed the stairs. "Did you see the way he was looking at you?"

"He was being polite," I countered, though her words revived that down low tingle, now complemented by a swarm of butterflies in my belly.

"Was he?" She winked at me, and I grabbed her wrist before she could burst into the media room.

"Don't say anything."

"What? Why not?"

"I just ... I ... please? Can we tell them about the pizza and leave it at that?"

"Yeah." She shrugged. "Yeah, sure. If that's what you want."

"Thanks."

She gave me a quick conspiratorial smile. "But he really is super cute."

"I know, right?" And we both burst into giggles, only to fall into total hysterics when our friend Carrie pushed open the door with a scowl.

"Hello? Waiting the movie on you two. I mean, rude."

We clapped our hands over our mouths to bite back another flood of laughter, took our seats, and settled in until the pizza came. And even though Alex was the one who delivered it—and even though he stayed to watch the second half of *Aliens* and sat right next to me—Brandy never said a word. Not then. Not ever.

Which is a big part of why she's my best friend to this day.

After that, Alex was around a lot. Peter had a home office, but he did most of his work at construction sites or in the offices of the apartments and hotels he owned. He'd hired Alex to do administrative stuff, which meant that Alex was at the house most every day.

I turned down beach and movie offers from my friends, choosing to stay in and fetch Alex water and snacks and coffee. Each time I'd linger a bit, asking what he was doing, and he'd never blow me off. He'd even invite me to stay. Then one day he asked if I wanted to help.

"Not as interesting as spending the summer with your friends," he'd said, "but I'd love the company." He smiled then, and that tiny little motion—nothing more than muscles around lips—had melted me.

"Good. Because I'd rather be here."

"Would you?"

I nodded, my heart pounding with such ferocity I was sure he must be able to hear it.

"That works out great, because I like having you here."

I met his eyes, and something deep inside me roared. For the first time in my life, I felt the hard punch of true, sexual desire.

"Right." I swallowed, trying to overcome my desert-dry mouth.

So that's what I did, helping him when I could, taking up space the rest of the time. And we talked. About anything and everything. I'd never been as comfortable with anyone in all my life, and that was despite the humming, buzzing, crackling in the air whenever we were near each other.

"Have you done anything?" Brandy asked when we were back in school months later.

"No! He works for my uncle, remember? Besides, he's eighteen. Me, sixteen. And he knows it."

She waved away my words. "Yeah, but so what? You act older. Ever since ... well, my mom says you raised yourself."

Honestly, Mrs. Bradshaw wasn't wrong. My uncle may have sheltered and fed and clothed me these last few years, but that was about it. Nurturing, I got at Brandy's house. And the rest? Well, I guess maybe I did raise myself.

"Eighteen," I repeated firmly. "Nineteen next week."

"That's perfect." Her blue eyes twinkled. "Wrap yourself in a bow, and you can be his present."

I didn't give myself to him, of course, but when he turned nineteen, I gave him a leather friendship bracelet with a Celtic knot. "That's called a love knot," he said, and I felt my cheeks burn hot.

"I—I didn't know."

"Didn't you? Well, it makes it all the more special to me."

"Oh."

He held out his arm to me. "Fasten it?"

I did, lightly stroking my thumb over his wrist as I manipulated the clasp.

"This is fucked up," he said, so soft I could barely hear him.

"What?"

"Us," he said, the words like ice.

"I'm sorry. I should—" I turned to go, but he grabbed my arm and pulled me back. We were alone in Uncle Peter's study, and he held me in place.

"You're sixteen." He practically growled the words. "Why the hell are you only sixteen?"

I shook my head, blinking as I tried to prevent the flood of tears.

"We can't," he said, and I didn't have to ask what he meant.

"I know," I whispered. I'd been talking to the ground, but I told myself that wasn't fair. He deserved the words. He deserved to see my heart. I looked up and met his eyes. "But I want to."

His head tilted in the slightest of nods. "I know," he said. "I want it, too."

MY FALLEN SAINT
CHAPTER THREE

For months, being with Alex was both torture and bliss. It was like living in a pressure cooker, and I think we both knew that the day would come when we couldn't fight it anymore.

Then, right after Christmas break, Brandy's dad pulled up stakes and moved the whole family to San Diego with barely any notice at all. We'd been devastated, and the day before she left, I helped her pack her room and stayed until her mom said I had to go because the movers were coming at five in the morning. I'd left reluctantly, fighting back tears so that Brandy wouldn't lose it all over again.

I got home to find Alex waiting up for me, ostensibly catching up on Uncle Peter's paperwork. I'd hurried up to my room, unable to even talk to him without risking more tears.

I'd been about to doze off when I heard the light tap at my door. I propped myself up, assuming it was Uncle Peter coming to say goodnight. Instead, it was Alex.

He shut the door behind him, then stood on the far side of the room. "I wanted to make sure you're okay."

"I'm sad," I admitted, and it was as if the words were permission for the tears to flow. "I don't think I've been this sad since Daddy died."

"Oh, Ellie..." I barely registered the fact that he'd crossed the room to me. That he was sitting on the edge of the bed, and I was upright and clutching him, sobbing against his shoulder.

I don't know when he slid into bed next to me, but he did. We were both fully clothed, him in jeans and me in PJs, and he held me tight as I snuggled against him. He stroked my hair, and I cried myself to sleep. Not only because Brandy was gone, but because I knew that one day soon, Alex would leave for college, and I'd lose him as well.

Nothing happened that night. Nothing sexual, anyway. But emotionally? Well, whatever bit of my heart I'd held back was fully his by morning. He snuck out before Uncle Peter arrived, and we shared a secret smile in the kitchen as I made toast to eat on the way to school. Just a normal day. Except it would never be normal again.

After that, every day held smiles and shared glances, and I floated on a cloud knowing this wonderful guy had become my rock. Someone solid and real in a world where everyone I loved kept getting ripped away.

I didn't have a party on my seventeenth birthday. With Brandy gone and Alex out of town for some work thing, I couldn't muster the enthusiasm. Instead, Uncle Peter took me out to dinner, and when he went out later that night, I took a twilight stroll down the beach to the tidal pools.

I sat on the rocks, careful not to slip into the pool and disturb the tiny ecosystem. The moon was full, so there was enough light to see the silver fish, brown anemones, and all the rest of the sea life that lived in that fragile little world.

I was bent forward, watching a hermit crab navigate its way across the pool, when I heard the soft pad of footsteps behind me. A spike of fear shot through me, and I jumped to my feet, not even thinking, and lost my footing. I started to go down, certain I'd either squash all the critters in the pool or scrape every bit of exposed skin on the rocks.

But then suddenly I wasn't falling. I was flying, being pulled off the rocks and into Alex's arms.

"I've got you," he said as my blood pounded in my ears. Not from my near miss, but from his proximity. From the sensation of his body pressed against mine as he held my upper arms tight in his clenched hands.

Our eyes met, and though I've never considered myself particularly bold, I moved first, tugging my arms free so I could wrap them around his neck as I rose on my toes and closed my mouth over his.

There was no fear, no worry that he'd push me away. I'd known in the instant before our lips met that this was the way it had to be. This perfect, intense moment that ignited a firestorm inside me as he cupped the back of my neck, pulling me closer until I felt like I could crawl inside of him.

"Ellie," he murmured when we broke apart, and hearing my name on his lips was like throwing gasoline on a fire. I wanted him. All of him. And once again, I

lifted myself onto my toes and lost myself in the taste
of him.

He hesitated only a moment, but in those few
seconds, I feared he'd push me away. But then he made a
low noise in his throat and thoroughly claimed my
mouth, his tongue tasting and teasing, dancing with mine
as his hands slid down to cup my ass.

He pulled me close to him, and I moaned when I felt
his erection against my belly. I'd never been this close to a
guy, and the proof that he wanted me that way burned
inside me, making my inner thighs ache and my core throb.

Then suddenly he wasn't cupping my rear anymore.
He had one hand down the back of my shorts and I was
spreading my legs, offering him all of me.

"Please," I begged, gasping for air. I wasn't even sure
what I was asking for. His finger? His cock? Did I want
him to lay me down in the sand and make love to me?
Did I want him to take me home?

All I knew was that the answer was *yes*. All I wanted
in that moment was to be his, however and wherever he
wanted.

When he looked down at me—when I saw the wild,
raw heat in his eyes, I knew that's what he craved, too.

*This was happening. Oh, God, this was really
happening.*

But then something in his face shifted, and he pulled
his hand out of my shorts. I heard myself whimper as he
took a step back, breaking the contact between us.

"Alex?" I heard fear in my voice. Fear that he didn't
want me. Fear that I'd done something wrong.

"We can't," he said, taking my hand and holding it

close to his chest. "I've never wanted anyone as much as I want you, Ellie. But we can't do this."

I tried to swallow, but the knot of tears stuck in my throat. And when I asked *why* my voice was little more than a croak.

He cupped my cheek. "You're barely seventeen, El. And I'm almost twenty. Plus, I work for your uncle." Something in his face hardened. "Your uncle's not the kind of man who would overlook it. We've already been playing with fire. Push this, and we'll both get burned."

I wanted to shout back that I didn't care. I wanted to burn. I wanted to get lost in the flames with him until we were both reduced to ashes.

But I didn't say any of that because I knew he was right.

He shook his head slowly, his expression profoundly sad. "I never wanted—"

"What?"

"Here. I never wanted to come here."

"To Laguna Cortez?" My voice rose in surprise. "I thought everybody wanted to come here."

"My dad made me. Now, though... " He trailed off, running his fingers over his short hair. "God, Ellie, now this is exactly where I want to be."

"Please," I said, blurting out the word before I lost my nerve. "I want to."

The corner of his mouth curved up. "Me, too. Obviously. But we can't."

"Yes, we can. Uncle Peter's barely noticed that we're friends, much less that there's more."

"Fine. We can."

For a moment, my heart stopped, but then he continued.

"But, El," he said. "I won't."

He stuck to that, too.

Every night, I'd go to bed and slide my hand between my legs while I imagined him doing all the things I read in romance novels. Every night, I'd silently pray for him to sneak into my room and into my bed.

But he never did. He kept his word, even though each time we were alone the air was so charged, I was sure that one of us would crack.

We didn't, though.

Not then. Not yet.

For the next two months, our friendship grew even stronger. Especially with Brandy gone, he became my closest friend. We talked for hours that summer after he was done with work, mostly at the tidal pools. Sometimes he'd stay late at the house, because Uncle Peter was hardly ever home.

We'd talk or cook dinner or watch movies. Horror mostly, because it was an excuse to sit close and hold hands at the first scary scene.

And always, *always*, there was that greedy, guilty need that had me squeezing my thighs to relieve the pressure. I imagined crawling into his lap and doing exactly what the girls in those movies were doing.

And I didn't even care that if I did them, then surely the monster would get me, too.

Maybe I should have cared more. Maybe in the end, I really did bring the monsters down on me.

I don't know. But I vividly remember that September day when Chief Randall came to school and delivered the news that Uncle Peter was dead. Killed by a single bullet to the back of the head, shot from the gun of a monster.

In grief and fear, I'd run home, expecting to find Alex working in the office. But he wasn't there. Later, I learned that he'd been checking the books at one of Uncle Peter's properties when a detective had come to give him the news. They'd questioned Alex for over an hour, digging deep into Uncle Peter's business, searching for clues as to who might have held a grudge.

I didn't know any of that at the time. All I knew was that I was dying inside. That I needed to hear his voice in order to know that he was truly okay. Because everybody I loved—*everybody*—was taken from me. Over and over and over again.

All afternoon and evening I sat with my phone beside me, curled up under a blanket in the living room with Amy Randall, the Chief's wife, bringing me hot tea and cookies. I loved her for taking care of me, but even with Amy in the room, I felt alone.

Alex never called, and at ten o'clock Amy kissed my cheek and got herself settled in the guest room. I went upstairs to my room—and there he was, sitting on the edge of my bed.

I don't know how, but I managed to shut and lock the door behind me before I fell, sobbing, into his arms. "You're going to be okay," Alex whispered. "I hate that you're hurting, but you're strong, El. Never forget how strong you are."

There was an unfamiliar edge to his voice, and he spoke straight to my soul when he said, "I've seen your heart, and you will survive this. And I'll tell you something else, too. I love you, Elsa Holmes." His voice burned with emotion. "That's why I call you El," he added, his thumb and forefinger making the sign for the letter L. "Because it's the first letter in *love*."

Pure joy battled the loss and pain inside me as he cupped my cheek, his eyes locked on mine. "Promise me you won't ever forget that."

"Alex... " I could barely say his name though my tears.

"Promise me." The words were harsh. Demanding.

"I promise."

He closed his eyes, then took a deep breath. And when he opened them again, I gasped at the wild intensity I saw. The blatant hunger. "Tonight, Ellie. Damn me all to hell, but I've got to have you tonight."

"Yes," I said, though I wanted to cry with relief. "Yes," I repeated, only to have the word lost in the soft brush of his lips, that innocent, tender touch exploding into something much more passionate. Something raw.

Something wonderful.

He flipped me onto my back and straddled me, his mouth hard on mine as I clenched at his hips and pulled him down, craving a deeper connection. Needing skin on skin. I wanted everything I'd been fantasizing about, and I wanted it right then. But at the same time, I wanted this to go slow. To last forever. I wanted no one but Alex, and nothing except being in his arms.

"Ellie," he whispered, then trailed kisses down my neck and lower still. I wasn't wearing a bra, and his mouth closed over my breast through my T-shirt. I arched up, so startled by the intensity of the sensation that I had to bite the soft spot at the base of my thumb in order to keep from crying out. Amy was all the way on the other side of the house and a floor below us, but considering the magnitude of what I was feeling, if I let go, I was certain that my cries of pleasure would shake every wall in the place.

He moved lower then, his tongue teasing the thin strip of bare skin between my shirt and my PJ bottoms, making me writhe beneath him. I felt the brush of his fingers as he unfastened the string, then watched as he lifted his head to meet my eyes while he gently eased my pants down, along with my panties. A shiver ran through me—not fear, but anticipation and wild nerves.

"Okay?"

I nodded, then closed my eyes as he kissed my belly button, then moved slowly lower. His hands were cupped at my sides, his thumbs barely touching the swell of my breasts. The only truly intimate contact was his mouth. Such a small bit of skin to generate such incredible sensations.

He moved with wicked slowness. He probably wanted to make sure I was ready, but I was flying from the heat of him, from the wildness and need he was setting loose inside me. Even with all the times I'd made my own body explode, I'd never experienced this growing anticipation or the pure erotic pleasure of being tended and led down a sensual path toward an avalanche of pleasure.

It almost became too much. I whimpered, then shifted my hips as his lips pressed against my mound. He slid his hands lower, then gripped my waist, holding me firmly in place. Only once did he take his mouth from my skin, and that was when he spoke to me. My eyes were closed, my back arched as my body strained for more. "You should touch yourself," he said. "Your breasts. Your nipples."

"Why?"

"You'll like it," he said. "I will, too."

I swallowed, the thought that he'd watch as I did something so intimate making me more than a little nervous. Ironic, considering how intimately *he* was touching me. But I did as he asked, barely grazing my fingertip over my very tight nipple. And oh my God, the sparks that set off. I closed my eyes again, forgetting to be nervous, letting my hands tease my breasts as his mouth explored below, his tongue flicking over me in ways that had me biting my lower lip to prevent me moaning so much that he'd worry about me and stop.

And then—oh God, and then—my whole body tightened and exploded with way, way, way more intensity than I'd ever managed on my own, because on my own, I'd always stopped. But Alex was relentless, teasing and sucking until I didn't care about embarrassing myself, and I writhed and moaned and screamed until he finally slid up my body, put his hand on my mouth, and reminded me that the walls were thin.

He'd held me then, taking over the job of playing with my breasts, then helping me out of my bunched-up T-shirt so that I was naked and he was still fully dressed.

I bit my lower lip and asked, "Do you want...?" I held my breath, waiting for him to answer. I was warm and sated, but I still wanted more. I wanted *him*.

"Desperately," he said. "I want everything with you, El. I want a night that neither of us will ever forget. I want to bury myself inside you and feel it as you shatter around me." He kissed me gently. "Is that okay?"

I nodded, mute, and he kissed me again before sitting up and reaching for his back pocket. He pulled out his wallet and took out a condom, and I felt like an idiot, then, because I was so worked up it hadn't even occurred to me.

"You've done this before," I said, a bit accusatorially, but that was only to hide my embarrassment.

"No," he said as he peeled off his jeans and shirt.

I rolled my eyes. "I'm not naive, you know."

His smile was both teasing and sweet. "Sex, yes. But never with someone I love."

"Oh."

"I do love you, El, and it's destroying my reason."

I frowned. "What do you mean?"

"We shouldn't do this. Not tonight. Not when I—Not after—But dammit, I want you too much. I can't stand the thought that I might—"

"What?"

"Lose you?"

He made the words a question, and I nodded in understanding. Peter was the first person he'd lost. And I understood grief better than anyone. "You won't lose me, Alex," I promised. "How can you if we love each other?"

I thought I saw tears in his eyes, but then he kissed me, and once again I was lost as he swept me away, out to sea on a tide of passion. He moved slowly, every touch bringing me that much closer to begging until, finally, I did exactly that and showered him with pleas.

He didn't ask if I was sure—he knew that I was—but he met my eyes, and when he grinned, he was more than my new lover, he was my best friend. And I knew right then that no matter what, the night was going to be perfect.

He buried himself inside me, moving slowly, taking care to hurt me as little as possible, until I was actually whimpering with need. And when he exploded, I opened my eyes and watched the release play out over his face and body, amazed that I had the power to take him there —and then amazed again a few minutes later when he once more sent me off on the same journey until we were both utterly spent and limp as rags.

He slid up the bed, pulling me against him, and we clung to each other, whispering softly until sleep claimed us. I drifted off in his arms, knowing that I would survive this. Because with Alex by my side, I could survive anything.

That's what I believed, anyway, but I learned soon enough that it was a crock of steaming bullshit.

Because by the time I got up the next morning, Alex was gone, vanished with no word other than one crappy slip of paper telling me he was sorry and that I was strong. I'd loved him. I'd trusted him. And he'd walked away.

Everyone else in my life had been stolen from me. But Alex? He'd left of his own accord.

And that made him the worst devil of all.

Visit your favorite bookseller for your own copy of
My Fallen Saint

ABOUT THE AUTHOR

J. Kenner (aka Julie Kenner) is the *New York Times, USA Today, Publishers Weekly, Wall Street Journal* and #1 International bestselling author of over one hundred novels, novellas and short stories in a variety of genres.

JK has been praised by *Publishers Weekly* as an author with a "flair for dialogue and eccentric characterizations" and by *RT Book-club* for having "cornered the market on sinfully attractive, dominant anti-heroes and the women who swoon for them." A five-time finalist for Romance Writers of America's prestigious RITA award, JK took home the first RITA trophy awarded in the category of erotic romance in 2014 for her novel, *Claim Me* (book 2 of her Stark Trilogy) and the RITA trophy for *Wicked Dirty* in the same category in 2017.

In her previous career as an attorney, JK worked as a lawyer in Southern California and Texas. She currently lives in Central Texas, with her husband, two daughters, and two rather spastic cats.

Visit her website at www.juliekenner.com to learn more and to connect with JK through social media!